Hello, Doggy!

"Doesn't it make you uncomfortable to speak for an entire gender in that way?" Tory said.

Keenan laughed. "Speaking for my gender. I certainly don't think of it that way. I'm speaking . . ." He paused, rubbing a hand along one lean cheek. "I'm speaking as someone who cares about women burned by men."

Surprising herself, Tory laughed. "Well, you are unusual, Mr. James, I'll give you that."

She glanced at him and saw he was smiling. Just a little. Just enough to hint at those deep dimples and make his long eyelashes touch at the corners.

He was charming the pants off these women. Maybe even literally.

Could Keenan James be using his round table as his own personal dating pool?

She slammed on the brakes and pulled to the curb. "Sorry, this is as far as I can take you."

"No problem. I appreciate the ride. See you next week?"

"Oh you bet." It was as much a threat as a promise.

ELAINE FOX

Hello, Doggy!

A V O N

An Imprint of HarperCollinsPublishers

AVON BOOKS
An Imprint of HarperCollins*Publishers*
10 East 53rd Street
New York, New York 10022-5299

Copyright © 2008 by Elaine McShulskis
ISBN: 978-0-06-117569-5
www.avonromance.com

First Avon Books paperback printing: January 2008

Avon Trademark Reg. U.S. Pat. Off. and in Other Countries, Marca Registrada, Hecho en U.S.A.
HarperCollins® is a registered trademark of HarperCollins Publishers.

Printed in the U.S.A.

10 9 8 7 6 5 4 3 2 1

For Peyton,
you'll always be The Best Dog in the World.

Hello,
Doggy!

Chapter 1

"You've heard of Keenan James?" the publisher asked. His white eyebrows curved up at the ends so that they looked like little wings on his face. His eyes were faded blue, but sharp.

"Keenan James?" Tory Hoffstra repeated, trying to keep the scorn from her tone and disapproval from her face. "That television guy pretending to be a psychologist?"

"Yes, the man who runs the Just-Dump-Him Round Table." Franklin Fender walked around his desk to sit on the edge of it in front of her. "He's doing amazing things, according to reports. Helping women get out of bad relationships, develop self-esteem, take control of their lives."

"He—he . . ." Tory searched for something positive—or at least not negative—about the man she considered a dangerous charlatan. "He had that special on The Discovery Channel, right?"

It had been little more than an extended infomercial for his women-only get-mental-health-quick program. She'd been so disappointed in The Discovery Channel that she'd actually written a letter in protest.

"Exactly." Fender smiled as if they'd reached some accord on the man. "He wants to write a book. And we want to publish it."

He paused, let that sink in, and Tory realized that she was not here because of *her* proposal to write a book—*A Humanistic Approach to Cognitive Adjustment in Post-Teenage Women and the Attachment Theory*. Optimism seeped out of her.

"Oh?" she offered weakly. She pushed her glasses up higher on her nose.

"The problem is . . ." Fender looked upward, as if posing for his portrait to be painted for the Great Hall of Editors. "He has no credentials. He's not a doctor, or even a psychologist. He's not even a certified counselor."

Tory frowned at the "even a psychologist" remark. As if she were a lesser being for choosing the cognitive side of the equation instead of the medical.

"That is a problem," she said significantly.

"That's why we want you," Fender said with a smile that implied he was bestowing a Nobel Prize, "to cowrite the book with him. Give him some credibility, add the right mumbo-jumbo to some of his theories. Make a real psychology book, but one for the masses."

"Me?" Tory nearly flinched. "You want me to write *his* book?"

"Well, with him, of course. They're his ideas, after all."

She cleared her throat, cheeks burning, and willed herself to stay calm. She'd thought this was her shot. When she'd gotten the call from Franklin Fender's secretary about a meeting, she was sure it meant deliverance from her failed career in the form of a book deal. Recognition, appreciation, proof that all that school and all those articles were not just confirmation that "those who can't do, write."

Instead of throwing her a life raft, however, fate had sent her a shark. Her choice: to drown or be devoured.

"Mr. Fender, are you aware that I sent you a proposal for a book based on my own research and ideas? Containing sound psychological theories and verifiable case studies?"

"Of course," Fender said, looking at her as if reassessing her intelligence. "That's why I contacted you. You have the credentials, the education, the knowledge."

"And the ideas, Mr. Fender. My research into the psychological attachments of post-teenage women and the perceptual angst involved in—"

"Yes, right, of course. But that, you must admit, Dr. Hoffstra, has a much more limited audience than a book by Keenan James. I mean, here's a guy who dates supermodels, who appears regularly in the tabloids, who's known for moving in celebrity circles. He's Manhattan's hottest bachelor! Women would *love* to get inside his head."

He rose from his seat at the edge of the desk and moved back around to his chair. He didn't sit, but stood behind the mahogany edifice with his finger-tips on the surface.

She wondered if he did all that moving around to show off the excellent cut of his obviously expensive suit. It almost made him look as if he didn't have that giant, white-guy-behind-the-desk belly.

She lowered her eyes, afraid he'd see her less-than-charitable thoughts in them. She had to get a grip. Fender was a businessman and she had a product. This wasn't personal. She had to show him her mettle, her smarts. That's what business-men respected.

Fender continued, "He's a *name*, Dr. Hoffstra. Especially since that Discovery Channel special. And he's a damn good-looking guy, if you'll permit me. Those two things alone will sell books."

Tory's eyes flashed up to his. "So you want to sell

women a book on how to get better relationships by convincing them a good-looking guy famous for dating models can set them straight." Her tone was deadpan, but Fender didn't notice.

"Sure. What better way to get them to pick up the book? If they're drawn to that type of man, they'll be an easy sell. But inside, Dr. Hoffstra," he said in a seductive tone, "inside will be *your* writing, *your* educated take on James's methods and successes. They'll be taking your advice as much as his."

Tory paused. This was a point, she had to admit. She would have some control, she presumed, on what went into the book as well as on how it was presented. She could make sure it wasn't psycho-tripe. A spark of interest flickered.

"It'll be like that book," Fender continued, "*He's Just Not That Into You*, with not just the television credentials—you know of course that James wrote the smash HBO series *Sex at Midnight*—but the fame. He's a known man-about-town, handsome, suave, worldly. If anyone could clue women in about the male side of relationships, and empower them to be equal partners, he could."

Tory sighed. Her vision of molding this venture into a scholarly tome of some worth popped like a soap bubble. "Yes, he does have a reputation for being with *a lot* of women."

"That's right. And with you giving him the academic credentials, Dr. Hoffstra, the book is bound to do well. What he has is a formula, a proven strategy. And he has that round table."

"Ah yes, the round table," Tory repeated. "Proving that there is such a thing as a free lunch."

"Dr. Hoffstra," Mr. Fender said, sharply enough that Tory straightened in her chair. "I sense that you don't approve of Mr. James's methods. But I assure you, he has seen tremendous success. And he is out there, every day, helping scores of women. They flock to his round table lunches, and he doesn't even charge them. Just—as you said—the price of his lunch, which, let's face it, is a small price indeed when you're talking about therapy."

"By a television writer," Tory added.

Her practical side—the one she called by her first name, Engelberta—closed her eyes in exasperation. This was an *opportunity*, Engelberta insisted, no matter how second-rate. This would get her name out to millions, not to mention it would probably bring in a helluva lot more money than her own attachment theory.

"But your line of books, Mr. Fender," she said, giving it one last shot, "it's one of the best in the business for putting out mainstream psychology materials with some worth. You're not the celebrity type; that's why I sent my proposal to you."

"You're right," Fender said. He tented his fingers over his chest. "And it's gotten us nowhere. We've got books by doctors, PhDs, licensed social workers, you name it, they're coming out our ears. And are we making any money?"

He looked at her with winged brows raised.

Tory swallowed.

"We are not," he said flatly. "And neither are the authors. But rather than throw our principles to the wind, Dr. Hoffstra, we have an opportunity here to put out a book by a celebrity with bona fide credentials behind it. James came to us for the same reason you did. He wants to write a serious book with serious solutions. What we need is a meeting of the minds, across the board, from the practitioners to the readers."

"You do know that I wrote the article 'No More Psychobabble' that I included with my proposal."

He grinned. "Yes. It was excellent."

She paused, unsure if she could go on without being insulting. "Did you read the, uh, the whole thing? The part about—?"

"About charlatans like Keenan James raking in money off the perceived mental instabilities of others?"

She smiled wryly. "Mental inconsistencies," she mumbled.

"I read every word, which is another reason you would be perfect for the project. Built-in skepticism will prove the theories even more conclusively. This will be a book even academicians will appreciate. That's what *you* bring to the project, Doctor."

Tory's heart lifted. "But . . . what if I punched up

my proposal a little? My attachment theory. What if I gave it a better title, and—and—"

"Save your energy, Dr. Hoffstra," he said, sighing. "The article was good, but it was in a small psychology journal. Not even one of the big ones like *Psychology Today*. You're essentially unknown to the general public. I don't mean to hurt your feelings, but we are not going to buy a book by you alone. There's just no percentage in it."

Tory gazed at him, fearing that if she opened her mouth she would cry. He was rejecting her to her face. Flat-out saying that her own ideas were not what they wanted. Not what the public wanted.

How was she ever going to succeed? She was in a practice now, but she was never going to distinguish herself there. She wasn't good enough with the patients. She'd tried radio, but that had been a disaster. She'd tried magazine articles, but while many of her colleagues read them, they didn't pay. She was no good at the one-on-one a successful private practice required. And while she was an excellent researcher, she could never make a living doing that.

Apparently all she was good for was her skepticism.

She wanted to make a name for herself, but not like this. Not on the coattails of some celebrity chick magnet.

She shifted in her seat, looked down at her hands, pushed her glasses up, then glanced back at Fender.

"Look," he said, his tone more conciliatory than Tory's would have been in his position. "Why don't you go to a few round tables yourself and see what James is doing. If you still think he's up to no good, you can turn me down. But I think you'll like what you see. The man is sincerely trying to do some good."

Tory took a deep breath, then asked, "Why me, Mr. Fender? With all due respect, the proposal I sent you was very academic and complex. Why would you choose me to write Keenan James's book? Especially after reading my psychobabble article, where I essentially derided everything he's doing. Surely you can find some other skeptic. Besides"—she smiled ruefully—"I'm being a bit difficult about it."

This brought a smile to Fender's face. "Because you can write, Dr. Hoffstra. That proposal you sent us was, as you said, complex to the extreme. But it was written beautifully. Even a bunch of boneheads like our ed assistants plucked it out of the slush pile. You reached them, despite the overblown academia of the subject. You'll be perfect for this project, if you'll take it."

Tory frowned. If they'd picked it out of the pile, didn't that mean it was worth publishing as it was? Why did she have to attach herself to someone like Keenan James? No one would recognize her sincere and educated efforts behind the glibness of James's notoriety. She might as well be giving advice through the mouth of Mr. Ed.

"And don't forget, we're offering cowriter, not ghost. You'll be published, Dr. Hoffstra. As I understand it, that's quite a coup in the academic world." He sat down in his chair, wearing a self-satisfied smile.

She felt as if she were being asked for her soul by the devil. The man's winged eyebrows and high-priced suit didn't help dispel the image either.

Would this be selling out? Would her work be embraced or shunned by the psychiatric community? Would Fender's offer catapult or catastrophize her career?

"I'd like to attend some of the round tables," she said finally. "As you suggested."

Fender started to beam.

"But I'd like to do it anonymously," she added firmly. "As one of the, uh, 'patients.' I want to see what he's doing without putting him on guard. If he's not doing any harm, and if I think I can contribute in a meaningful way, then I'll do it. Is that all right?"

She'd just see if Keenan James was doing what everyone claimed. And if he wasn't, she'd set him straight, somehow or other. Because a book deal was about the only way she was going to be able to make a decent living.

She was an excellent researcher, a theorist of the first order—but her people skills stank, she hated being in the public eye, and she'd never make it in radio or television. She was no Dr. Phil and she never would be.

Becoming an author was her only hope.

"Is it all right?" Fender repeated. "It's perfect. It'll give you the exact perspective you'll need for writing the book. And trust me, Doctor, you'll want to write it once you see this guy in action."

He stood. Tory did too, and they shook hands.

"We'll see," she said ominously. Engelberta sighed. "We'll just see."

"A *golden doodle*?" Keenan's brother looked at him sideways as they made their way up Connecticut Avenue toward Keenan's hotel. "Give me a break. There's no such thing."

"In fact there is," Keenan said. "Half golden retriever, half poodle. A golden doodle."

"No way." Brady's mouth curled. "It sounds like a snack food."

"Well, it's not," Keenan said, wishing that were the worst of the news he had to break to his brother. "Though it wouldn't say no to a snack food. It's Mom's dog, Brady, and you've got to take it. I've had it for three months now, and she can't keep it in the nursing home."

Brady stopped, his face set and his arms folded across his chest. Around them, the Washington, D.C., street clanged and groaned and heaved with life. Keenan had driven from New York to D.C. for business—he'd been invited to speak to a women's group—but mostly he'd wanted to see his brother in the hope that he could convince Brady to take their mother's dog off his hands. Even as they walked back from lunch, the pup was waiting in Keenan's room, leash, food, and toys packed up and ready to go.

"Is that why you came down here? To scrape the dog off on me?" Brady asked.

Keenan stopped walking, turned, and looked at his brother's dark expression. Brady, he knew, could be one stubborn son of a bitch if he wanted to be. Still, Keenan thought he could see the little brother—half brother, to be precise—of years past, wanting his older sibling's approval but not willing to cave on anything to get it, and it made him pause.

"Partly," Keenan admitted. "Once you meet this dog, you're going to love it, I promise."

"You have it *here*?" Brady's brows shot up, comprehension showering his face.

Keenan felt like the worst kind of heel. Brady'd sounded happy to meet him in the city, despite living an hour south, and now he looked as if he'd been had.

"I told you on the phone I can't take the dog," Brady said, shaking his head and moving forward. "You could have saved yourself the trip."

"Come on, Brady, it's *Mom's dog*. She'd be so

happy to know you had it, especially since you don't visit that often—"

"Stop right there, Keenan." Brady's expression darkened further. "Guilting me isn't going to help your case at all. I *do* visit Mom, when I can. Is it so hard to remember that I live five hours away?"

"I didn't mean it that way. I meant *because* you live so far, she'd be glad to know—"

"I'm not taking the dog, Keenan. I can't take it. I don't want to take it. I won't do it, so just give it up."

Keenan tilted his head. "I'm sensing some indecision."

"Very funny."

"What if I told you she came with a free forty-pound bag of dog food and three squeak toys? Not to mention the goodwill of everyone she meets." Keenan gave his laziest smile and put his hands in his jeans pockets. The early fall day was chilly.

"You're not going to jolly me into this, Kee," Brady said. "Not this time. I'm already living with the dog from hell, who would no doubt massacre Mom's little mutt after first diabolically driving it insane."

Keenan turned and they resumed walking. He gazed toward a small park next to the hotel. Washington was so green, that was one thing he liked about the city. Across the grassy expanse, an old woman walked a portly Pomeranian, the two of them moving at a glacial pace.

Keenan knew that was the sort of dog Brady was picturing. Something small, perhaps old, definitely slow. It wouldn't do to have him shocked when he laid eyes on the real thing.

He cleared his throat. "Actually, Mom's little dog isn't quite so little anymore." He glanced over at Brady's face. "It's more your kind of dog. A real guy's dog."

Brady stopped walking again. "What do you mean, 'a guy's dog'? Aren't you a guy?"

The narrowed eyes, the stiff-legged stance, all said Brady was not moving another inch toward Keenan's hotel until he knew he wasn't leaving it with the dog.

"It's a babe magnet." Keenan laughed. "But it's too much for me."

"Oh what, you have too many babes as it is?" Brady laughed, but he hunched his shoulders in his leather jacket at the same time. The little boy cold in his brother's shadow again. "You get a little too famous for your own good?"

Keenan shook his head. "That's not what I meant. *The dog* is too big. That's one of the reasons you have to take it. It's close to forty pounds, and I can't keep anything bigger than twenty-five in my building."

"Forty pounds!" Brady burst. "I thought it was one of those yappy little dogs like, I don't know, Reese Witherspoon had in that movie."

One corner of Keenan's mouth kicked up. "You saw *Legally Blonde*?"

Brady made an impatient gesture. "I was on a date. So what have you been feeding this thing? How big's it going to get?"

Keenan sighed and prepared to deliver the next bit of bad news. Which unfortunately was not the *last* bit. "The vet said it should top out at about sixty-five."

Both of Brady's brows shot upward. "*Pounds?*"

Keenan nodded.

"There's no way. Absolutely no way. There'd be a war at my house." Brady's face clouded with obvious visions of the carnage such a scenario would produce.

"Not with this dog. It's a pushover. And it's cute. Kind of got that Tramp look going for it. But it's getting big and I can't keep it."

"Sixty-five pounds," Brady repeated, shaking his head. "What was Mom thinking?"

"I don't know if Mom knew how big it would get when she got it, and I don't want to ask her now. Being in the nursing home is bad enough without her having to give up her dog too. She really would be glad to know you had it, Brady." Keenan turned and started walking again.

Brady scowled, waiting a beat before slumping along behind him. "If it was a puppy when she went in, she couldn't have had it very long. How attached could she be? Couldn't we give it to some-one who wants it?"

Keenan angled his head and sighed, giving Brady the look.

Brady rolled his eyes. "Okay, okay. You don't want to give it to someone else. But I'm telling you, I can't take the damn thing. I've got Doug."

"Doug?"

"Lily's dog. You have no idea how much I have to do for Doug to tolerate me as it is. The last thing I'm going to do is piss him off by bringing home competition."

"You don't want to piss off *Doug* so you're will-ing to give Mom's dog away? Are you sure it's not Lily you're worried about?" Keenan looked at him incredulously. He couldn't wait to meet the only girl ever able to make his reckless brother settle down. Surely this was her doing, not her dog's.

Brady scoffed. "Are you kidding? Lily *loves* dogs. If it weren't for Doug she'd probably jump at the chance of getting another one. But trust me, Keenan, you don't piss off Doug. And this new dog, what's her name? She wouldn't want to piss him off either." Brady's head turned at a passing woman. "Did you see that? She couldn't take her eyes off you. Man, if one Discovery Channel spe-cial can do that for a guy . . ."

"I just look familiar. They can't place me." Kee-nan frowned and looked at the sidewalk in front of him.

"They'd *like* to place you," Brady laughed. "You bring that babe magnet you got out here and you'll be beating them off with a stick."

Keenan shot him a sidelong glance and was glad to see Brady grinning. This girlfriend of his must be making him pretty happy, Keenan thought, or he'd be dishing out more grief than that on Keenan's celebrity personality.

"As appealing as that sounds," Keenan said, "I'd just as soon stay as anonymous as possible."

Brady eyed him. "Oh. So. The book project?"

Keenan nodded. "Right. The book project. Much easier to stay anonymous as an author than a speaker. All you need is name recognition, not face."

"Shouldn't have done *Oprah*, then, huh?" Brady chuckled. "Almost everybody I ever met called me up after seeing you on that."

"I know." Keenan shook his head. "I don't know what I was thinking. I was kind of on a roll after The Discovery Channel thing. But . . ."

"Oh yeah, what was that called? The Discovery thing?"

"*Straight Talk from a Straight Guy.*" Keenan suppressed the wince he invariably felt when talking about it.

"Right." Brady chuckled again. "Hey, at least they didn't say a straight, *single* guy or you'd really have problems, diehard bachelor that you are."

Keenan glanced at him. "I'd say the pot was calling the kettle black, except for the Lily surprise."

Brady laughed. "Commitment's not as scary as it seems from the outside, my friend."

It was Keenan's turn to raise his brows.

"So the book deal," Brady continued. "That should be a no-brainer. Since people already know your name from writing that TV show. I mean, Jesus, *Sex at Midnight* couldn't have gotten any bigger, could it? And now they know your face from that *Straight Talk* special and then Oprah's thing. What was that? *Just Dump Him?*"

Keenan rubbed a hand over his face. Why had he ever felt the need to be *on* television? Writing for it was much more fun. Becoming a personality had been scarier, and a lot more work, than he'd ever dreamed.

It was just . . . after doing so much informal counseling he'd thought he could help people. And television seemed like a great way to help a lot of them at once. Naïvely, he'd had no idea the powers-that-be would want him to continue doing that and not focus on the writing. They'd wanted to hire a *ghostwriter* and slap his name and picture on the cover.

"That was great," Brady continued. "The *Oprah* thing. Lily loved it. Said all her friends had a crush on you after that. So the books ought to fly off the shelves, right? Why's the publisher holding back?"

"It's not the publisher. Or rather, it's *this* publisher. I could find one who'd publish a book by me, just not the kind of book I want to write. I don't want it to be another celebrity vanity book. I don't want *Keenan James Tells You How to Live Your Life*." He made sarcastic quote marks in the air. "I want it to be real. And I want it to really help people."

"Well, women," Brady said. "I don't see you offering a whole lot of help for guys. Besides, think how many women would pick up a book with a picture of you *and* your babe magnet on it."

"Brady, I'm serious. I can't keep the dog. You live in a small town in a house with a yard. How is it harder for you to take her than me? I'd have to *move*." Keenan exhaled, glad to be back on a safer topic.

Brady twisted his shoulders as another woman walked by with eyes only for Keenan. He shook his head. "I told you. Doug. I know it sounds crazy but it's true. Doug would make all of our lives a living hell. Otherwise I would take Mom's dog, Kee, I really would."

"I'm sure Doug will like Barbra Streisand." Keenan nodded to the porter in front of the hotel.

"Mr. James," the man said, opening the door.

Keenan strode through, Brady following him into the marbled foyer.

"*Who?*" Brady demanded.

Keenan pushed the button for the elevator and looked at the numbers overhead. He could feel Brady's eyes on him.

"You named the dog Barbra?" Brady asked.

"*I* didn't name it. Mom did. And the name's Barbra Streisand," Keenan said. He kept his eyes on the lit numbers. *Eleven, ten, nine. . .*

It took a moment, but Brady's whoop of laughter echoed around the stone-and-fern lobby. "You're joking."

"I'm afraid not."

"But she lets you call her Barb around the house, right?" Brady snickered.

"Actually," Keenan winced at the words, "she won't come unless you say the whole name."

Brady's expression grew disbelieving. "So . . . you're outside, walking around Central Park, the dog runs off, and you have to yell . . ."

"Barbra Streisand," Keenan confirmed. "At the top of my lungs."

Brady's laughter exploded as they stepped into the elevator. "Then I *definitely* can't take it. I'm more of a Pearl Jam kind of guy."

Keenan leaned back against the wall and watched the elevator numbers again. Brady would take the dog, he told himself for the dozenth time, and he could get on with life again. He didn't know why, but the dog had seemed to take up an inordinate amount of space and time in his days. Maybe it was because he'd never had one before, or maybe it was because she was still a puppy, but it seemed like the thing always needed to be fed or watered or taken out or petted.

Or rescued—but that was another story. One he hoped never to have to reveal to Brady.

They got off the elevator and Keenan pulled the card key from his wallet. Brady eyed the white door with the gold trim, then turned and looked down the hallway.

"I can't believe they allowed you to bring a dog in here. All this white carpeting. It's a wonder they let you wear shoes," he said.

"I'm paying extra. Besides, she's pretty clean. These dogs don't shed, you know. I'd have kept her if she'd stayed small." Keenan opened the door. "Trust me, you'll like her. She's cute."

They stepped into the suite. Keenan shut the door behind them and paused. Usually she was right at the door to greet him, wagging her whole body and licking his hands.

Except for the time she'd locked herself in the bathroom at his condo. And the time she'd somehow gotten stuck in the dishwasher. And the time she'd tried to run over to him with an end table complete with lamp cord tangled in her back legs.

As they stepped into the hotel suite, both of them scanning the room for the missing Barbra Streisand, he supposed in good conscience he ought to mention to Brady the last bit of bad news about his mother's dog.

He opened his mouth to speak when he spotted her. There, in the dining area next to the windows with the view of Rock Creek Park, was Barbra Streisand, her head stuck between the slats of a mission-style dining chair.

The dog's mouth opened into a bearded doggy grin, and her tail started to wag.

Brady's laughter returned. "Well, hello, doggy!"

"That's the other thing." Keenan let out a slow breath. "She's not real bright."

Brady grinned at Keenan. "I'm not taking that dog."

Chapter 2

Tory stepped around the movers' dolly and squeezed between a leather sofa and a bookcase on the sidewalk to make her way to the front door of Stewart's co-op. Clearly someone was moving in, and yet she hadn't heard Stewart talk about a new resident. Or had she been so wrapped up in her book project that she hadn't paid attention to his comments about the board meetings? Sometimes Stewart's voice took on a tone that she found hard to follow. She wouldn't call it a *drone*, exactly, but his voice would hit a register that made her mind wander to other things.

Though Tory and Stewart had been in a relationship for eight years—Tory hated referring to it as "dating"—they had ended it six months ago. Mostly it had been Tory's idea, because she kept thinking there should be more . . . passion, if one were to take the leap into marriage. Not that anyone had proposed. But she still struggled with the decision. She and Stewart were best friends, they got along beautifully, they understood each other, they had just ended up living something of a celibate life the last seven or eight months of their relationship. Tory had had her doubts that you should marry someone who felt more like a brother.

Then again, with the divorce rate at fifty percent, weren't you better off marrying someone you felt close to, as opposed to someone you wanted to sleep with?

In any case, they had stayed friends. Indeed, their routine had hardly altered, except that neither one made the pretense of spending the night at the other's house.

Even when they were a couple, Stewart had been to her apartment in Brooklyn Heights only a handful of times. He didn't like taking the subway, the cab ride was too expensive, and his place on the Upper West Side was so much nicer, and roomier, that Tory had never minded.

Today, however, she wished they had gone to her place. With someone moving in, the elevator was bound to be going nonstop, and Stewart's front door was right next to the elevator bay. She didn't need that kind of distraction, not today, not when she needed to talk to Stewart about what to do with this latest twist in her quest to write a book.

She was determined not to let Fender's proposal get her down. She had been given an opportunity, she told herself. She hadn't been robbed of one. It had just been exchanged for something unexpected. Surely she could make something good out of the new scenario.

She nodded her head, determined to rise above, as she clip-clopped down the sidewalk in her low sensible heels.

She was just nearing the building when the door jerked partially open, then shut. It happened again, once, twice more, making her think someone with an armload of something must be trying to get out. She was hurrying the last twenty feet or so to grab the handle when the door pushed out and a thin dog with long blond hair and an enormous, toothy mouth bounded free.

Tory froze, her heart rocketing into overdrive. She'd never seen this dog before. And it was *big*. Panicked, she pressed herself against the side of the building. Maybe it wouldn't see her. Maybe its owner was right behind it, with a thick, sturdy leash or a pocketful of steak. Maybe the dog was extremely obedient and would stop the moment the owner said its name.

Maybe the dog would eat her alive.

The dog paused, nose in the air, as if trying to decide which way the more delicious scents led. Tory didn't breathe. Her eyes shifted toward the door, but she didn't move her head. *Why* didn't someone come out? *Where* was the dog's owner?

Her heart hammered in her chest, and her entire body went cold with sweat.

Then, as if in a bad dream, the dog's head swiveled over its shoulder and it caught sight of her.

A scream lodged in her throat, the wind knocked out of her by the sight of the giant animal's attention. She gulped a mouthful of air just before it ran toward her.

Tory found her breath.

"Help!" Her voice was high, so high it was probably in a range only the dog could hear. And the dog clearly thought it was an invitation.

It leaped upon her. She felt its feet against her arm as she shielded her face with her hands. She moved so quickly, so clumsily, her fingers hit her glasses and they flew from her face.

"Stop! No!" She waited for the feel of its teeth, the warm sensation of her own blood dripping down her limbs. It would go for her legs next, she was sure of it. Her knees wobbled.

"*Barbra Streisand!*" someone yelled. A man's voice. Loud. Imperative.

Tory wasn't sure she'd heard right. Was *Barbra Streisand* there? Could this possibly be *her dog*?

Great, she had the presence of mind to think. Her

ignominious demise would probably end up in the newspaper.

"*Bar*bra *Strei*sand! Come here! *Come!*"

She felt the animal's feet push off her body, heard the click of its talons move off down the sidewalk, but for some reason she could not remove her hands from her face. Every inch of her, from her hands to her spine to her knees, was shaking like she was plugged into an electrical outlet.

She sincerely hoped Barbra Streisand wasn't nearby, to make her humiliation complete.

A moment later a man took her forearms and pried them gently from their protective position.

"It's all right," he said, looking at her with great concern. His face appeared friendly and his eyes were an impossibly clear blue, she could see even though her glasses were somewhere on the sidewalk.

She swallowed. "I—I know, I'm fine." Her entire body shook.

"No, you're not." He took her elbow and started to lead her to the door. "Let me help you inside. Were you going in here?"

She stopped, legs frozen again. "Wh-where is it? The dog. Is it inside? I can't go in there. I'm afraid of dogs."

There was an understatement, she thought. Not to mention a needless statement.

"It's okay," the man said. "My friend took it upstairs. I'm so sorry she got loose. She's really very friendly, but when she gets out she behaves like a bat out of hell. She'd never hurt you, trust me."

She looked at him askance. "That's what they all say. Before their dogs' teeth end up in your neck."

The guy chuckled. "I doubt that dog even knows it *has* teeth. She's more likely to lick you to death."

"Not an impossible scenario, technically." She took a quavering breath and glanced around the ground. "My glasses . . ."

"Oh." He let go of her arm and looked at the ground, turning first one way, then the other. "Here they are."

He jogged over to a spot a yard or two from the attack and picked up her glasses. He moved back toward her, looking at them critically. "They might have gotten scratched. Give me your name and I'll buy you a new pair."

Tory took the glasses with trembling hands and shoved them onto her face. Through the smear of her own handprints and the input from the sidewalk, she looked up into the kind blue eyes.

It took her a moment—during which time she noted that (a) her rescuer's eyes were kind, (b) he appeared genuinely sorry, and (c) he did not simply seem worried that she might sue him—but she eventually realized whom she was looking at.

The face was familiar. More than familiar, it was *known* to her, in a dreadful but certain way.

The face belonged to Keenan James.

She had pored over that face before writing her "No More Psychobabble" article, finding in its cocky expression and piercing blue eyes the duplicity of a star trying to sell snake oil to the afflicted masses. She had watched Keenan James's *Straight Talk* DVD thinking he was being anything but straight and seeing in him everything that was wrong with the world's attitude toward mental health.

And now here he was.

She pushed her glasses up again and remembered that she was to attend his Monday round table—anonymously. Fender had it all set up so she could evaluate him objectively before committing to the book. How would that work if he met her now? Saw her before she attended? Realized she practically lived in his building?

She didn't have time to work it out. She dipped her head, causing her hair to fall into her face, and headed for the door.

"I'm sorry. I have to go."

He took a step with her. "Are you sure you're all right? You don't seem very steady."

"I'm fine. Really. I know it may seem irrational to you, to be so affected, but I was mauled as a child and I . . . I just never understood the, uh, fascination of a pet that some people have."

"I'm with you on that," he said, causing her to turn a brief glance on him. He was walking with her and shaking his head. "This is my first dog, so

I'm not used to having to think about it. I'll keep better track of it in the future. Promise."

"Great." Tory tried to wipe one side of her glasses with a sleeve without taking them off.

She had to get out of there. If she was going to attend this man's round table she did *not* want him seeing her like this first. Not to mention that she didn't want him knowing anything about who she really was. She had planned to go completely anonymously, fake name and everything.

He kept up with her easily, his long legs eating up the sidewalk that her trembling knees were having trouble negotiating. "Please, won't you at least give me your number so I can get you some new glasses? Or wait, I'll give you mine and you can send me the bill."

"No, no. It's all right." She shook her head, at the same time thinking how much a new pair of glasses was going to cost. "I really have to go. My, uh, someone's waiting for me."

She always ran into trouble when a sentence required the word "boyfriend." It sounded so silly and immature. Not to mention that it was inaccurate at this point, something she sometimes forgot.

"I'll leave my information at the front desk," he said as she reached the door.

"Fine." Why didn't he just go away? Why couldn't she just deal with people's pets like a normal person? Why did people even *have* pets?

But there was no getting around Keenan James.

He reached out and grabbed the handle. As he pulled the door open, irrationally, a part of her balked at entering, still sure the animal was inside, lying in wait for her.

"She's upstairs, locked in the bathroom, several doors and an elevator ride away. Please don't worry," Keenan James said, having the effrontery to read her mind.

She made herself step into the foyer. "Thanks," she said without looking at him.

Thankfully, he let the door close behind her and stayed outside.

She stopped, catching her breath and putting two fingers to her wrist. Her pulse fired like a machine gun.

"Good afternoon, Dr. Hoffstra," the desk clerk said.

"Good afternoon, Mr. Perkins," she said. The voice that emerged was shaky and weak. She took another deep inhalation, then turned to the man behind the desk. "This may seem like a crazy question, but was Barbra Streisand here?"

"You didn't tell me Keenan James was moving into this building," Tory said, walking into Stewart's living room and unwinding the scarf from around her neck.

She was still twitching from the encounter with the dog, and the star, so her tone came out more accusatory than she'd intended.

Not that Stewart noticed. He looked up from the sheet music he was studying, his eyes meeting hers over the small half-glasses he used for reading. He frowned irritably. "What?"

Sometimes, when he wore those glasses, Tory thought he looked far older than his thirty-eight years. Maybe it was the thinning blond hair, in addition to the glasses. His face was certainly youthful enough.

His eyes cleared as he came out of concentration. "Oh, yes. Keenan James," he said casually. "Do you know him?"

She wasn't fooled. Stewart, for all his high-society pretensions, was a celebrity watcher par excellence. If they were in a restaurant with someone famous, he could spot them within two minutes and would go out of his way to say something to whoever it was. Usually it was something commiserating about how hard it was to have a private meal as a public persona that left the celebrity puzzling if Stewart was someone they should reciprocally recognize.

As a cellist in the New York City Symphony, however, Stewart was not nearly as well-known as he seemed to think, despite being profiled once, five years ago, in *New York Today* magazine. The exercise invariably embarrassed Tory, though she knew enough not to say anything to him.

"Of course I know him," she said. "I mean, I know who he is. Like everyone else in the country. Did he interview with the board?" She laid her coat on the arm of the sofa.

Stewart's eyes trailed to the coat and he frowned. Tory picked it up, walked it to the closet, and hung it up, all the while keeping an eye on Stewart.

"Yes he did. He was quite charming, actually. Not at all the demon you made him out to be in your article." Stewart gave her a smug smile.

She crossed her arms over her chest. "You could tell he was a good psychologist from his co-op interview, could you?"

An impatient look flitted across his face. "Of course not. But he was intelligent and sincere. A likable fellow. I'd have a hard time believing he was doing anything unethical."

Tory sighed. "Why, because he's famous?"

"Don't be ridiculous." Stewart took his glasses off and gave her his full attention. "Just because he's famous doesn't mean he's *not* ethical. You really have to get over this reverse prejudice you have, Tory."

She resisted the urge to roll her eyes. "Did you know he has a dog?"

Stewart managed to look simultaneously annoyed and abashed by averting his eyes while raising his chin. "It's the reason he's moving here. The dog belonged to his mother, I believe, but she died. Or moved, or something." He perched his half-glasses back on his nose and studied the sheet music. "I trust it won't be a problem. He lives on the top floor. We'll never see him or the animal."

"How can you know that? I just saw it out in

front of the building. The thing nearly took my arm off, if you must know."

He looked up at her and frowned skeptically. "It attacked you?"

She took off her glasses and tried cleaning them again on the hem of her shirt. "It didn't attack, exactly. But it was all over me. It ruined my glasses!" She held them up. "You *know* how I feel about dogs, Stewart."

She wished he would get up, ask her how she was, make a little bit of a fuss over her ordeal. It was immature, she knew, to be so needy, but just once she'd like him to be a little bit protective of her.

She put her glasses back on her face and scowled. They would definitely have to be replaced.

"I don't know what you expected me to do about that, Tory," he said, rising from the couch. "I could hardly refuse him residency because my girlfriend, or rather my *former* girlfriend, is afraid of dogs." He put an arm around her shoulder and kissed her on the top of the head. "The building does allow them, you know."

She didn't mean to, but she remained stiff in his embrace. He let go.

"I don't see any blood," he said, looking her over in mock-concern. "Are you all right?"

"I'm fine. But there's another problem," she said, sounding pouty and hating it. She cleared her throat and tried to adopt a more objective expression. She knew she was only making the day worse by complaining so much.

"And what's the other problem?" He moved toward the bar, a large, marble-topped affair near the windows overlooking West Eighty-sixth Street. He held up a short tumbler. "Bailey's?"

She let out a breath and nodded. After a second she went to the bar and sat on one of the tall leather stools. She didn't know why she felt so angry with Stewart. Maybe it was the adrenaline rush from the dog attack making her edgy. Not to mention nearly meeting Keenan James face-to-face.

"You know the meeting I had today with the publisher?" she said.

"Oh yes!" He looked at her with renewed interest. "How did that go?"

She slumped. "He didn't want my idea. He actually said he'd *never* want my idea. Or any of my ideas. He's got psychologists coming out his ears, apparently."

"Well, you can see where that might be true, what with Dr. Phil being so popular." He nodded, agreeing with himself. "So why did he want to see you?"

She leaned an elbow on the bar and put her cheek in her hand. "He wanted me to write someone else's book, and you'll never guess whose." She paused. "Keenan James."

Stewart's mouth dropped open. "But that's perfect! With him right here in the building, it couldn't be more convenient! We can have him over for dinner. You two can work in my den. Think of the exposure. Honey, you'll have a best-seller."

Tory leaned back on the stool. She should have anticipated this. Stewart looked at her as if she'd suddenly become some sort of celebrity herself. B-list, maybe. Or more like D-list, but still. A celebrity to him for potentially bringing one into his home.

He certainly wasn't seeing this from her point of view.

But then, shouldn't she be seeing it from *his*?

"But Mr. Fender didn't want *my* idea," she persisted. "And you know how I feel about Keenan James."

Stewart made a sound reflecting a close call and said, "*I* do, yes. But let's hope Fender doesn't."

He slid her Bailey's across the bar to her.

"He does," she said miserably. "That's one reason he wants me to write this. For balance. He likes my skepticism. So I'm supposed to go to one of James's round tables for a few weeks to see what he's doing. *Anonymously*. That's another reason it was so awful to be mauled by his dog just now. He can't know who I am."

Stewart mixed himself a martini, carefully wrapping the shaker in a fresh bar towel as he'd done ever since he'd heard about a man getting frostbite on his fingertips from the frozen side of a martini shaker. Stewart was very protective of his finger-tips.

"Why? He didn't know who you were." A strand of Stewart's comb-over came loose as he vigorously shook the martini.

Tory explained how she might look familiar at the first meeting now that James had seen her, and how awkward that might be if he thought she lived in his building.

"So I need to look like someone else when I go to the round table. I don't want him to make the connection. And I should go by a different name. Maybe my first name," she mused.

"Engelberta?" Stewart laughed. "I'm not sure that's a good idea."

"Oh right." She looked at him gratefully. "That's the name I used on the 'No Psychobabble' article. In fact, I use it on all my articles. How could I forget?" She laughed.

"That's not what I meant," Stewart said. "I just meant, my God, what a name. You sure you want someone like Keenan James thinking your name is Engelberta?"

"My name *is* Engelberta. Engelberta Victoria Hoffstra, as you should know by now."

"Well, sure. But Engelberta's not the one you use." He sipped his drink, closing his eyes and savoring the taste. "Mmm."

"It's the one I use professionally, including the very article that used him as an example of every-

thing that's wrong with pop psychology. As I said."
She sipped her Bailey's but it was hard getting it
down her suddenly tight throat.

"Oh honey. Don't worry about that." Stewart
rounded the bar and ran a hand along her back
comfortingly. "There's no way *he'd* have heard of
you."

Tory slowly put her glass back down on the bar,
her day now officially worse than it had been even
ten minutes before. Stewart was right. Of course he
was right. There was no way Keenan James would
care or even remember who the mousy little woman was that his dog had attacked today. Nor would
he know who she was from her article. She'd bet
her life he'd never read a magazine—or anything
else—about psychology.

She wasn't nearly as well-known as she thought.
She and Stewart were quite the pair, she surmised
glumly. Both of them suffering delusions of gran-
deur. The only difference was, Stewart managed to
hang on to his, while hers were disproved, sometimes multiple times in one day.

Chapter 3

"Oh my." The woman behind the cosmetics counter at Saks frowned at her. "Of course I help you. We have excellent product, and you have lovely skin. Just little bit pale, yes?"

She could have been Spanish or Polish, all Tory knew was that the woman had an accent. More importantly, however, her dark curly hair surrounded a flawless complexion, rich dark eyes, and a wide, deeply colored mouth, all of which was accented by layers of deftly applied makeup.

She was pretty in a way that would have looked better without the makeup, Tory thought. And her perfume was way too strong. But based on her looks alone Tory was confident she'd know how to take Tory's less dramatic gray-eyed blondness and turn it into something . . . different. Hopefully something that wasn't clownlike.

"Yes, I'm always a little pale. I don't wear much makeup," she said, "but today is kind of a . . . a special occasion."

Such a special occasion, she'd gone to the eye doctor and had been set up with contacts. It had taken her forty-five minutes to get them in, but the optometrist had assured her it would become second nature in no time.

They felt a little strange—or maybe it was just strange not to feel her glasses on her nose—but she liked the way she looked. Her face didn't look so small and insignificant without the giant lenses. And, most importantly, because she was going to the Just-Dump-Him Round Table, she could *not* look like herself.

For one thing, she didn't want Keenan James making the connection between her and the woman he'd rescued from his vicious dog last week.

For another, she wanted to look like a woman in a dead-end relationship, with no self-respect, who felt the need to color herself with synthetic products to be attractive to men.

"And you are wearing that?" The saleswoman's eyes raked over Tory's suit.

Tory looked down too. "Well, yes." She returned her gaze to the saleswoman. "Why?"

The woman tilted her head and held out her hands with a shrug of the sort Tory considered "European." Italian, maybe.

"Well," she said, doubt dripping from her tone, "is the color, you know . . . is rather . . . dead, yes? Makes you look dead. Nobody should wear that. Like a computer, yes? But with a little green, like sick stomach."

Tory looked back down at her suit—which had cost a significant amount. She was not one to skimp on clothes, if for no other reason than that she expected them to last for decades. The color was "bone," but perhaps it did edge a bit toward "putty." It went with everything.

The woman relented and smiled again, holding out her hand. "My name is Katya. And you are?"

"Tory."

They shook hands.

For just a second she wondered what it must be like to be a "Katya," with an exotic accent and that voluptuous body. Despite the fact that she worked in a department store, the woman for all her make-up and perfume looked dramatic and interesting, as if she'd had lives and experiences a practical Tory would never know. She could as easily have been standing in front of an apartment building on the Upper West Side clutching a small dog and dripping diamonds, as behind a cosmetics counter in a department store. Tory would have taken her for an heiress, maybe an ambassador's wife.

"Okay, Tory. I call my sister. She will help you." The woman turned on her heel and headed behind the counter.

"Wait! Don't bother, please. I don't have that kind of time." What in the world was the woman thinking? That her sister would come here from God knows where and—and *dress* her?

Katya waved a hand. "Is not bother. She works in misses. She can be here in"—another shrug— "two minute."

Sure enough, before Tory could even settle herself on the swivel stool at the makeup counter, Katya's sister—Sasha—was there eyeing her like a headmistress on inspection day.

"You are size six, I think, yes? Maybe four sometimes?" Sasha wore her dark hair cut bluntly at her chin, with thick bangs that hid her eyebrows. Her dark eyes were rimmed with black so that she looked like an exotic doll, dressed in dark tights, short skirt, platform shoes, and a tiny, low-dipping shirt in what looked like tie-dyed silk.

Tory shook her head. These women were born to flatter, she guessed. "I'm a ten."

Sasha looked at her as if she'd confessed to wearing men's clothing. "No! Absolutely not. You will swim in ten. Look at this suit, yes?" She pinched some fabric near Tory's waist, and Tory felt the skirt tighten across her hips. "Much better. You have cute figure. You don't need to dress in bags, you know."

Tory felt her face get hot. *Bags?*

Sasha took one last look up and down Tory's body, clicked her tongue behind her teeth, and said, "I will be back." Then she turned and left.

Tory was reminded of the Terminator's *I'll be back* and felt nearly as threatened.

"Okay, first we do your face, yes?" Katya said brightly. "A special occasion! You are meeting a man?" She rounded the glass counter to come to Tory's side and indicated the tall chair next to what looked like a surgeon's palette of instruments, jars, cotton balls, and swabs. "Please sit."

"I'm going to a luncheon," Tory said. "And I don't want to look like myself. At all. In fact I want to look like the complete opposite of myself."

"Ah yes. I understand." Katya smiled knowingly. "All right, we get to work." She picked up a bottle of clear liquid that smelled like rubbing alcohol but was probably called something like youthening serum and sold for a hundred dollars, wet a cotton ball, and began circling it over Tory's face. "You have wonderful features and good clear skin. For me, this is treat, you know? A blank canvas for Katya, the artist, yes?"

Tory had the mean thought that she'd rather be blank on the outside than the inside, then mentally kicked herself. *You're just threatened by women like Katya. You don't understand their preoccupation with beauty.*

Katya picked up another bottle and poured a little of its contents on a triangular sponge. She wore a half-dozen gold bracelets that clanged together as she patted the stuff onto Tory's chin.

Katya's breath smelled like mint. She stepped back again and studied Tory's face with a critical expression. Then she picked up a small jar and poured its flesh-colored contents onto a sponge.

This was one reason Tory didn't like makeup. This soft, smeary feeling of laying something on top of her skin to lie there all day was unpleasant. For one thing, she was sure she'd forget it was there and end up with the stuff all over her hands, neck, hair, clothes, whatever, and look ridiculous all day.

Well, it was for a good cause. She wanted to look like a woman who would get involved with stupid sleazy men, instead of the woman she was: a sensible, intelligent professional, who was content with her steady, stalwart Stewart Reasoner, concert cellist for the New York City Symphony.

Or had been content, she reminded herself. And would be content again with someone *like* him whom she also wanted to sleep with.

Katya worked for what seemed like forever, applying layer after layer of lotions, potions, and powders. Look up, look down, close your eyes, turn your head. Tory felt as if she were a prize pony getting ready for a show. Would she even be able to eat with all this stuff on her face? She imagined opening her mouth and her face cracking like a New York sidewalk after a hard winter.

After an eternity, Katya stepped back, beaming. Tory started to turn toward the mirror, but Katya held up her ringed hands and said, "Stup! You wait a moment, yes?"

Then, with a conspiratorial smile, she crossed the cosmetics department on her high-spiked heels and disappeared.

Tory sat on the stool. Around her, perfectly coiffed, porcelain-faced women chatted and moved with graceful efficiency in pseudo-lab coats of varying but serious shades of black, gray, and white.

It was a foreign land, but one Tory could see the sisterhood of. Women of all shapes, sizes, colors, and styles approached the salespeople behind the counters, some tentatively, some with confidence, seeking help from these chic benefactors of beauty.

They left with a lilt in their step that spoke of a problem solved. Tory reached for her purse, pulled out a pad of paper and a pen, and noted the phenomenon. "Makeup as confidence, surface solutions, moments of hope. Ultimately destructive?" she wrote. When those women arrived at home with bags full of merchandise they'd spent a fortune on and still saw the same person in the mirror, were they better off or worse? When the product did not turn them into a Katya, did that spring leave their step in a bigger way than when they'd entered the store?

A moment later Katya reappeared with Sasha, who clutched a fistful of hangers from which clothing flowed like banners.

"Here, try, please," Sasha said, then leaned her head toward her sister and muttered something in a foreign language.

Katya stood back with a brilliant smile, and, just as she had advised Tory, her red lipstick really did make her teeth look astonishingly white.

Sasha held a shirt of pale peach, a type of knit pullover that Tory never wore. With that she had a dark brown skirt, a pair of pants in a similar shade, and what looked like an alligator-skin belt.

"You try?" she said again as Tory stared. "I had another beautiful skirt, very short, but I think you are more conservative, yes? This is very pretty stuff. You will like it, promise."

The look on Sasha's face was commanding, but the expression Katya wore was so hopeful, Tory felt like taking out her pad again and noting that the experience of imparting beauty might hold some therapeutic benefit for the benefactor as well.

"All right," Tory said and held out her hand. The clothes were light on the hangers and she fingered the belt. It was a rich, thick leather that was somehow supple at the same time. She caught a glimpse of the price tag and nearly choked.

"I'm sorry, but there's no way—"

But Katya and Sasha were off and running.

"This way," Katya sang as she sailed across the store with a stride that Tory could match only because she wore flats. How Katya did it in those stilts she wore—not to mention Sasha in her platforms—was a mystery.

They reached the dressing rooms, and it seemed Katya was ready to step right in with her.

Tory turned and held out a palm. "I'll come out."

She closed the dressing room door and turned to the mirror. There, reflected back at her, was a face she honestly did not recognize. It was as if a surrealist painter had done her portrait—right on her face. Tory couldn't help it, she laughed out loud.

"Something is wrong?" Katya called from the other side of the door.

Sasha added ominously, "If size is wrong I will get another."

"Don't give up," Katya added. "You are beautiful girl!"

Oh yeah, right, she thought, still laughing to herself.

"No, I'm fine. I just . . . didn't recognize myself."

She heard Katya's low chuckle. "Is good, yes? This is what we want, when we come to store. To have 'new me.' Yes?"

Tory shook her head and watched her painted lips curve upward. *New me, indeed.* "Yes. It's new all right."

As the sisters chattered in the unknown language

outside her cubicle, Tory pushed out of her "bag" suit and pulled into the clothes Sasha had picked out. Slowly, miraculously, Tory felt something amazing happen. She felt lighter, somehow. Comfortable. Like she did in her pajamas. But when she looked at herself in the mirror, she was not the frumpy, flanneled woman she was in the morning; she was tall, trim, and graceful-looking.

The peach shirt highlighted the color Katya had put in her cheeks, and the skirt draped over her slim hips so perfectly, she almost felt as if she were wearing nothing. The hem hit her just at the knee, but was so tailored that she felt as if she were wearing something deliberately sexy.

Katya knocked on the door. "You like?"

Yes, Tory had to admit. She liked. It wasn't her, she reminded herself, but was it someone who would go to a Keenan James round table? She more thought it was someone who'd lunch at Lutece and go shopping in the afternoon.

"Tory?" Katya knocked again. "Sasha can look for other things. You must not give up."

Sharp words from Sasha in that foreign language had Katya shushing her.

Tory opened the door and stepped toward the three-way mirror.

Katya beamed. "Yes."

Even Sasha looked satisfied.

Tory looked at herself from all angles. "Yes," she had to admit. "I do like it."

"Wait." Katya went to the dressing room to retrieve the belt Tory had forgotten. She helped her put it on, then stepped back. "Excellent."

"We get shoes to match. And bag," Sasha determined.

Tory took a deep breath. Alligator shoes and bag. Would she look like someone looking for schlock therapy? She didn't care. She wouldn't look like herself, that was for sure. And she was so darn comfortable.

"You have time to curl hair?" Katya asked, touching the bun Tory wore. "Is beautiful color. Like butter."

"My hair doesn't curl," she said, not sure she could handle much more change. It was nice, it felt good, but she felt like a traitor to herself for liking what the sisters had done. At least there was no risk of her being able to replicate it at home.

"Okay, we get you nice, classy barrette and let some down your back, yes? You look like beautiful, classy woman." Katya nodded in satisfaction.

Tory began tallying the costs in her head. Even if she bought none of the makeup—which she had no intention of doing anyway—it came to several hundred dollars. For clothes she wouldn't wear again. Would she?

She looked at her watch, then back at herself in the mirror. She didn't have time to go home and search her closet for something other than the bag suit.

"Okay." She expelled a breath. "I'll take it. I'll take it all."

Katya beamed. Sasha nodded.

What the heck, Tory thought. Maybe she could write the expense off on her taxes.

⌖

Lunch at the Metropolitan Grill was something Keenan never got tired of. Which was a good thing, considering it was something he did a lot. Once a week with two different groups of women.

The lunches had started innocuously enough. He'd taken one of Brady's castoffs out to lunch to help her deal with Brady's dumping, and he'd talked some sense to her. She was a gorgeous woman, with a brain, and a future, someone who had no business sacrificing herself to grief over losing his once-insensitive brother.

Not that he didn't love his brother. Of course he did. Brady was sharp, witty, adventurous, and never dull. And he was good-looking. Women got roped in by his charm, frustrated by his emotional unavailability, then heartbroken by his short attention span.

And for a while there—before this new woman had turned his brother into someone Keenan had always hoped lurked inside—Brady had a habit of dropping women by taking up with a new one before telling the old one it was over.

Keenan, who believed in honesty above all things,

had made friends with a few of these women and told them exactly what had happened and why. Including why the women had fallen for the man in the first place.

They liked a challenge. Brady was unavailable, a little bit untamed, and each thought she was the woman to change that. So why couldn't they take that courage, that belief in themselves that *they* were the ones capable of that difficult job, and turn it to something more productive? They were more than slaves to the unattainable man, weren't they? They had more to offer the world than just taming an asshole.

It was tough talk like this that led that first woman to invite some friends to her next lunch with Keenan. Then those women invited friends. Then they decided to make it a weekly thing. Before he knew it, the first woman had moved on and he had three groups he met with regularly.

From there, the lecture circuit was a natural. With his experience as a television writer—and in particular a television writer who wrote about a psychiatrist—he knew how to hold and control an audience. And it paid off. His seminar recorded for The Discovery Channel was one of the most watched of their programs the previous year.

Keenan got out of the cab in front of the Met Grill and straightened his jacket. He had to admit that sometimes it was a daunting idea to go into the restaurant, knowing he was going to be bombarded by women's tales of perpetual woe. Sometimes he wondered what on earth he could say to the women who put up with the same thing, day after day after day, then came to him to complain about it.

Today wasn't one of those days, though. He had a new woman joining the group, a favor to the man he hoped was going to publish his book. Vicky Smith was a friend of his wife's who'd been struggling in a dead-end relationship for years, apparently. She was a pretty girl, Fender had said, who didn't realize it, and didn't know how to play it up or take advantage of it. She was also smart as a whip, Fender had added a bit wryly, and didn't know how to tone it down around others. Maybe she antagonized the boyfriend with it and that's why he wouldn't commit.

Keenan thought she'd fit in well with his Monday group, who also thought they knew everything yet came faithfully to these meetings in the hope of fixing their men, or finding their men, or leaving their men, depending.

The entry to the restaurant was crowded, as usual, but William, the maître d', spotted him over the heads of the others and waved him forward.

"They're all here, sir," he said with a smile, "along with one extra. We made room for her at the table. I hope you were expecting her?"

"I was, William, thanks. I should have warned you about that."

"Not a problem, sir."

Keenan made his way through the crowded room, aware of the eyes upon him. His round tables had gotten famous of late. It was lucky there was a large table toward the back of the room that allowed for some privacy, as, according to William, some people requested seating nearby in order to eavesdrop on the conversations. The skilled maître d' did not oblige those people, of course, but others were more subtle. Keenan had seen an article or two in the paper quoting things overheard at the table, which was why he advised the women to use false names for their significant others, and only first names for one another.

The group was there and chatting animatedly when he arrived. The new woman—not chatting with anyone—looked at him sharply, assessing him from head to foot with pale, disdainful eyes.

This will be interesting. Keenan smiled right into those eyes and said, "Hello, ladies. I see that I'm the late one today."

Fender had been wrong. This new woman wasn't plain. Her large gray eyes were immediately arresting, and not just because they were so direct. They were fringed with long, dark lashes and highlighted by well-defined cheekbones. Though her hair was drawn back rather severely, the pastel shirt she wore softened the look and showed off a trim figure.

"You're not late, Keenan, you're right on time," Angelica said, looking at her watch. As usual the tall black woman's hair was done up in a high, elaborate style, with tendrils and swirls and ornaments that made her even taller and more dramatic than her clothes and bearing already did. Keenan loved seeing what Angelica turned up wearing every week. She was an artist, and it showed.

"You do *not* want to date a guy with a Doberman," Jan was saying. She was a stocky woman with short brown hair and sensible shoes who had a habit of judging a man by his dog, or what kind of dog he might be if he happened to be one. This held new appeal to Keenan since he'd inherited Barbra Streisand, but he hadn't been sure he wanted to hear the verdict on a man who owned a golden doodle, so he had yet to confess his newfound status as a dog owner.

Though she wore no makeup and walked like a truck driver, she had a no-nonsense way of talking that he liked.

"What's wrong with a guy who has a Doberman?" He sat, straightening his jacket as he did so, and laid his forearms on the edge of the table.

"Major macho issues," she said. "All those big guard-dog types have 'em. Be especially careful if they've got their ears cropped. The dog's ears, that is. That's the mark of a man who doesn't care who he hurts, as long as he looks good."

"What if he adopted the Doberman?" Martina, another woman in the group, asked. "If it was a rescue."

"Doesn't matter," Jan said, shaking her head. "He could have adopted a Lab. You want a good relationship? Look for a guy with a retriever. That's a guy who knows about give and take."

"He may ask you to fetch him a beer, however," Keenan said.

Jan laughed, and her eyes showed confidence. Keenan felt a small bloom of gratification. When she'd arrived at the round table for the first time four months ago, she'd been so prickly and defensive, a joke like that would have set her off. Now that she'd gained some self-esteem, she felt less threatened by those around her and trusting of the group; she was positively easygoing.

"So what held you up?" Jan asked him.

Keenan blew out his cheeks, thinking back on the wrestling match he'd just endured. "Long story. I couldn't get a dog out of my shower. But I'll tell you more about that later."

"A dog?" Jan said brightly. "I didn't know you had a dog, Keenan. What kind?"

He grinned. "Not a Doberman."

Chapter 4

There were five of them, with the new woman, a number that Keenan liked. He wanted five women so that if opinions were split on a subject there was never a tie, and he himself was not asked to weigh in. He'd learned a thing or two in the years he'd been doing this and knew it was better for him to point things out conversationally. Let the others take a stand in opposition if they wanted.

"Okay. We've got someone new joining us today, as I'm sure you all noticed."

All eyes shifted to Vicky Smith, who, for all her

assessing looks, appeared uncomfortable under the scrutiny.

"This is Vicky," Keenan continued. "Why don't you tell us about yourself, Vicky. Just the basics, what you do, your relationship status, and why you're here. You don't need to get specific, and don't forget, we use false names for our significant others."

She shot him a look, and he could tell she wanted to say something she thought she shouldn't. She restrained herself, though. With some effort, he thought, suppressing a smile.

There was no doubt in his mind that this woman was a plant put here by the publisher. Why else would Fender have asked him to take her on before finalizing the book deal? So he wanted to check out what Keenan was doing, that was fine. Though he wasn't sure why the *Straight Talk* TV program wasn't enough.

Vicky glanced around the table, her head back as if she could pull into her shell like a turtle.

"Hi." Her eyes swept the circle. "My name's Vicky and I'm a dentist. I'm here because I recently broke up with my boyfriend but I'm not sure it was the right decision. I had been thinking he took me for granted, but he's steady and reliable, and I know he cares about me. The problem was, we just weren't passionate, but maybe you don't need that past a certain point. We were together eight years."

She nodded once in punctuation of this rundown.

Keenan studied her a moment, sure she was lying about something, but unfazed by it. Chances were she was lying about everything. But even if she wasn't, most of the women who came here fudged things at first, and why wouldn't they? Who would trust a bunch of strangers right off the bat?

Well, Martina would, and she was the one who spoke up now.

"So you're here because you're not sure you should get back together with your boyfriend or not sure you should marry him?" Martina asked, leaning forward over the table.

"Well, both," Vicky said.

"Does he hit you or anything?" Martina asked. "Throw stuff? Threaten to leave you?"

"No, nothing like that," Vicky Smith said, unrattled. "He doesn't have that kind of passion either."

"Passion," Martina snorted. "I guess you can call it that. My Rex once threw a frozen lasagna at me."

"Oh stop, Martina," Jan said. "Did it actually *hit* you?"

Martina angled her shoulders at Jan and put one hand on her hip. "It damn near broke my foot."

"You didn't answer my question. Did it *touch* you? Did even one drop of tomato sauce land on your person?"

"Well . . . no," Martina said, with an indignant pout, flipping her long dark hair behind her shoulders, "but it came damn close and if it had it *would* have broken my foot, believe me."

"Hmph." Jan smirked.

"Why did he throw a lasagna at you?" the new woman, Vicky, asked.

"Because I said I wasn't in the mood for Italian. We'd been arguing about what to eat. I wanted to go out for Chinese and he's too cheap to go to a restaurant more than once a month."

"What did you do after he threw it?" Vicky continued.

"I put it back in the freezer." She shrugged. "It was still good."

Vicky tilted her head, focused intently on Martina. "I meant, what did you do to Rex?"

"Oh, Rex." She laughed. "I didn't sleep with him for a week. Not that he noticed." She mugged for Jan.

"Martina," Keenan interrupted, "that was a good question. How did you react to the lasagna at the moment Rex threw it? Did you *say* anything to him? Tell him to get the hell out, threaten to call the police, anything?"

He glanced at Vicky and noted her expression going from disapproving to suspicious. An improvement, he thought. She obviously thought he was going to be an idiot.

"Were you afraid? Or angry?" Vicky added.

Martina sighed and glanced at Vicky. "I guess I was intimidated. When he gets like that, if I say anything at all he blows up. I didn't want to risk it. I mean, like I said, it didn't really hit me."

Jan shook her head. "I could have predicted that from the start if you'd told us about the Doberman."

"He doesn't even have it anymore," Martina said. "That was years ago."

"But hadn't he already blown up?" Vicky asked. "Isn't that why he threw the lasagna?"

Martina shook her head. "No, throwing things is usually the first step. If he misses me—and he usually does—and I don't react, a lot of times it blows over. Then later, after he's calmed down, I can get mad."

"So you can only express your feelings on his schedule," Vicky surmised.

Good point, Keenan thought.

Martina's eyes looked inward a moment. "Yeah, sort of. I guess so."

"Wait a minute," Jan interjected, looking at Vicky. "We were talking about your issues, not Martina's. We all know all about Martina's. I want to hear more about why you're here. Your boyfriend won't marry you?"

Keenan interjected. "Martina, were you through?"

Martina, still looking pensive, nodded. "Sure."

"So, Vicky." He turned to her. "Tell us about your boyfriend. And what should we call him?"

"Louis," she said promptly, looking at him in a businesslike way. She took a deep breath. "He's not very passionate or romantic, and even though we were together a long time, marriage didn't ever come up."

"And are you passionate and romantic?" He had to ask. She looked like a ballbuster.

That made her gaze drop to the table. "Well, sometimes. I try to be."

"And what does he do when you try?"

She shrugged. "He doesn't notice. I don't think. And I end up feeling foolish."

"Honey," Angelica said, "it sounds like you need to be at Victoria's Secret instead of here."

The group laughed. Vicky Smith didn't.

Keenan glanced over at the last member of the group, Ruth Bitterman. Ruth was by far the quietest member, as well as the oldest. Somewhere around sixty, she came because she had some of the same issues Vicky Smith did. Ruth's husband made her feel invisible, and it was hardly surprising, considering how invisible she usually made herself when she came here. She was little more than a shadow of a presence.

"I believe an intimate relationship should be possible without playing those sorts of games," Vicky said archly. "I don't want to have to dress up in a costume in order to be appreciated."

"Actually, game playing can be pretty hot," Keenan said. Though the group howled, he gave Vicky a gentle smile. "A lot of guys I know are into it."

"What do you do, Keenan, dress up as Batman or something?" Martina asked.

Keenan shot her a quick grin. "We're not here to talk about me. So Vicky, did you ever say anything to Louis about his lack of passion? Ask him if there was something he was missing, something he'd like you to do?"

She shrugged. "I don't think he was missing anything. It was me who wanted more. He seemed content to leave things pretty . . . platonic."

"That doesn't really answer my question. Do you ever say anything to him about it specifically?"

"What are we talking about here?" Angelica asked. "Will he not give it up, or is it just not romantic enough for you?"

"Yeah, how often did you all have sex?" Martina asked. "A lot or a little?"

Vicky looked like a deer caught in the headlights; those pretty gray eyes bounced from one to another in the group, and he saw her attempting to calculate an answer.

"It's up to you how you answer, Vicky," he said, "but I've found that if you respond quickly, with the first thing that comes into your head, we get closer to the truth than if you think about it too much."

"We had sex on, uh, Fridays," she said on a huff of breath.

Angelica raised a brow. "Just Fridays?"

Vicky nodded.

"Every Friday?" Martina asked.

Vicky nodded again. "Like clockwork."

Angelica laughed. "That sounds exciting."

A considering expression crossed Vicky's face. "At least it was regular."

"That's right," Martina agreed. "Some people don't get it that often. Did you ever try to get him into it on another day?"

Vicky thought for a moment. "Yes. Once I tried on a Saturday, after a dinner party we had."

"What did he say?" Martina asked.

Vicky hesitated. "Well, it was before the dishes were cleaned up. And it was very late. I guess I'd had a few too many glasses of wine, and he does hate it when I've done that—"

"Why are you making his excuses for him?" Angelica asked, her tone incensed.

"I'm just telling you what he said—"

"That's what he said when you tried to get him into bed?" Martina asked, aghast. "That the dishes weren't done?"

"Among other things. Mostly I think he just wasn't in the mood." Vicky shrugged again.

"Vicky," Keenan said, "why do you think you stayed so long with a man who wasn't interested in you sexually?"

The table went silent. Vicky Smith's cheeks went pink.

"That's not true," she said quietly, but firmly. "He *was* interested."

"On Fridays," Martina added.

Vicky glanced at her. "That's right. But then he was *very* interested."

"But he didn't want it any other time," Keenan confirmed. "Like a Wednesday. Right after work, say, when he wasn't tired and you hadn't been drinking?"

"That's right." She inclined her head slowly. "He . . . he said it wasn't Friday. And that I'd just have to wait."

"You'd just have to wait!" Angelica spouted. "Get real, girl! You're a dentist, why didn't you drill him a new one?"

"Sounds to me like he's using sex as control," Keenan said.

For a second, it almost looked as if she was going to smile. "Well, he certainly controlled the sex."

The group laughed and Vicky did smile then.

"Tell me, Vicky," he said mildly, "did you control every other aspect of the relationship?"

Just as he'd suspected—as he'd *intended*—the smile dropped from her face.

After a long moment of silence, Jan said, "He doesn't own a dog, does he?"

Vicky shook her head. "No, thank God."

"I didn't think so," Jan said. "He sounds like a basset hound to me."

Vicky frowned in Jan's direction. "All I know is he's a good friend, and a dear person, and we get along perfectly. Isn't that what marriage is supposed to be? So am I too concerned about passion?"

"Honey," Angelica said, "you might as well be living with your mother as with this man, it sounds to me. Or get yourself a roommate. You don't need to marry someone just because you get along."

"Yes but . . . children," she said, lifting one shoulder. "What if you want a—a family?"

"You're not going to get children either if you're not sleeping with him," Martina said. "Keenan, what does it say when a guy won't sleep with you?"

Keenan leaned back and looked at Vicky. "It could say a lot of things. Could be a medical issue, he could have low levels of testosterone, a naturally low libido, or maybe he's lazy. He's not attracted to Vicky anymore but he doesn't want to break up and have to find someone new."

Vicky turned a glare on him, but Angelica laid a hand on her forearm. "Take it easy, honey, he does this all the time. He's not trying to insult you."

"He's not insulting *me*," Vicky said, her back straightening. "I just don't see how such simplistic advice can help me, or anyone."

"You know, this brings me to something I've noticed," Keenan said, leaning his arms on the table again and looking around the group. "What is it about women that they have to complicate things all the time? Is it because the more convoluted they make things, the easier it is to get away with not making a decision? Because I could come up with a hundred lame reasons why this guy won't sleep with you, but none of them would help. The bottom line is, you were in a relationship that wasn't satisfying, so you got out. Good move."

"Number four!" Jan crowed. "Gotta have that bang!"

Vicky frowned. "What?"

"It's the acronym," Martina said, looking at her as if she hadn't heard of the president. "*Seal The Deal, Baby*. Sex, Trust, Dedication, Bang!"

"Bang?" She looked incredulous.

Keenan smiled lazily. "Ah, a woman who hasn't experienced the bang."

The group groaned on her behalf. Keenan laughed. Vicky turned bright red.

He softened his voice. "Listen, Vicky. It sounds like you had sex with this man, and you definitely had trust. You received and felt dedication to him and to the relationship. But there was no *bang*, no pizzazz, no excitement." He shook his head. "You gotta have the bang."

"'Pizzazz'?" she repeated, her voice dripping with disdain. "You're telling me to give up a guy with a thousand good qualities because of 'pizzazz'?"

"Hey, I'm not telling you to do anything," Keenan said, leaning back in his chair. "But it sounds to me as if you already did."

"See," Jan said after a moment, "that's what a Labrador will get you. Pizzazz. A basset hound?" She shook her head. "Not so much."

❮❮❯❯

This was a joke, Tory thought. It had to be. Surely Franklin Fender, publisher of such classics as *In*

Search of the Real Dr. Freud and *Darwin or Disaster*, thought she'd get a kick out of coming to amateur hour at the Metropolitan and then offer her a book contract.

He could not possibly, *conceivably* want her to write a book with a psychological underpinning like *Seal The Deal, Baby*.

She was tempted to look around for television cameras. Could it be some kind of reality show? Take a degreed and licensed psychologist, throw her into what felt like a teenage soap opera, and see how she handles it. Except people loved crap like this. Nobody would get why she was so appalled.

She took a deep breath and managed to keep a straight face, instead of running howling for the door.

"I'm not sure that dogs have any real relevance here," she said slowly.

Chapter 5

"So what did you think?"

Tory turned to find Angelica, the tall, thin black woman in the group, looking at her through calm, heavy-lidded eyes. Her hair stood high over her head, making her look like a sculpture of an ancient goddess.

They stood on the sidewalk outside the restaurant, Tory pawing through her purse for her parking stub and Angelica putting black leather gloves onto her long-fingered hands.

"I'm sorry?" Tory asked, one hand still deep in her purse.

A slight smile turned up the woman's coral-colored lips. "I asked what you thought of your first round table. He was a little tougher on you than most, for your first time."

Tory's cheeks pinkened. "I, uh, it was interesting. And I'm fine. He can be tough if he wants."

Heck, *she* could be tough. Ask anyone.

Angelica gave an elegant lift to one shoulder. "He doesn't like to mess around with too much information. He gets the basic story, then makes a decision."

Tory couldn't help scoffing. "Yes, it's much easier to make a decision without all of the information."

Angelica gathered her coat around her neck and tilted her head, the small smile still in place. "You seem pretty determined not to trust him. Did you think he was wrong about you and Louis?"

Tory thought a moment. She didn't want to appear too skeptical, as then it would make no sense that she was there. And she'd like to get to know some of the women individually, at least to hear their opinions on his "counseling."

In keeping with her strategy, she decided to stick close to the truth.

"I'll give him the sex-as-control thing," she said, thinking how much worse his assessment would have been if she'd admitted they hadn't even had sex on Fridays in something like seven months before they broke up. "That was on target. I admit, I was impressed. But turning the control around on me was nothing but a psychological parlor trick."

"You sound like you've been in therapy before," Angelica said.

"A little." Tory shrugged evasively. "But I don't think what went on here today was therapy so much as advice, or opinion sharing."

"Therapy comes in many different forms," Angelica said. "Don't you think?"

Tory looked back into her purse as her fingers found a small piece of paper. "In the colloquial sense, sure." She pulled the parking stub out with a triumphant "Aha!"

Angelica laughed. "You *drive* in this city? Where do you live?"

"Brooklyn Heights. And no, I don't normally drive, but I'm going out to my parents' for dinner tonight so I borrowed a friend's car."

Angelica nodded. "Have a nice time, then. I'll see you next week."

"Thanks. Yes," Tory agreed.

Angelica turned and started to walk away, then turned back. "Unless . . . ?"

Tory stopped and turned back too. "Unless?"

"I'm having a show, downtown, on Friday night. Would you be interested in coming?"

"A show?" Tory's mind leaped from wondering if Angelica was a singer to a performance artist to a Rockette. All seemed equally possible; the woman was nothing if not mysterious. Tory wished Angelica had said something about the reason she was in the group today.

"I'm an artist, a painter. Most of my work is carried by the Bender-Glass Gallery on Spring Street, and they're bringing out some of my new work on Friday. A few of the girls will be there." Her expression was casual, but friendly. "Just a thought. Don't worry if you can't make it."

Tory's mind went on alert. "A few of the girls? From the group, do you mean?"

Angelica nodded.

Tory thought quickly. She was supposed to go to dinner with Louis—er, Stewart—but this was more important. This was an opportunity to speak to some of the girls in the group, get their take on Keenan James's advice without the man himself anywhere in sight. That could render invaluable information.

"I'd love to," Tory said. "I had no idea you were an artist. What time?"

"Any time between seven and ten. It's an opening, so there'll be wine." She smiled conspiratorially, then glanced at her watch. "See you then, Vicky. Got to run. I've got an appointment for a manicure in ten minutes. Another form of therapy." Angelica winked, then turned, curled four fingers in a wave over her shoulder as she sauntered off down the sidewalk with all the grace of a runway model.

Tory exhaled slowly and let loose a genuine smile. Perfect. She was in.

"You should do that more often."

Once again, she turned toward the voice behind her and found Keenan James looking at her with a pretty darn nice-looking smile of his own.

"I smile often," she said, wiping the current one from her face. "Not usually when I'm being told I'm a control freak, though."

He wagged a finger. "I never said that."

An attendant from the parking garage, obviously spotting the ticket in Tory's hand, approached her, and she handed him the stub.

Keenan's eyes lit. "Ah, you have a car."

Despite herself, she smiled again. "My, you *are* perceptive."

He grinned. "I hate to ask, but I'm late for an appointment. Any chance you can give me a ride uptown? I need to be somewhere in about fifteen minutes, and it's impossible to catch a cab at lunch around here."

She hesitated. Did she really want to talk to Keenan James outside the confines of the group? She was, after all, playing a part at the round table. Keeping it up out here made it feel more like a lie. Why that hadn't occurred to her after Angelica's invitation, she couldn't say. Maybe because that was for a good cause. She had to know if what he was doing was harming those women in any way.

"Never mind, I can see it messes with your schedule," he said, surprisingly little judgment in his tone.

"No, it's all right. I was just calculating my route and my timing. But it's fine." What an excellent liar she was turning out to be, she noted. They turned back toward the parking garage and stood awkwardly side by side, waiting for the attendant to bring the prehistoric Mercedes she'd borrowed from her neighbor.

"So," Tory began, unable to bear the silence any longer, "couldn't get a dog out of your shower?"

Keenan's laugh was, literally, spine tingling, low and intimate. "Yeah, I inherited a puppy from my mother when she went into the nursing home. Turns out it's afraid of jackhammers and they're doing roadwork on my street."

"A puppy, huh?" she said wryly, remembering the giant dog that had nearly taken her arm off.

"More of an adolescent, really," he said. "You don't know anything about training dogs, do you?"

Tory snorted, then straightened and looked at him out of the corner of her eye. Vicky Smith didn't snort. She was too well-dressed.

"No, sorry, I don't," Tory said. "It sounds as though you could ask Jan, though. She seems like something of an . . ." *Obsessive.* " . . . authority on the subject."

"Oh my God!" A female voice shrieked, and half a second later a gaggle of young, well-dressed girls were rushing across the sidewalk toward them on precarious-looking heels. "Are you Keenan James?"

"Ohmigod, I loved *Sex at Midnight*. Are you going to write another show?"

"What about a sequel? Or a movie?"

"I saw you on The Discovery Channel. I dumped my boyfriend because of it."

Tory looked from the adoring girls to Keenan, who seemed to be basking in the attention. He gave them a megawatt smile and tried to answer their questions, even though they fired them without consideration of a reply.

Tory was feeling as invisible as the nearby fire hydrant when she heard the unmistakable sound of her neighbor's car in the garage. A moment later, its diesel engine rattling like a box of bones, the attendant accelerated the ancient car up the ramp to street level.

Tory tipped the man, moved around the car to the driver's side, and wondered if she should honk to get Keenan's attention or just drive away. She was leaning toward the latter when he noticed the car and backed away from the horde—but not before signing his name to the belly of one of the more scantily clad of the group. He opened the passenger door and slid his tall frame into the car.

He moved lithely, and she had a moment to contemplate the weirdness of having Keenan James in the car. If someone had told her a month ago she'd be driving this man somewhere, she'd have thought they were nuts.

"Her belly?" Tory arched a brow. "Couldn't have been an arm or a hand. Or—here's a thought—a piece of paper?"

Keenan laughed. "They think they're being outrageous. They're too young to know that women have been doing that since the sixties."

"And an illustrious era it's been," Tory said.

"You're a cynical person, aren't you?" He crossed one leg over the other so his right ankle rested on his left knee.

"Session's over, counselor, you can stop analyzing me now."

"Sorry." He held up his hands. "Sometimes I get carried away."

"So where can I drop you?" For some reason she felt nervous driving with him in the car, like she might forget how to drive and run into something.

"Can't wait to get rid of me?"

She turned her head fractionally toward him. "More analysis? Or just oversensitive?"

He laughed, told her where he needed to be, and said if she could get him within even a few blocks it would be great. Then he asked, "So what did you think of the lunch?"

She nodded slowly. "It was . . . very interesting. I'm not sure what I think of your methods, but they're certainly a lively group. And they seem comfortable with you."

He raised his brows. "I'm not sure I'd call them

'methods.' I mostly just try to get people to talk. Seems that most women don't get to do that with a man who will actually listen to them."

"So you're standing in for their men?" she asked.

He made a sound in the back of his throat. "God no. I'm just trying to give them a male perspective. And help them stand up for themselves some. I'm getting the feeling you don't have that problem yourself, though."

Tory checked herself. She'd forgotten this was not a professional conversation, that she was supposed to be the "patient" here.

"Not usually," she said, and wondered if that was true. Sometimes she worried that she let Stewart push her around, but then she thought they just agreed on everything. She turned her attention back to him, which was much easier. "I'm curious about you, though, *Doctor*."

She shot him a small smile to show she was kidding. Sort of.

He shifted in his seat to lay that robin's-egg gaze on her more directly. "Don't kid yourself, Vicky. Or me. I'm no doctor, and I make that clear to everyone who comes to the group. This is not 'therapy,' this is a discussion group. I give my opinions, that's all."

"Uh-huh." She glanced at him. "And what qualifies you to do that? I mean"—she softened her tone—"doesn't it make you uncomfortable to speak for an entire gender in that way?"

He laughed, and she noted what an easygoing sound it was. The man didn't appear to have any hang-ups.

Overblown confidence, she concluded.

"Speaking for my gender. I certainly don't think of it that way. I'm speaking . . ." He paused, rubbed a hand along one lean cheek. "I'm speaking as someone who cares about women burned by men who are, if you'll forgive me, assholes."

Surprising herself, Tory laughed. "Well, you are unusual, Mr. James, I'll give you that."

She glanced at him and saw he was smiling. Just a little. Just enough to hint at those deep dimples and make his long eyelashes touch at the corners.

Shit, Tory thought, turning abruptly back to the road. *Shitshitshit*. He was taking her in with that pretty-boy celebrity crap and she was falling for it. A handsome man listens to you and suddenly he's God's gift to women, she thought, wishing she could write it down. That's what was making this round table thing work. He was charming the pants off these women. Maybe even literally.

Startled, she wondered if that could be true. Could Keenan James be using this organization as his own personal dating pool? No, that would be too low. And surely it would have gotten out by now if that were the case. It would, however, be something worth keeping an eye on. She shot her eyes toward him again, saw that he was looking at her.

This was not good. The guy was altogether too charming.

Then she realized that she was supposed to be on his side, writing his point of view, not investigating him for fraud.

Unless, of course, he *was* a fraud.

She slammed on the brakes and pulled to the curb. "Sorry, this is as far as I can take you," she said abruptly.

He took his hands off the dashboard and gave her a surprised look.

"No problem." He unbuckled his seat belt. "I appreciate the ride. You've cut off at least half my trip. See you next week?"

"Oh you bet," she said, and this time she didn't even try to disguise her tone. It was as much a threat as a promise.

Keenan James got out of the car, and Tory watched him move down the sidewalk. He appeared oblivious to the stares that trailed after him from the women he passed. Heck, even the men seemed to notice him, stiffening their walk and jutting their chins as he passed, as if his very proximity questioned their manhood.

Tory took a deep breath and let it out slowly. She had no idea she'd be so vulnerable to the charms of a guy like him. He was tabloid fodder. She was a serious person, a scientist, a woman not easily taken in by eye candy.

Well, it just went to show how his round table had gotten so popular.

It was probably all that sex they'd talked about. She'd gotten her sexual id all riled up, then sat next to a man brimming over with testosterone. It was only to be expected that she'd react to it.

She sighed and headed for New Jersey. It was lucky her parents chose today to ask her to come for an early dinner, as she had taken the day off for the round table lunch. Of course, ideally she would be home jotting down notes about her first session, but with the confusion Keenan James produced in her, it was probably best that she let the experience settle before writing anything down.

Just the thought of Keenan James made her pause again. She pictured his eyes, their directness and seeming candor. They crinkled at the corners when he was amused, and he looked perpetually amused, now that she thought about it. Which was pretty unprofessional, in her opinion. Why didn't that irritate the others in the group? In fact it was just the opposite; they all seemed gratified when they made him laugh.

She pressed her lips together, then jumped when a cacophony of car horns sounded. She refocused her eyes and saw that traffic had begun to move ahead of her.

What was it about Keenan James that brought about this fugue state in her? He wasn't such a complex subject. Certainly not fascinating. He was as two-dimensional as his pictures in *People* magazine.

You're not being fair, Engelberta said.

Tory sighed. She *wasn't* being fair. She straightened in the car seat and put her hands in the proper ten and two o'clock positions on the wheel. "Keenan James is no less a person just because he is famous and fortunate in his looks. Just because he is pretty does not mean he is lesser. He might, however, be more manipulative because of it. Isn't that what charm is? A form of manipulation? And there's no denying that Keenan James is charming."

A simplistic formula, Engelberta spat. *Perhaps we should look at how charm plays on you, as that seems to be the issue.*

"Nonsense," Tory said automatically. She didn't even know why she imagined Engelberta would say that. "I am not the issue. I am never the issue because I am immaterial to the subject. But—aha." She smiled, amazed yet again at the power of the subconscious. "Yes, I see your point. I was losing track of that. It doesn't matter how I respond to Keenan James. Or if I respond at all. My focus was diverted from my true purpose. It doesn't matter that I've been momentarily distracted by Keenan James's good looks and celebrity. That will pass. I am irrelevant and only here to observe both what he is doing and how it is affecting the women he is treating."

She expelled a sigh of relief and smiled, content once again. Keenan James and her response to him was nothing more than weather—clouds over the landscape—that she had forgotten to ignore. It was the landscape itself—the work—that was her concern.

"I'll bring it tonight," Keenan promised, stepping off the elevator onto his floor. He held the cell phone to one ear as he pushed at the keys on his key ring with one thumb.

"Please don't forget," Fiona said, her voice gentle and cultured-sounding, with its proper British accent. "I need it for my shoot tomorrow. I wasn't supposed to take it to begin with because it's a one-of-a-kind Lagerfeld, but Lionel said I could wear it if I was very, very careful."

"And were you very, very careful?" Keenan teased.

"Until I was accosted by a brute in Armani," she threw back. "Lionel would be horrified. He much prefers Dolce & Gabbana on you. Ooh, got to go. See you at seven, right?"

"Silk in hand," he promised, and flipped the phone shut, smiling to himself.

He loved it when Fiona came to town. She was the least high-maintenance model of any he'd ever known. And he'd known a few. Plus she was fun. Somehow she'd made it to twenty-eight without any baggage, and that showed in her face, adding, he was sure, to her appeal in front of the camera.

Keenan slid the phone into his jacket pocket and stopped in front of the door to his co-op, taking a deep, bracing breath.

These days he couldn't come home without intense trepidation before opening the door. It had become a crap shoot, whether the place would be chaotic or calm. Anything from mayhem to destruction to the status quo was possible. He'd at least learned the hard way to stand sideways when greeted by speeding dog muzzle and leaping limbs. Much less chance of damage to the private parts that way.

Yesterday he'd begun locking the dog in the bathroom to avoid all of the above, but first he'd had to tie the shower door closed, and even that hadn't stopped her from chewing the molding off the base of the door frame or unraveling the toilet paper all over the room. And though it wasn't logical, he didn't put it past the devil dog to somehow chew her way through the bathroom door and wreak havoc on the whole place.

He stepped into the foyer cautiously. "Barbra Streisand?"

No response. Was that good or bad?

He crossed the granite foyer to the living room, eyes scanning everything from the large sectional couch to the flat-panel TV mounted high over the gas fireplace. Hey, you never knew. The dog seemed to understand what was expensive. Either that, or expensive things just happened to be tastier.

He glanced into the kitchen. Dishwasher still closed tight—good. Stainless steel appliances mercifully unbitable.

He moved through the dining room—unscathed—and down the hall to the bathroom, where the door remained shut. He exhaled for the first time since entering the apartment.

"Thank God," he breathed, and opened the door. "Okay, come on out."

Nothing stirred. He stepped into the large, ceramic-tiled room. Nothing in the shower, he could see that from here as the stall was completely transparent. Nothing in the wide Jacuzzi tub. A pile of wood chips lay on the floor next to the already-destroyed molding. Nothing new there; the dog could just take off the rest of that trim if she wanted. He wasn't replacing it until the animal was trained. Or gone. Though he wasn't sure how he could pull that off without a stealth mission to his brother's place in Virginia. Drop her off and disappear before Brady knew what was happening.

But where *was* the animal?

He stood in the middle of the bathroom. "Barbra Streisand?"

Nothing. He sighed. God help him if he had to employ the other ruse his mother had told him to make the dog come. For the umpteenth time he thanked God he lived alone. Though if he didn't there'd be a chance he could make the other person deal with the dog.

How had his mother handled the thing? Then he remembered, it was thirty pounds smaller when she had it.

One thing was certain, it wasn't in this bathroom any longer.

Maybe someone had stolen it. Despite thoughts of his mother, his heart lifted.

Then he spotted the cabinet under the sink, mentally measuring its dimensions against the size of the dog. It wasn't impossible. If Barbra Streisand could get into a dishwasher, she could get into a bathroom cabinet. Now *there* was a sentence he never thought would cross his mind.

He strode across the tile and threw the doors open.

Nothing. In fact, everything in it looked untouched, which was a stroke of luck, as he'd forgotten to secure those doors this morning.

He turned back toward the hallway and put his hand on the doorknob, noting the tooth marks in the chrome. Had they been there yesterday? Surely they had. But the fact remained that the dog was not in the bathroom, so she must have gotten out somehow.

He stepped into the hall and went to the bedroom. It occurred to him the dog might have left the building. She seemed devious enough. Then he came to his senses. The front door had still been locked, for God's sake. The pup wasn't mystical, after all.

The bedroom looked untouched as well, and fear of something having happened to the dog replaced his fears of the dog having happened to something he owned. How could he tell his mother he'd lost her dog? Or worse, killed it? What if he'd let her die in some let's-chew-the-electrical-plug accident? His mother asked about the dog every time he went to visit, and he was a notoriously bad liar. Plus he didn't believe in lying, though that might have started when he'd realized he was no good at it.

Panic made him resort to her last tip.

"*People*," he began to croon, off-key and low in a paranoid attempt to keep the neighbors from hearing what he'd sunk to. "*People who need people . . .*"

He heard something stir and stopped, ears as alert as any canine's.

"*Are the luckiest . . .*" He crept toward the walk-in closet. "*People . . . in . . .*" He pulled open the door.

Nothing.

"*. . . the wooorrrlllld.*"

A small whine escaped from under the bed.

Keenan crouched to the floor and lifted the covers that draped over the edge.

Two button eyes shone out of the darkness at him.

He blew out his cheeks. "Barbra Streisand," he said, and heard the *thump thump thump* of her tail. He smiled in genuine relief. "Come on out of there."

She moved slightly in his direction, then stopped.

Guilt surged in his chest. The little thing was afraid of him. He pictured his mother cuddling with Barbra Streisand as a puppy and hated himself. He guessed he'd been pretty angry when he'd discovered the torn-up bathroom molding yesterday. But he hadn't hit the dog or anything. He'd just ranted a bit. And he'd left her with a stern warning this morning that he was sure she hadn't absorbed or cared about.

But now here she was, cowering away from him.

"Come on, Barbra Streisand," he said, in the friendliest tone he had, snapping his fingers. "I'm sorry. Come on out. Hey, if you come out I'll put on Barbra Streisand's greatest hits CD."

He continued beating himself up with guilt until he realized the dog was stuck. While she had fit under the bed easily when he'd brought her home, she'd apparently grown just enough that she could get underneath, but now could not wriggle out.

With a relieved laugh he stood and lifted the bed from the bottom. Before he could hum another Streisand bar the dog scuttled to freedom.

"Good girl!" he laughed.

He glanced under the mattress once before putting it down and stopped.

There, in tatters, lay Fiona's silk shirt. The one he was supposed to bring her tonight. The one with which she was to be *very, very careful.*

"That's it," he said, giving the dog a hard look. "You've crossed a line. *Now* you're messing with my love life."

Chapter 6

"Tory! Oh my God!"

Her sister, Claudia, had answered the door and was staring at her.

For a moment, Tory panicked. "What's wrong? Where are Mom and Dad?"

Claudia's pretty blue eyes narrowed with an impish smile, and Tory let out a relieved breath. "They're in the kitchen, silly. I'm just amazed."

"Amazed?" Tory's heart labored to slow. She was in a state today. How rare for her to assume something bad had happened just because her sister had emoted inappropriately, as she always did. It had been too long since she'd seen her family, she guessed. She'd forgotten how over the top they could be.

"Yes. Amazed. At you!"

Her sister's eyes swept down her body and back up to her face. Tory looked down as well. Ah, the clothes. Tory had forgotten about Sasha and Katya and her earlier transformation for the round table. She wondered if the makeup had migrated around her face yet.

Claudia tossed her blond, shoulder-length curls and called behind her, "Mom, Dad, you won't believe who's here!" She laughed, and the sound tinkled out like the chime of a crystal bell. Claudia was like a fresh breeze on a summer day. Cool and refreshing to most people, but blowing Tory's hair into her eyes and spraying her with sand.

Tory found herself caught up—as she was every time she saw her sister—in the good-Claudia/bad-Claudia game. It was a game that had originated in their childhood and entailed Tory trying to discern whether her sister was being sincere or manipulative. If Tory guessed wrong, she was treated to an emotional tirade from which she could not escape without full-scale surrender.

"You look . . . absolutely amazing!" Claudia enthused.

"It's nothing," Tory said, squeezing by her sister to enter the house. Claudia, in her exaggerated shock, had neglected to move from the doorway. "I had a lunch meeting."

Claudia laughed again. "Some meeting. I don't think I've ever seen you in makeup. And *where* did you get that belt? And those shoes! They're to *die* for!"

Ah, compliments on the outfit and expressions of envy. Simon must be here, Tory thought. Claudia usually tried to sound sincere in front of her boyfriend.

Footsteps sounded from the kitchen, through the center hall, and her parents—Berthold and Liezel Hoffstra—emerged into the foyer, followed by— sure enough—Claudia's boyfriend, Simon Morgan. Tory had never quite warmed to Simon, though she appreciated his grounding influence on Claudia. He was a serious person, which she usually admired, but in his case it translated as dull. And he seemed patently wrong for her sister. Simon seemed only to be Claudia's latest accessory, one that provided her with everything she wanted, including the audience to watch her enjoy it.

One of the good things about Simon was that Claudia tried to be more serious around him, but Tory could never be sure if it was a condition that happened to Claudia or if it was an act Claudia put on for some reason of her own.

"Tory, honey, you look beautiful!" her mother exclaimed, coming to give her a Shalimar-scented hug. Tory hugged her back, comforted by the powdery refuge of her mother's affection.

"Well, well, well." Her father beamed. "What's the special occasion? Surely not dinner with your old folks."

He embraced her too, his hug large and enveloping.

It had been too long since she'd been here, Tory realized. The moment she saw her parents, she felt nourished in a way that nothing else made her feel. Sure she was the black sheep of the family, the one nobody understood, but they loved her. She never had to question that.

She only wished they didn't make such a big deal over how she looked. Surely they knew her better than to think this truly changed her.

"I had a meeting. This . . ." She gestured down at her clothes and thought about washing her face before dinner. "It's a kind of . . . disguise. I had to look like someone different."

"Well, you don't," Claudia said. "You just look more beautiful."

Tory glanced at her sister and couldn't help laughing. "You must want something really big out of me."

Claudia frowned. She hated it when Tory saw through her.

"What happened to your glasses?" Claudia demanded.

"Oh, I, uh." She put a hand to her face as if to

push her glasses back up her nose; inexplicably felt mildly surprised when they weren't there. "I'm experimenting with contacts."

"You've *got* to be kidding," Claudia said.

"Hello, Victoria," Simon said, holding out his hand.

Tory took it, shook it once, and dropped it quickly. "Simon."

Simon had picked up calling her "Victoria" from her parents, who did it every now and again for no particular reason. Tory chalked it up to Simon's pretentiousness that he chose to use it as well, a way for him to insinuate himself into the family. He also sometimes called Claudia "Claudia Rae" as her parents did, and it annoyed the heck out of her.

Not that it really mattered. As far as Tory could tell, Simon was merely a phase for her sister. After years of dating wildly irresponsible, handsome, and disrespectful men, Claudia was experimenting with a totally different sort. "The Cold Fish," Tory had dubbed him in her mind. Well, okay, once she'd said it to her brother and he'd begun using it too.

Not that Simon wasn't handsome. He was, in a Clark Kent kind of way. And who knew? Maybe he had a smile that transformed him, but Tory wouldn't know because the man never used it.

"Let's get out of this hallway," her mother said, waving them into the kitchen. "Come inside and let me get you something to drink. Simon and Claudia brought champagne, isn't that nice?"

Tory's eyes snapped to her sister's. "Champagne? On a Monday?" Something uncomfortable dropped in her stomach.

Claudia winked at her. "Sure. Why not? Simon and I decided we're all just too set in our ways. Champagne on a Monday seemed the perfect way to shake things up."

Well, if anyone would know about being set in his ways, it would be Simon, she thought. And Claudia would be the one to know how to shake things up.

Now, now, Engelberta whispered. *Your sister loves him. Try to see why*.

She doesn't love him, Tory thought in exasperation, wondering why she had to imagine all of Engelberta's more irritating assessments—she was, after all, just a figment of Tory's imagination. *Simon is another experiment, nothing more*.

"Is Conrad coming?" Tory asked, remembering something about her mother wanting the whole family together. She wondered if her parents had something to tell them. It was unusual for them all to get together outside of the holidays.

For a second, Tory worried. If her brother Conrad was coming too, then something momentous must be occurring, and for some reason, this idea filled her with dread.

"Oh we tried to get Conny," her mother said, "and for a while there it looked like he'd make it. But he had some client he had to fly out to San Diego for at the last minute, and that was that."

Tory exhaled a pent-up breath. What was wrong with her? She didn't believe in premonitions, so this sense of unease had to have something to do with being thrown by Keenan James earlier in the day. That, and she was dressed like a stranger to herself. That would have a disorienting effect on anyone.

Tory's eyes landed on the back of Simon's perfectly trimmed hair—he could be a Ken doll with that short, unmovable, side-part style—and had the thought that Keenan James would be the perfect match for Claudia. With his reckless dark hair—she pictured that thick lock dropping over his forehead as he'd gotten into the car—his breathtaking smile, and his disconcerting eyes, they would be the perfect complement to each other. Both were gorgeous, exuded charm like an industrial smokestack, and had that spark of charisma that knocked people flat on their butts if they weren't prepared for it.

She spent a moment wondering who would win the charm-off; Keenan with his celebrity looks or Claudia with her love-me! exuberance.

The Hoffstra kitchen was large, warm, and filled with old German country artifacts. The counter was stone, the table a thick slab of ancient wood formerly used as a pig-slaughtering block, complete with ax marks discreetly covered with stain and polyurethane, and the walls covered with tin cookie presses, cast-iron skillets, and other old cooking instruments. Today it smelled like sauerbraten and spaetzle—Tory and Claudia's favorite.

At the first strong whiff, Tory's tension left her like a second skin.

"Have a seat, everyone," her father said, gesturing broadly to the table, set with the family china and surrounded by enough silverware to hoist a ten-course meal to the mouths of an army. He picked up a champagne flute and filled it for Tory, handing it to her across the table.

She sat in the seat she had occupied since she was a child, at the left hand of her father, and looked across the table at Claudia. She was beaming like she held the punch line to a joke and winked at Tory again.

Should she be getting something? Tory wondered. Claudia looked at her as if they were in on something together. She passed her a frown of incomprehension, and Claudia laughed.

"Oh I can't stand it," Claudia finally said, leaning toward Simon, next to her.

Simon put an arm around her and passed her a look that—it had to be admitted—was tender. Tory gave him grudging points for probably loving her sister. She just wondered how well he knew her.

"I'm about to explode," Claudia continued.

"Oh, Bert," her mother said, excitement in her tone too. "I knew it! Didn't I tell you?"

Tory felt as if she were waking from a dream. A horrible sense of doom descended upon her. She put her hands on the table and clutched a spoon with her right hand.

"What? What is it?" she asked, more sharply than she'd intended.

Claudia stood up and raised her glass, her face shining like a child's exuberant drawing of the sun. "Simon and I are getting married!" Then she shrieked in a way that only Claudia could shriek—light, happy, and infectious instead of shrill and jarring—and all chaos broke loose.

Both of her parents stood up; her mother leaned across the table to hug her older daughter, knocking over her glass of champagne to the laughter of all. Her father rounded the table and clutched her in one of his smothering bear hugs. He kissed her repeatedly on her temple and swung her back and forth.

"I'm so happy for you, baby doll," he said, loosing one hand to shake Simon's, behind her.

Her father never called Tory "baby doll." She was "honey" or "sweetie," generic names like that, but nothing so personal and perfect as "baby doll." Claudia had always known just how to manage their father. One time, in a moment of sisterly goodwill, she'd shown Tory how she could cry on cue, a trick she often used on their father after breaking curfew or getting caught with beer or a boy in her room in high school.

Tory's eyes shifted to Simon, whose lips were actually curved into a tight smile. He was looking down, his cheeks pink, and he looked as pleased as Tory had ever seen him.

"Tory?" her sister queried, her eyebrows raised,

her gaze expectant. "My God, we've really shocked you, haven't we? Well, that has to be a first." She laughed and glanced at Simon, who clasped her shoulder. "Tory always seems to know us better than we know ourselves."

Which was patently untrue, Tory realized. She just talked as if she knew it all, but she really knew nothing. Nothing at all.

She lurched out of her chair and moved on stiff, surreal legs around the table. "Claudia," she croaked, "I don't know what to say."

Except that this was a colossally huge mistake. Claudia would run roughshod over Simon their whole married life, and hate him for it. It could only end in disaster.

Then, because she really didn't know what to say other than what she shouldn't, Tory leaned forward and gave her sister a hug.

Claudia leaned into her and hugged her harder than she ever had before. Tory felt tears prick her eyelids. If only they were the close sisters they so often appeared to be.

"Congratulations," Tory choked, squeezing back just as hard.

"Someday this will happen to you too," Claudia said. "Don't worry, Tory. I'll make sure of it."

Tory pulled out of the embrace.

"Tell us all about the plans!" her mother interrupted. "Have you got a date in mind? A location? Oh, this is so exciting!"

Claudia looked smugly at Tory again and turned to their mother. "We're thinking spring. It's Simon's favorite time of year and . . ."

The talk swirled while Tory stood in a daze. Dates and dresses, honeymoons and caterers, a world of considerations that had never once entered into a conversation Tory'd been involved in. She moved unnoticed back around the table, only then realizing she still clutched the spoon in her right hand. She sat and put the spoon on the table.

"I have a friend who plays piano beautifully," her father was saying. "He could play at the wedding, the, uh, what's it called, Liezel?"

Her mother slapped him playfully on the arm. "The wedding march, silly."

They all laughed as if this were the height of humor.

"What about Stewart? He could play," Tory said.

"Stewart?" Claudia said, as if she'd proposed he hum the wedding march through a kazoo. "We don't want that stuffy old kind of music he plays—"

"We'd like him to be a *guest*," Simon interrupted.

"Never mind," Tory murmured.

"We must go to the bridal sale at that place in the Garment District," her mother said. "The gowns there are always the best and you'll have time to get one at their annual sale. The prices are amazing. Leslie Adams's daughter got a Vera Wang there for five hundred dollars. Can you believe it? A *Vera Wang*."

"Oh I should definitely be married in a Vera Wang, don't you think?" Claudia looked at Tory. "And we'll get you something nice too. After all, this might be the only wedding you'll be in!"

So much for making sure it happened for her too, Tory thought.

"Nonsense!" Tory's father objected.

"Dad," Tory said, shaking her head. "Forget it."

"Well it's true," Claudia insisted. "She doesn't *have* any girlfriends. You'll see," she said to Tory, "this'll be the most exciting thing you've ever done. It's so much fun to be a bridesmaid. Not as much as a bride, of course." She trilled a laugh.

"Speaking of exciting, I'm going to write a book with Keenan James," Tory blurted.

They all turned to look at her. "What?" Claudia asked.

Tory was immediately ashamed of herself. What was she thinking? She didn't want to steal Claudia's thunder; she really didn't. And God knew she didn't want the emotional response she was sure to get from her.

"Keenan James," she repeated weakly. "I met with him today. We're going to write a book together." She paused, hating herself. "But that's not important right now. Sorry," she added to Claudia, who looked at her with narrowed eyes.

"Nonsense!" her father said again, looking uncertainly toward his wife. "What a wealth of good news we have today. Looks like both of our girls have snagged eligible men!"

True to history, personality, and luck, however, Tory thought, Claudia was marrying hers.

❦

"Mom," Keenan said, rounding the pink curtain to where his mother lay propped in the adjustable bed. "Hey, it's me."

It disturbed him when he found her lying in bed like this, staring at the wall. What was she thinking about? Was she depressed? How could she not be? Did anyone pay any attention to her at all when he was not here?

His mother turned her face to him and smiled, her eyes losing some of their dullness at the sight of him.

"Keenan, is it Sunday already?"

"No, Mom, it's Thursday. Remember I come Thursdays too?" He hated this. Hated that she didn't even know what day it was. He made a mental note to bring her a calendar. One with big, bright pictures of Ireland on it.

She nodded, her face not losing its smile. "Of course. Of course."

As usual, one of the candy stripers had dogged his heels as he'd come down the hall and entered the room, and she now fluttered around his mother as if she did it all the time.

"Would you like something to drink, Mrs. Cole?" the candy striper said, using the last name his mother had taken during her second marriage, the one that had produced Brady. "Can I get *you* something, Mr. James?" she added, not listening for his mother's reply.

"What do you want, Mom? Coffee?" he asked. All she ever drank was coffee. Throughout his entire childhood, he could swear he saw her drink nothing else.

"Oh, the doctor said she can't have coffee anymore," the candy striper said. "But we've got Ovaltine!"

He turned to the girl. "Why no coffee?" he asked sharply.

She looked startled. "Be-because she's not sleeping. That's what he said. She shouldn't have any caffeine at all."

Keenan studied her a moment, then checked his watch. "It's ten o'clock in the morning. Get the woman some coffee, all right?"

The girl backed up a step toward the door. "I don't know. I'll have to check."

"Fine. You check and if somebody else says no you send them to me." He turned back to his mother, dismissing the girl.

"My hero," his mother said softly.

Keenan had to lean forward to hear her, some days she was so weak she could barely achieve any volume, then he leaned back and grinned. "Hey, I'll

slay any dragon you put in my path, Mom. How
are you feeling? Are you really not sleeping?"

"I never did sleep. They only just noticed." She
shook her head.

He chuckled. "It probably is the coffee. But why
shock your system now by getting rid of it?"

"Exactly what I said." She lifted a thin hand and
brought it down in an old gesture Keenan recognized. She was always patting a hand decisively on
her thigh, or the table, whatever was handy, when
she made a point.

"Hey, I brought some cards today. Thought we
could play casino, or gin. What do you think?"

"Gin," she said, leaning her head back and closing her eyes a moment. She needed to rest frequently these days, but if you ignored it she could
manage a conversation pretty well. Stopping and
starting, but keeping the thread.

He dealt the cards, knowing this one hand would
probably last the entire visit.

"How's Brady?" she asked, lifting her eyes. "I
thought you said he was coming to visit again."

Keenan dropped his eyes to the playing cards.
He'd tried to get Brady to come here, God knew
he'd tried. But Brady had cried work and begged
off his last two trips. He had some kind of phobia
about it, said he couldn't stand the smell or the look
of the place, couldn't stand seeing his mother in a
place like this, waiting to die with a bunch of semi-
corpses strewn around the halls in wheelchairs.

Keenan understood. He understood far better than Brady would ever know, in fact. Keenan couldn't stand coming here either but he made himself do it, literally forced himself, twice every week. Because his mother had no one else, and he couldn't imagine being stuck here without anyone he knew or loved day after day, week in and week out, waiting, as Brady had said, to die.

That didn't change the fact that Brady was his mother's favorite, Keenan knew. Always had been.

"He's fine. Busy." Keenan arranged the cards in his hand, mentally damning Brady for putting him in this awkward position again. "He doesn't get that many flights up here, it turns out. His boss has more contacts in Chicago than New York. I did make him break his racquet on the racquetball court the other day, though, when I was in D.C." He chuckled, hoping to change the subject from Brady's neglect.

"You should let him win once in a while," she chided.

"No, I shouldn't, Mom. His head's big enough as it is already."

"Is he dating anyone?"

Keenan picked a card off the pile. Why hadn't Brady told her all this? Why didn't he pick up the damn phone once in a while? A little news would go a long way toward making their mother happy.

"Yeah, actually. A real nice girl named Lily."

"Lily. That's pretty." His mother's gaze drifted somewhere far away.

"He said it might actually be the real thing this time," Keenan added, thinking he'd believe it when he saw it. "Brady's calmed down a lot. You'd be surprised. He's stopped tearing up the town and breaking hearts as fast as he can find them."

"Really?" his mother asked weakly, her eyes hopeful.

Keenan chuckled mirthlessly. "Yeah. Leave it to Brady to find the perfect woman the moment he decides to stop being an ass."

Immediately he regretted the words. He knew he shouldn't say things like that, but still they popped out. His frustration with the old Brady was different from his mother's and didn't need to be shared with her.

She shook her head as he discarded. "That boy. I do worry about him. He's just like his father."

"Nah, he's not bad. And he's happy, Mom. Don't worry about him," he added.

"He'll happy himself to death." She frowned, her gaze going inward.

"No, he won't. I told you, I think this girl is it. He's in love." Keenan picked up her cards and arranged them into a fan facing her.

She looked at him over the cards, hope lighting the faded blue irises. "Do you really think so? Do you think he'd bring her to visit sometime?"

Keenan looked down again, unwilling to meet her gaze as he lied. "Sure."

"How's Barbra Streisand?" she asked, letting her hand droop.

He smiled wryly. "She's fine. You didn't tell me she was such a handful."

"She's not. She's the sweetest little thing. All she needs is some good cuddling every now and then. Are you cuddling with her?" Her smile was nice to see. Engaged and light. No worries about her dog-child. That one was pure joy.

He smiled. "I'm trying, but she's hard to catch."

His mother frowned. "I thought Brady was going to take her. She won't get enough exercise in the city. She should be with Brady."

Keenan sighed silently. "He couldn't take her. Not yet, Mom. Soon, though." He vowed to himself that this would not be a lie.

Silence reigned for a few moments while Keenan waited for her to notice the cards in her hand.

"How is your book coming?" she asked.

He was always surprised when she remembered things like this. Some days all she could talk about were events that happened in his childhood or even before. Sometimes she talked about a whole community of people whose names he didn't recognize at all. On those days he contributed by telling her anything that came into his head, the smallest happenings in his life, thoughts he'd had, things he figured she'd never remember. But then she'd surprise him by bringing up some detail. Like now.

"I guess it's coming along," he answered. "It's with the publisher and he seems to like the idea. He said there's a couple of things he needs to work out before he can make an offer. I'm getting a little impatient, though."

"You need to push him, Keenan." One of the cards fell unheeded from her hand and lay face-up on the faded pink blanket. The two of clubs. "It's important. Women need to hear what you're saying. They . . . they shouldn't waste their life like I did, waiting and wondering, hoping, putting up with all that . . . that . . ."

"I know, Mom, don't worry." He looked her in the eye, forcing her attention. She could wear herself out with anxiety. He wondered for the hundredth time if the regrets she harbored were so monumental, or if this distress was some by-product of her diminished mental faculties. "It'll get published, I'm sure of it. And in the meantime, The Discovery Channel special is going strong. They've replayed it three or four times. And the round tables are packed. I'm saving women from jerks all across the country." He grinned.

She gave a wan smile in return. "I know you can't save the world, Kee. But if you can change even one woman, keep her from being the fool I was . . . well, that's more than most men would do."

He looked back down at his cards, then picked up the one that had fallen from her hand and returned it to her fan.

"You weren't a fool, Mom. Hey, my Monday table got a new member. The publisher sent this new woman to the group, asked me to take her on as a favor even though it was full. I think that's a good sign. He wouldn't do that if he didn't like what I was doing. So this woman . . ."

Keenan kept up a steady conversation as his mother's energy faded, trying to inject some anecdotes he knew would make her laugh.

But even while he did this, his thoughts about the round tables strayed to how ready he was to be rid of them. Listening to women's problems—some of them truly seemingly insurmountable—twice a week, sometimes for more than a few hours, was exhausting. He felt himself burning out.

Not that he didn't still care; he just couldn't take in so much. He couldn't give the thought and attention and certainty to so many, so often, without feeling as if he were too often faking it. And he couldn't help wondering if he was really doing any good. Or if he'd *ever* done any good. The women seemed to enjoy the lunches, but had any of them changed? Or was it just entertainment for them?

He had no way of knowing. The only thing becoming increasingly clear was that he wasn't cut out to be a therapist. Lately he'd been thinking he had reached far more people with his television show— *Sex at Midnight*—than he would ever reach with the round tables. If he could write another show based on what he knew now, it'd probably run forever.

Which was why the book was so important. He wanted to say what he had to say once and for all and let people decide if he was a quack or not on their own, with only a book to throw away instead of hours and hours of their lives.

He had determined to start cutting back on the clients, not filling a space when someone left, when Fender had asked him to take on the new addition to the Monday round table. Vicky Smith.

He had wondered if he could engage with one more woman on that level, but his fears had been unfounded. There was something about the new woman that had demanded attention, and it wasn't just that he was sure she was a plant. There was something about her sharpness, her confident, combative attitude. She didn't act like the typical woman who joined one of his groups. There was no vulnerability. No uncertainty. In fact, she told her story as if it belonged to someone else. She was either dissociating completely, or she was making it all up.

But even if she'd made it up to test him, there was something else, something she was hiding, about herself. There was a bit of defensiveness, and the prickliness didn't seem so much a part of her personality as something she forced herself to adopt.

The only crack he'd seen in her façade was when he'd asked her for a ride that day. Then she'd been thrown, clearly not expecting to have a conversation with him one-on-one.

Despite his fatigue with the role, despite his growing concern about the good he was doing, he made another mental note: to talk to Vicky Smith alone again. Find out if she really was sent to test him, and if she was, what she was going to tell Fender.

If she wasn't . . . then there were a whole lot of questions that came with that too.

Chapter 7

"Ah! A gallery opening," Katya said, sweeping blush across Tory's cheek with a brush so large it looked like a small animal. "I love art galleries! In my home country I would go to art school and be a model, you know? I would pose for students. I felt I was part of something important, yes?"

Tory's eyebrows rose. "You posed for the students?"

"Oh yes," Katya said, then leaned close to her ear. "Sometimes in the *nude*." She cackled merrily and put the blush away, then picked up a square of eye shadow. "This is called Hypnotic, this color.

Your eyes hypnotize tonight, you will see. Maybe you will meet someone special, yes? Close eyes."

Tory closed her eyes. "No. I'm meeting my boyfriend, um, ex-boyfriend, afterward."

She paused. That didn't sound right.

She'd actually had a devil of a time getting out of their dinner. Stewart had not understood why he couldn't come to the opening. Even after Tory explained to him that since Keenan knew him from the co-op, he'd need to introduce her as his girlfriend, he refused to believe her anonymity was that important. He only acquiesced after she told him she'd made up so much stuff about her fictional boyfriend for the group that Stewart might be embarrassed to be attached to it.

"Look up," Katya sang, making it sound like a game played with a toddler at mealtime.

"*Here.*" A dress was thrust into Tory's field of vision. Before she could even raise a hand to take it, a pair of shoes was thrust out by another hand. "You buy these things for opening. You will look splendid." The words were flattering but Sasha's tone sounded more like a threat.

Tory swiveled her eyeballs toward Katya's sister while trying to keep her lids up for Katya to line her bottom lashes.

"I ring them up now." The clothes were snatched back before Tory could even graze them with her fingers.

"Wait!" she called.

Katya sucked some air between her teeth. "Please, you are moving."

"Sorry," Tory said, "but Sasha . . ."

"Clothes are perfect," Sasha stated from the vicinity of the register. Tory heard the machine crank out a receipt.

"But—" Tory began.

"We have your card on file," Sasha added, in the same tone as if she'd said, *We have snipers watching your every move.*

Tory experienced a moment of irrational panic, envisioning Sasha in a Russian soldier's uniform, her blunt hair and bangs rigid under her hat, her eyes devoid of compassion. *Vee haf vays of making you buy. . .*

"You will look beautiful, like work of art yourself," Katya said. "Look down."

Tory did as she was told. It wasn't as if she wouldn't buy anything the sisters recommended, so there wasn't much point in insisting she see Sasha's choices. Still, it seemed wrong.

"Stup frowning," Katya pleaded. "You crease your face."

Tory tried to iron out her face.

Minutes later, Katya stepped back, beaming. "There."

Tory turned to the mirror beside her. "I don't know how you do that," she said with a sigh. Who was that person in the mirror? And why did Tory like her so much more than her regular self?

"Is easy, I keep telling you. You can do yourself."

Tory looked at her, noted her hopeful face, and something inside her relented for the first time. "Okay. I think . . . I'll take that blush."

"Excellent!" Katya's face lit up.

"And, um, the base stuff too. The foundation." She looked in the mirror again. "And maybe the eye shadow?"

By the time she had finished, she'd bought the whole palette, telling herself she was doing it to make Katya happy. After all, why should Sasha be the only one selling her stuff when Katya was so much nicer?

It wasn't until she got home that she saw the outfit Sasha had chosen. It was the most beautiful set of clothes she had ever owned.

Vicky Smith flowed into the room in a diaphanous white outfit that made her look like a fairy. Though it appeared to have layers, it clung to her slim body while hinting at supple pleasures beneath. Her eyes were dark and sultry as original sin. A marked contrast to her hair, which was light and shiny as a child's.

Keenan couldn't take his eyes off her. She glowed. She was like some small, beautiful, cream-colored moth caught in a web of New York black. All around her women in "little black dresses" spilled over and under their tight bodices and short hems, stuck like kabobs on their spiked heels, but Vicky Smith seemed to float in a spotlight all her own, her slippered feet not even touching the ground.

He excused himself from Martin Balm, a producer he'd been wanting to speak to for weeks about a *Seal The Deal, Baby* follow-up to *Straight Talk*, and made his way across the room toward Vicky.

She was studying one of Angelica's abstract pieces when he approached.

"Is it a goat, or a tornado?" he asked, standing next to her.

She looked up at him, startled. It was a good look for her, with those wide gray eyes and delicate features. Something about her seemed so vulnerable, he was taken in every time.

"Oh, *you're* here," she said.

Taken in, that was, until she spoke.

"Hello to you too." He grinned. There was also something appealing about how difficult it was to get a smile out of her. It stimulated his creativity, and felt like quite the reward when he won one.

"I think it's rage," she said, looking darkly at the painting.

He studied it anew. "Rage? It looks like sex to me."

He thought he heard a little laugh. Or maybe it was a scoff.

"I'm sorry," he said, leaning down. She smelled soft, like honeysuckle. "I didn't catch that."

She turned to him. "I said you must be a Freudian."

"No, actually, I cheated." He pointed to the tag, where the title of the piece, *Sex ###14*, was typed.

Keenan was surprised to see her cheeks color slightly. Who could be embarrassed about not guessing what a blob of color and texture on a canvas were? He actually *had* thought it was a goat the first time he'd looked at it.

A tall, thin waitress with cocoa-colored eyes and long false eyelashes brought a tray of glasses filled with champagne. In the oblique spot-lighting the bubbles looked like tiny jewels floating to the surface.

Keenan took two and handed one to Vicky. She hesitated and that she was weighing something flashed plainly across her face, but she took the glass and thanked him. She started to turn back to the painting but he stopped her.

"Cheers," he said, holding out his glass. "To free expression."

She gave a slight but gratifying laugh and touched his glass with hers. They moved sideways to the next painting.

Keenan's mouth dropped open. There on a six-foot-tall canvas, in bright oranges and yellows, was the body of a voluptuous woman with—it could not be denied—his head. His eyes darted to the tag. *Phantasie at Midnight*. He started to laugh.

Vicky's head swiveled toward him, her eyes clearly alarmed. "Did you know about this? What do you think it means?"

He shrugged, amused beyond measure. If it hadn't cost eighty-five hundred dollars, he might have bought it. "I think it means Angelica has a sense of humor. Now I know why she was so anxious for me to come tonight."

"But . . ." Vicky's eyes were intent upon him. "Don't you think it *means* something?"

"Sure. Something different to everyone, like all the works." He tilted his head. "If you narrow your eyes it looks a little like the grill of a truck with my head as the hood ornament."

"But what does it mean to *you*?" she insisted.

"Well," he said, "I can tell you right now it's not a very good likeness from the neck down."

She studied the painting intently, barely registering his joke.

"All right. I actually think it means," he continued, adopting a more serious demeanor. After all, he wasn't *sure* she was just a plant in the group from Fender, and if she thought something wrong was going on, he should set her straight. Still, it was fun to watch the obvious thoughts playing across her face. "That I'm missing quite a bit of what Angelica really wants. Though perhaps she sees something in me that isn't totally distasteful. If, that is, it's really me."

Vicky rolled her eyes. "You think the clock in the background set at midnight might not mean anything?"

He looked up. "Oh yeah. I hadn't noticed that."

"And the title of the piece? *Phantasie at Midnight*? Clearly referring to your show," she said, over-enunciating each word.

He slanted his eyes at her. "Yeah, I got that part."

She planted her hands on her hips. "This doesn't *bother* you?"

"No, not really. Why should it? Now, if it had been a woman's head on my body . . . I might have worried about that, but . . ." He chuckled again. Angelica was full of surprises.

"Oh my God," Vicky muttered.

"What?"

"So now you've seen it," Angelica's voice purred as she approached. "What do you think, fantasy man?"

"I think I need to start working out." He tipped his glass to hers and they clinked. "You've obviously idealized me; I need to work on my, uh, pecs."

She laughed low in her throat. "There's no amount of exercise you could do, Keenan, to get yourself in the shape I want. This . . ." She swept a long-nailed hand up and down before the canvas. "This fantasy has a little something for everyone."

"I'm flattered." He gave a half bow. "But I'm sure you could have found someone better than me to top your masterpiece."

"That," she said, turning, "would depend on whom you asked." She glanced once at Vicky, gave a wink, and left them.

What the heck did *that* mean? Tory wondered. Did Angelica think *she* was one of the groupies fantasizing about Keenan James? Granted, she had again noted how charming his smile was when he was chuckling over the painting. And she had again been feeling the intensity of his eyes, that clear blue, so penetrating somehow, when he looked at her, asked her questions about the first work. *Mentioned sex.*

Her faced burned again just thinking about it.

Good God, she thought, she needed an intervention. How could she be falling into the same trap all those other, less educated, women fell into? How could she be taken in by good looks and a little charisma, even knowing all she did about how superficial they were?

And had Angelica *seen* it in her? Her humiliation would be complete if she had.

She pulled herself together. This was not about her. This was about Keenan. How was this painting okay with *Keenan*? How could he not see the danger in one of his "patients" fantasizing about him? Not just fantasizing, but creating actual works of art about him? In the psychiatric world, it would be scandalous.

Keenan moved toward the next painting and Tory followed, struggling not to say anything too judgmental. It would reveal too much, she thought, if she were to point out ethical problems in his brand of "therapy." She was here on reconnaissance only.

As they studied the next work, Tory tried not to feel distinguished by the fact that he was staying with her so long. She was not unaware of the other women's eyes trailing them around the room, no doubt wondering what sort of help Keenan was trying to offer the stray girl in the funky clothes.

She didn't care. She loved this outfit and she had things to find out about Keenan. That she suddenly felt like the popular girl in high school meant nothing.

"So, what do you make of this one?" Keenan asked, covering the tag with his palm and grinning.

"I'm not the one you need to cover that for," she said. "You got the first one."

"I also got the second. Your turn."

"We could probably debate the second one's meaning." She gave him a significant look. It was hard keeping her mouth shut.

"Vicky," he said, in such a way that she wished it really were her name, "I'm not sure you're aware that Angelica . . ." He leaned close, and her nerves stood up and took notice. " . . . is a lesbian."

Tory drew back. "What?"

He straightened and smiled, but it was gentle, not mocking. "That painting didn't mean anything. Or it didn't mean what you thought it meant, at any rate. Angelica has no feelings for me other than friendship, of that I am sure."

Tory's lips parted. So he knew her concerns? More importantly, he knew to *be* concerned? Maybe he wasn't so unprofessional after all.

"I—I had no idea."

"I didn't think so. And I can see why you'd have been worried if she were expressing any kind of real desire for me. Or anyone in the group, for that matter."

Anyone in the group? That brought up a whole new host of issues.

"Is her, uh, partner here?" Tory asked, wishing she could ask what Angelica's issues with her partner were, but knowing that would be asking for a breach of confidence. Then again, chances were Keenan wouldn't care about that. But *she* did. She would probably find out at the next meeting anyway.

"Next to the bar." Keenan raised his chin toward the corner, where a woman with jet black hair and extremely pale skin, dressed head to toe in leather, leaned against the wall. "Her name's Suzanne. Want me to introduce you?"

Tory shook her head. "No, that's all right. Angelica might not want us all to meet her, since she talks about her in the group."

"Is that why you didn't bring Louis?" Keenan asked.

She turned back to him, the lie on her lips that he was working, but the look in his eyes stopped her. How did he do that, look at her as if more was going on besides their seemingly innocuous conversation? It made her not want to lie to him.

She stood, tongue-tied and unable to think when someone joined them. Tory was only just aware of a third presence when something pushed past her leg and wedged itself between Keenan and her.

She looked down to see the animal that had attacked her on the street. She swallowed a gasp, and took a quick step backward.

"Is everything all right?" Jan, who was suddenly right beside Keenan, asked.

"Fine, yes," Tory said, her voice an entire octave higher than normal. She was acutely aware of Keenan's eyes upon her. If he recognized her terrified expression from that on the woman's face a couple weeks ago, she'd be outed as the one he'd met that day.

Would that be the end of the world? her mind screamed. *Can't we just let him recognize us and get the hell out of here?*

"I walked her around the block a few times," Jan was saying, "but she didn't do anything. So I thought I'd bring her by and ask if you wanted me to give her dinner."

"You walked her all the way down here from my place?" Keenan looked down at the dog. "No wonder she's finally calm."

"I needed the exercise. Besides, it's nice out." Jan smiled and shrugged.

Tory noted the sheen of sweat on her forehead. If

you could work up a sweat in fifty-degree weather, you were not just out for an enjoyable walk.

"She really only needed to be out for a minute after work," Keenan said. "You didn't have to put this much time in. One stop at a tree and she could have gone right back in."

Were they really talking about the dog's excretions in the middle of an art gallery? What was wrong with these people?

"They allow dogs in here?" she asked shrilly.

The expression on Keenan's face was unreadable but dark, as he passed his gaze from Jan to her. "Angelica said it would be all right, though I hadn't intended to bring her. Jan kindly offered to let her out after work. Instead," he added, perhaps pointedly.

The dog was pulling at the leash in Tory's direction, nose sniffing the air as if Tory smelled like a particularly good brand of sausage.

She stood stock-still, heart hammering, trying to keep her face from showing her fear. Her eyes were locked on Keenan's hand, the leather leash wound tightly in what looked like a firm grip, but you never knew. Surely he wouldn't let the thing near her. If nothing else she was dressed up.

"I was going to feed her when I got home," Keenan told Jan.

"Oh, okay. I'll take her back then," Jan said with a laugh. "But look at all the attention she's getting!"

Because people are afraid she's going to attack them, Tory thought. What was the matter with dog people that they didn't know when their dogs didn't belong?

"Ooh, she's so *cute*," a woman in a little black dress cooed, coming over to them and bending over to let the animal sniff her fingers. "Is she yours?" The woman looked up coquettishly at Keenan.

"She is indeed," he said, his tone more than a little wry.

"I just *love* dogs," the woman breathed. "Not to mention guys who love dogs."

Tory took a shallow breath and said, in an unnaturally deep voice this time, "Excuse me, I'm going to get some more champagne."

Her head was light from holding her breath by the time she got to the bar, and she exhaled in a huff, drawing the attention of Angelica, standing nearby.

"Vicky," Angelica said with a smile. "I'm so glad you could make it. Are you enjoying yourself?"

"Yes, yes I am having a good time," she said quickly.

She was having trouble keeping her eyes off the tall blond dog in Keenan's fist.

"You look lovely," Angelica said. "Where on earth did you get that dress?"

"I, uh, got it at Saks, I think. Yes, Saks. Thank you. Oh and your work is—is lovely. Uh, too." She kicked herself for repeating Angelica's word and searched her mind for another. "It's extraordinary, really. I've been very impressed."

"Is everything all right?" Angelica asked, moving closer so nobody nearby heard her question. There was something extremely comforting about Angelica, Tory noted. Something that made you want to open up.

"I'm fine," Tory said, fighting the urge to reveal her phobia. "I was just, uh, looking at that painting you did, with, uh . . ." She motioned in the direction of *Phantasie at Midnight*.

"Ah, you're afraid I might have inappropriate feelings for Keenan," Angelica said calmly.

"Well, no, I just, well," she stumbled, trying to figure out how to say, *Yes, that's right* without actually saying it. "It does seem to be saying something, uh, that is, aren't you worried about making Keenan uncomfortable?"

Angelica smiled. "I'll let you in on a little secret . . ."

"Oh Keenan already told me," Tory said quickly, waving one hand. "About your—your girlfriend. But still . . ."

Angelica laid a hand on Tory's forearm, and Tory instantly felt reassured. "You have to trust me on this," she said, with a slight smile still on her lips. "There's nothing to worry about. One of these days you and I should go out for a drink; I can tell you just how far I am from having inappropriate feelings for Keenan James."

Tory exhaled. "Oh, that would be . . . nice. I'd really like that." And she would. In fact, right now she thought there was nothing she'd like better than to be someplace quiet and calm with this reassuring woman.

"You look *gorgeous*," Martina said, butting into their conversation with champagne glass in hand. Her eyes were a little brighter than usual, and Tory suspected she'd been there awhile. "*Where* did you get that dress?"

"Saks," Tory said again. "Thank you."

"Is everything okay here?" Martina asked. "You guys were talking awfully close. Any gossip I should be in on?"

"No, no," Tory said, laughing. "I never know any gossip."

She glanced again across the room at the dog. It was still in the same place, thank God, and was even sitting by Keenan's feet. No doubt scouring the room for its next victim.

"So are you having a good time?" Tory asked Martina, but she and Angelica had turned to see what she was looking at.

"Oh Lord," Angelica murmured. "I was afraid she'd figure out a way to end up here."

"Is that Keenan's dog?" Martina asked.

"Yes," Angelica drawled. "She's volunteered to

walk it after work, anytime Keenan's not going to be home."

"I heard about that." Martina chuckled smugly.

"She volunteered to walk his dog every time he's not going to be home?" Tory asked. "*Why?*"

Angelica's eyebrows rose significantly. "Yes she did. And she doesn't live anywhere close to Keenan's neighborhood."

Jan was now scratching the dog's head, gazing up into Keenan's face.

"Last time she got leather burns on her palms when it dragged her down the sidewalk after another dog," Martina said to Angelica. "But she isn't about to quit."

It dragged her down the sidewalk? Tory thought. What was to stop the dog from dragging Keenan across the room to kill her?

"I'm not surprised," Angelica said.

"She said she'd do anything to see inside his apartment," Martina continued. "Now I guess she has. Think she's gone through his underwear drawer yet?"

This actually jerked Tory's attention away from the dog for a moment, as Angelica and Martina laughed together.

"Would she *do* that?" Tory asked.

"I wouldn't put it past her," Angelica said, with a shake of her head.

Martina leaned across Angelica toward Tory.

"I'll tell you two but you can't tell *anybody else*. She's got a major *thing* for Keenan."

Tory's mouth dropped open. "She has? What about her boyfriend?"

"Oh no," Angelica murmured.

Martina dissolved into peals of giggles. "She doesn't *have* one! Can you believe it? She made one up so she could come sit at the table with Keenan every week!"

Chapter 8

Tory decided to return to Saks the evening before the next round table instead of right before it. She was determined to learn how to apply the makeup herself, so she didn't have to keep coming to the store and getting tempted to buy more clothes.

"You have a night meeting?" Katya asked, stifling a yawn behind one beringed hand.

"No, no. I just had some time and I was hoping you could show me what to do here." She fanned her hands out over the palette of makeup on the glass counter. "I'd like to try doing it myself."

Katya glanced at her watch, looking worried. "I can give you quick lesson. You are lucky, you know. If you arrived later, maybe I would not be here. I leave at six today."

Tory glanced at her watch too. Five-fifteen. Surely it wouldn't take longer than a few minutes to learn how to apply a little makeup.

As Katya gathered her tools—brushes, tissues, cotton balls, small triangular sponges—Tory noticed that she looked tired. Dark circles appeared under her eyes when she tilted her head and she sighed several times as she searched for something in a drawer.

"Is everything all right?" Tory asked. "You seem a bit . . ." Subdued? Would Katya know that word? Her English was pretty good, but not perfect. "Sad," she finished.

Katya looked up at her, and for a moment Tory thought she might cry. "It is my boyfriend." She shook her head and came around from behind the counter, holding some brushes. "I think . . ." she started slowly, "he cheats on me."

"Oh Katya." Tory gave her a sympathetic look. "Why? What makes you think so?"

Katya shrugged one shoulder and unscrewed the cap from a small jar. "He has done before. I find out, he says, 'Sorry, sorry, I'm so sorry,' and I forgive him. But now . . . I don't know. He is doing it again, I am sure."

"Is it with the same woman?"

Katya gave her a wry look. "Is a different woman, every time. He says it means nothing. But it does to me."

"Of *course* it does." Tory laid a hand on Katya's arm.

Katya smiled wanly. "You think probably I should leave him, I know. Sasha says so all the time. But . . . I love him. I am with him a long time, you know?"

"I know," Tory soothed. What was it with people thinking you just cut and run when a relationship hits a rough patch? No wonder the divorce rate was so high in this country. "You have to try. You can't just throw it all away."

"Yes! This is it. Sasha doesn't understand."

Sasha and Keenan would get along quite well, she thought. "Have you tried counseling?"

Katya tilted her head. "What do you mean?"

"I mean like a therapist. Someone both of you can go talk to, to find out why he keeps doing this. Do you think your boyfriend would do that with you?"

Katya laughed sadly. "If it is a woman, he will do."

Tory smiled. "A man or a woman, a good therapist might be able to set him straight. I'll get you some names, okay?"

"You know therapists?" Katya laid out the foundation, eye shadows and blush in a line in front of Tory.

"It's kind of my business." Tory turned to the products. "I know a good couples counselor."

"Okay." Katya let out a deep breath and smiled at her, looking hopeful. "I will do it. Now you will do this." She laughed, sounding better, Tory thought. "First you take this and shake . . ."

Twenty minutes later Tory was looking at herself and feeling quite proud. She'd transformed her own face! She looked just like she did when Katya did her face, and yet she had done it all herself.

"Vicky?"

Granted, Katya had told her every step to take, but Tory thought she could remember the order for next time.

"Vicky? Is that you?"

As Katya rang up her purchases, Tory fiddled with the lip glosses. Stroking lines along the back of her hand to test the colors with her skin tone.

Someone touched her shoulder. "Vicky? It *is* you!"

Tory turned to see Angelica looking at her inquiringly, and it dawned on her that she'd been saying her name, the fake one, and Tory had been oblivious.

"Angelica! I was just in my own little world here." Tory stood up. "How nice to see you."

"Were you getting a makeover?" Angelica asked, looking over her face. "Perfect colors."

"Yes, well." She laughed nervously, though why she should be nervous was beyond her. "To tell you the truth, I get a makeover before every round table."

"Do you really? Why that's brilliant. What a perfect way to lift your confidence before going to counseling." Angelica beamed.

"That's one benefit," Tory agreed. "But the reason I started doing it was because I didn't want to be recognized. Isn't that funny? I never used to wear makeup, so I was using it as a disguise. Now, though, I kind of like it. I wanted to learn how to do it myself."

Tory didn't know why she was telling Angelica all this. There was just something about the woman that made her want to confess. Maybe because Angelica made everything seem all right, like nothing was a big deal.

"It looks very natural," Angelica said. "Though I'm sure you're just as pretty without it."

Tory snorted. "Oh no. It's Katya. She's a genius."

"Is she the one who picked out that gorgeous dress you wore to the opening?"

"Actually that was her sister, Sasha. She works here too. I should introduce you." Tory turned as Katya returned with her bag of potions.

"Here you are," Katya sang, handing her the bag and smiling at Angelica. "I put receipt inside."

Tory introduced Katya to Angelica and asked if Sasha was working.

"No, never on weekend. Her husband, he doesn't

like it." Katya shook her head. "*Men*," she added in a tone that was not the least bit light.

Angelica raised her brows.

"I'll get you those names," Tory promised.

"And I will give to Sasha too," Katya said with a laugh, heading back to her station.

"Have you got some time?" Angelica asked. "I was just thinking maybe we could have that drink we talked about now."

"Oh I'd *like* that," Tory said, feeling her spirit buoy. She was making friends, she thought. *Girl* friends. She was no longer the workaholic with only her boyfriend to talk to. Of course, she had no boyfriend now either, so this was extra special.

They went to the bar at the Palace Hotel, which was right next door, and each ordered a martini. Tory couldn't remember the last time she actually went out just for a drink, but she settled in comfortably.

Conversation with Angelica was easy, and not just because of the alcohol. Angelica was the type of person who asked a lot of questions and seemed genuinely interested in the answers. While that could have made it difficult for Tory to keep track of her deceptions, Angelica didn't ask typical questions, and they rarely touched on the facts Tory had had to fudge for the round table.

They talked about books and movies and families and, of course, relationships.

"Can I ask you something?" Tory asked, in the middle of her second martini, feeling all glowy and warm from the first. "What do you get out of the round tables? I mean, we talk about men, and Keenan gives his opinions because they're"—she rolled her eyes—"*male*. How does that help you?"

Angelica smiled. "Well, it's certainly interesting, isn't it?"

Tory laughed. "Oh yes, I'll give him that. He's interesting."

"Keenan is actually a good friend of mine. I go to his round tables for him, mostly, as support, you know. But occasionally I find myself asking advice of him or the other members. Relationships all have similar evils." She laughed.

"A friend?" Tory scanned back through the conversation, hoping she hadn't said anything too insolent about Keenan. "So you, uh, respect what he does?"

"Tremendously. Don't you?" Angelica looked at her curiously, her fingers grasping the olive skewer and stirring it around in her drink with one hand.

"I'm—to be honest I'm not sure yet." What a relief to be *honest*, she thought.

Angelica nodded encouragingly.

"I mean, I'd heard good things about what he was doing, but I wonder if some of the women aren't there for reasons other than his counsel."

She twisted her glass on her napkin and looked at Angelica askance. "Like Jan, for example."

"Yes, I was afraid of that with Jan." Angelica sipped her drink thoughtfully. "It's happened before. Keenan usually knows how to handle it, but he might need to be warned about this one. I don't think he saw it coming."

"So . . . in your opinion, his motives are . . . pure?" Tory asked.

"If you're asking if he really wants to help women, the answer is unequivocally yes. Is that what you meant?"

Tory nodded. "And, well, I just wondered if you ever thought he, you know, did it to meet women?" She tried to make the question sound less accusing than it was, but there was no way to do it.

To her surprise, Angelica laughed.

"Vicky, if you were a man, looking for a woman, would you go out of your way to find one who needs therapy?"

Tory wanted to be offended—after all, there was nothing *wrong* with being in therapy—but the way Angelica said it made her laugh. "I guess not. And from what I know of Keenan, he doesn't need something like *this* to help him find women."

Monday morning, Tory caved. She was getting dressed to leave for her second round table when she found herself facing a closet full of navy, gray, and putty-colored suits that rendered pointless the new makeup she'd acquired. She needed something new to wear. Something *not her*.

The sleeve of the pale peach shirt peeked out of the folds in the closet like a daffodil in February— sweet, soft, and vulnerable. Exactly how she should have acted at the first round table. Or even the art opening. But she'd blown both fairly decisively. She had to put on a better front today. A more feminine front.

So instead of putting on one of her old outfits, or rerunning the new one she'd worn last week, she threw on some jeans and a shirt, wrestled the damn contact lenses into her eyes, and bolted for Saks. She wasn't sure why it suddenly seemed so vitally important to look as good—and as different—as she had the first time, but it did. If Sasha was there and they hurried, she could get a fresh outfit and maybe still make it to lunch on time.

Fortunately, both sisters were there. Unfortunately, they were feeling more confident in their opinions—no doubt because Tory kept returning— and Tory didn't have sufficient time to resist their more assertive ministrations. "Feminine" to them meant "sexy."

Which was how she came to be standing in front of the Metropolitan Grill wearing a skirt that was considerably shorter than she was comfortable in, heels considerably higher, and her hair considerably looser in the early fall breeze.

She felt naked, and not in the good way she had in the light, drapy fabric of the last two outfits.

Well, okay, she thought. She was someone different, someone who dressed for men and hoped to manipulate them by their testosterone into a long-term committed relationship.

She took a deep breath, and from the corner of her eye, felt a presence unlike any of the others on the crowded sidewalk. She turned and was not surprised to see Keenan James walking with his loose-legged stride toward her. Today he wore blue jeans and hiking boots—in New York City!—with a brown shirt and tweedlike jacket. But this wasn't any tweed like Stewart's elbow-patched professorial-style jackets were tweed. This was somehow more outdoorsy, yet stylish, with a hint of disregard for convention and a dash of ready-for-anything action.

Or was the jacket just tweed and the man all of the above?

He had his hands in his pockets, pushing the jacket out behind him and revealing the trim way his shirt tucked into the front of his well-worn jeans. No soft belly there, and she'd bet no tweed-covered love handles either. Her eyes rode up his chest, past the open collar and masculine throat to the gently quirked mouth and the eyes looking right at her.

Shit, she thought involuntarily. Looking right at her roaming eyes. She would concede this one thing, this thing that possibly dictated his success: that he *paid attention*. He paid attention like no other man she'd ever known, studying whomever he was talking to, listening with an engagement that was fully involved, right in the moment with them. When she talked to him she had a thousand thoughts running around her head—*What was he thinking? Had what she just said sounded stupid? Was he noticing her ridiculous makeup?*—and he looked at her as if he were completely unaware of anything but her.

It was a gift.

And a curse to those who were not interested in being seduced by it.

"Vicky," he said as if he couldn't have seen anyone who'd give him more pleasure. That damnably warm celebrity smile didn't help either. Did he practice it in the mirror? "Glad to see you back."

"Hello, Keenan." The name was weird on her lips, an unusual name that was tough to get out naturally in any circumstances, let alone these. If he'd been a "Bob" she might have been able to forget he was famous.

"You look nice today," he said.

She nearly scoffed. *Nice?* She looked like a hooker. But then he probably liked that in a woman.

She raised her chin. "Thank you, Keenan. You look ready for the Adirondacks," she said, tempering it with a smile. "Heading off for the mountains after lunch? Or are you just back from a weekend away?"

One side of his mouth kicked up and he shook his head, removing a hand from his pocket to rake that lock of hair off his forehead. "The latter. I'd have changed clothes but I guess I wanted to hang on to the feeling of being in the mountains. I walked here from my apartment and tried to convince myself I was still hiking a mountain trail."

She glanced around the concrete jungle in which they stood. "That must have been difficult."

He laughed at himself and nodded ruefully. "Took a lot of imagination."

For some reason she felt hot. She glanced at the pavement beneath her new high-heeled shoes, then realized she was avoiding his eyes and looked back at him directly. "Well, I hope you're here now. You've got some patients who need your undivided attention." As if she'd ever seen anything less from the man.

"You're not a patient, Vicky. Please remember that."

She bit back an *of course I'm not* just in time. "I was being facetious. I just meant that these women seem the type to require complete concentration."

"I find it difficult to give them anything but." His eyes were cool, but amused. He held a hand out toward the door. "Shall we?"

She inclined her head and preceded him to the

door, nearly jumping when she felt his hand graze the small of her back—a gentle guiding motion she'd only seen other people do and never experienced herself. It was pleasant, if somehow patronizing. As if she needed herding. No doubt it was the clothes that made him think she couldn't reach the door without this help.

Once inside, Tory strode across the room ahead of his hand and tried to keep her head high, even as she struggled to keep the short skirt from riding up and the shoes from collapsing sideways. How on earth did women do this without feeling like they were about to reveal everything to everyone around them? When they arrived at the table Angelica and Jan were engaged in conversation, and Ruth Bitterman was sitting quietly, a small gray shadow across the table from them.

"Hello," Tory said, smiling cordially at each of them. She almost couldn't look at Jan, knowing what she now knew about her made-up boyfriend.

The women answered her warmly but when Keenan appeared from behind her, they all lit up like pinball machines on tilt.

"Hi Keenan!" Jan burst, her round face even rounder with the smile she gave him. Suddenly it was so obvious; Martina had been right. Jan definitely had a thing for him.

Though she might have guessed that just on hearing that she walked his dog.

"The man of the hour." Angelica was more subdued in her tone, but her face did seem to glow.

Even Ruth Bitterman, who barely said a word in the sessions, blushed timidly and said, "Hello, Keenan."

Was this group therapy or mass infatuation?

"How is everyone today?" Keenan pulled out a chair, and Tory moved toward one on the other side of the table. Too late, she realized he'd been holding out the chair for her. He gave her a quizzical look, a tilt of his head and considering eyes, and sat down.

She tried to add that formality to his list of chauvinistic actions but she knew it was simply gentlemanly. How unused she was to those little courtesies. Stewart had taken the finer points of feminism and used them to abandon all such gestures, even while thinking, she suspected, he was superior to women. To be fair, though, she believed he considered himself superior to most men too.

Moments later Martina arrived and they were all assembled. Menus flipped open, talk shifted to crab cakes and chicken salads, before, with no warning Tory could discern, Martina burst into tears.

Talk around the table ceased as all eyes turned to her. These were no delicate sniffles, no muted cry for sympathy and assistance; these were full-throated sobs of the sort that came straight from the gut.

Jan rubbed Martina's back, asking her to calm down, to please tell them what was the matter. Jan's ministrations were so frantic in themselves that Tory wondered if she wasn't simply egging the poor girl on. Martina's long dark hair swung over her face and pooled on the table in front of her. When she finally lifted her head, several strands stuck to her wet cheeks and neck.

Tory looked at Keenan, who was leaning forward in his chair, his elbows on the table, hands clasped in front of him. His eyes were intense, a laserlike blue that shot across the table and snared the sobbing girl with their power.

Tory glanced furtively around and saw a couple of nearby tables watching too. She glared at one man until he noticed, flushed red, and turned back to his dining companion.

"Martina," Keenan said finally. His low voice sent a tingling up Tory's spine and commanded the attention of the weeping woman. Tory watched him, wondering why she herself felt the urge to blush. It was the intimacy of the tone, she finally concluded. As if his head were next to hers on a pillow, his hands. . .

Then she did blush, and turned her attention to Martina.

"It's Rex," she said, choking the name over several syllables. "He's never going to marry me. I—he—he's not even thinking about it."

"Did something happen?" Keenan asked. "You've suspected this for some time."

"No," she said, shaking her head wildly. "That's the thing. I just suddenly realized. We were talking yesterday and he said he was going to join the board of his condominium. Just said it. Like in passing. Said he had ideas about how the place would run better and he didn't want that damn Oriental decor in the lobby anymore. And I just realized, it's never going to happen. I mean I think about this every day. Every single stupid day. I agonize and plan and wonder what he's thinking and feeling and planning. Sometimes I even pretend he's going to surprise me. Like maybe he just *said* he was working on the weekend because he was out ring shopping. And then . . ." Her voice threatened to break again but she caught it. "He says just oh-so-casually he's going to run for the board of his condo. And he *knows* I can't move in there. Not with Janice and Cucumber."

This caught Tory off guard and she glanced around the table to see if it did anyone else. Angelica caught her eye and mouthed the word "cats."

"We've talked about it," Martina continued. "He knows we have to talk about moving if we want to live together. And now . . . the board's term is a year!" she wailed.

More eyes began roving to Keenan, waiting for the oracle to speak, Tory thought. Normally so outspoken and opinionated, the group now sat virtually paralyzed, wondering what the Great Man would come up with in the face of this difficult and damning information. Would the sage speak truth or would he equivocate? Did he have any idea what to do in this situation?

Tory knew what she would advise. Communication, plain and simple. Martina needed to ask him what he was thinking, tell him how upset this made her. While Martina came here every week and talked out her problems with the man so that this group all understood her needs and wants perfectly, she suspected the same was not true of her dealings with Rex. If it were, he would never have been able to just toss off so casually that he planned to stay in his building another year.

It was obvious Martina had not yet made herself clear.

Finally, Keenan leaned back in his chair, considering Martina with a kind, pained look on his face. For a second, Tory wondered if this was acting, then remembered that Keenan only wrote for television, he didn't act in it. So was he really as concerned as he appeared? Why did she doubt it?

"Dump him," he said finally.

There was a collective gasp around the table.

"*What?*" Tory and Martina said it at the same time, with nearly the same appalled tone.

Keenan's eyes shot to Tory's a moment, lingered, then shifted back to Martina.

"Motivation," he began, "is driven by the balance of needs. And needs are governed by two things. If you want to get psychological about it, these two things are called 'homeostasis' and 'equilibrium restoration.' You, Martina, are suffering from Rex's homeostasis."

Tory let out a heavy sigh and nearly rolled her eyes. She stopped herself in time. This was so predictable.

Martina looked at him in horror. "Are you saying Rex is *gay*?"

Next to her, Jan gasped. Angelica laughed. Ruth gaped at Keenan.

For a second, Tory wanted to laugh too.

Keenan actually did, if gently. "Of course not. What I'm saying is, when a guy's needs are met, when he's happy with the status quo and not inclined to change anything, that's homeostasis. What you need to do is upset that. Turn over the applecart. Then he will be provoked into restoring the equilibrium. That is, he'll want to get you back, to get back to that place where he was so comfortable. And he'll do anything to restore what he had. So if you tell him marriage is the only way you'll come back, then that's what he'll have to do. But Martina, if he won't do that, then you'll know that he never would have come around to marrying you in the first place, no matter how long you stuck it out in this situation."

Martina chewed on her bottom lip and looked at Keenan. "That—that makes sense."

Tory couldn't stand it. "How long have you been with him, Martina?"

"Three and a half years," she sniffed.

"Plenty of time for Rex to know what he wants," Jan interjected. "Right, Keenan?"

"Sure." Keenan's tone was so offhand that Tory turned on him.

"She's been with him three and a half years and you're saying to trash the whole relationship?" she accused. "Cut and run? Don't try to work anything out, just tell him she's out of there?"

Keenan looked pleased, even as he leaned forward to shrug out of his jacket. *"Seal The Deal, Baby.* She's not getting any dedication. And he's got no reason to change anything. He's getting everything he wants, so why would he? Martina can stay in the situation and suck it up, while her self-esteem crumbles and her biological clock ticks down, or she can get out and find someone who makes her happy."

"Just like that," Tory said, seething. "Just go out and find someone who makes her happy. That's your advice? Like great single guys are wandering around the street waiting to be chosen?"

"I've got to go with Vicky on this one," Angelica said. "If Martina dumps him, she's likely to be alone awhile."

"And is that worse than being with someone who makes her do this?" He laid a palm out flat toward Martina. Exhibit A.

Keenan's eyes shifted to Martina. "Dump him," he said again. Confidently, definitively.

Tory couldn't believe it. He had no qualms telling the girl to make a major life change, without letting her come up with it or anything else on her own. If that wasn't dangerous, Tory didn't know what was.

Tory flashed him a furious look, then turned to Martina and said, "*Talk* to him, Martina. For all you know he's unaware of how deeply you need a commitment. Maybe he has something else in mind by joining the board. Like changing the pet policy."

Jan frowned at her. "Isn't that like thinking he's out ring shopping when he's working on the weekend? It's a fantasy."

"That's why I'm saying she needs to talk to him," Tory said. "Tell *him* all of this. Not just us."

"I don't know," Jan said, shifting her gaze from Tory to Keenan. "We can talk till we're blue in the face, but I don't think men take it seriously. I'm with Keenan. For men, there's cause and there's effect. They react to things that make them uncomfortable and that's about it."

"Exactly," Keenan said.

"I've said this for months," Jan went on. "You're

too good to him, Martina. Let him see what life's like without you for a while."

Martina sniffed and blotted the corners of her eyes with her napkin. "I don't know."

"It's game playing," Tory insisted. "That kind of thing hasn't worked since middle school. And it's not exactly treating Rex or the relationship with any respect."

"It's about *self*-respect." Keenan turned to Tory. "Something too many women set aside in their relationships. If nothing else comes out of it, she'll feel better about herself for taking control of the situation."

Tory glared at him, into those eyes that were at once uncompromising and probing. Why did he have to look at her as if *she* were the one needing help? He acted as if he saw right through her, even while she was the one with the answers.

All he had was that stupid *Seal The Deal, Baby* phrase.

"What if he finds he doesn't mind being without Martina?" Tory questioned, remembering at the last minute to turn away from those intense blue eyes to Martina's red-rimmed ones. "What if he finds someone who, because it's the initial stages of a relationship, makes him feel like he's a prince among men? It's always like that in the beginning, don't you remember? It won't matter to him at all that it's not real, not tested, Martina. There'll be all that initial passion to burn up any doubts."

Martina began to cry again. "I can't stand thinking of him with someone else. I'd rather he be miserable with me!"

"Of course you can't," Tory said sympathetically. "But if you give him an ultimatum, you have to be ready for the bad result as well as the good. And I mean absolutely prepared to accept it and live with it."

"What if Martina discovers she's happier without *him*?" Keenan said to Tory. He moved his focus to Martina. "All that stuff about passion, Martina, that could happen to you. You could well find someone who makes you feel as special as you are, not like someone who has to beg to be loved."

"I am begging to be loved . . ." Martina said softly.

"And she should trust that? Just like that?" Tory protested. "Heck, every relationship is perfect in the beginning. What about the trials her relationship with Rex has already been through? What about the tests and hurdles they've already scaled, the time they've grown together? Should that mean nothing? Surely they had that sunshiny phase already in their relationship. Now is time for the hard work."

"Spoken like a woman who spent eight years in a relationship with a man who wouldn't marry her," Keenan said.

A hush fell over the table. Tory's entire body went rigid.

"You guys are tough," Angelica murmured, frowning at Keenan.

"We're not talking about me," Tory pushed out through stiff lips.

"Maybe we should be," he said reasonably. "This is how we learn from one another. You might be the classic example of what Martina has to look forward to if she continues on the way she has been. Not that it's not a valid decision to do that. But is that what you want, Martina?" He turned back to her.

Martina scrunched up her face as if she'd been asked if she wanted anchovies instead of ice cream. "No way!"

Tory recoiled. It was made up, she reminded herself. Louis wasn't real. She wasn't real, not in this scenario.

But then, she had been in a relationship with Stewart for eight years. And he hadn't talked about marriage. Ever.

"Maybe *I* didn't want to be married," she blurted, hating the defensive tone of her voice. This was why psychologists liked to be the ones asking questions, their own personal lives off limits.

"*Aha*," Keenan said, satisfaction all over his smug, handsome face. "Now we're getting somewhere. I thought you were here because you were rethinking your breakup with Louis and thought maybe you should marry him, despite the lack of passion. Maybe it's time we talk about *your* ambivalence to the idea."

Her eyes darted to his, and she saw that his searching, concerned look had turned to one of skepticism. He was on to her. Or was she just imagining that?

But this wasn't about her, wasn't even about the made-up her. This was about *him*.

She leaned forward in her seat. "What about you, Keenan James?" she demanded softly. "They're— *we're* all here, listening to you, taking your advice. What has your most successful relationship been like? Are you in one now? Have you ever been married?"

Four expectant faces swiveled to him, in each of them a level of curiosity Tory was sure had been growing since long before she joined the group.

"I am here," Keenan said easily, "to offer the point of view of the male. And as someone who has successfully avoided marriage for years, I think I am uniquely qualified to explain to Martina, or anyone else, how a man dodges commitment." He turned to Martina. "He's comfortable. He's getting what he wants. *All* he wants. There is absolutely no incentive for him to change."

"Except that if he loves you, truly loves you, he will want to satisfy *your* needs," Tory added.

Heads pivoted, one by one, toward Martina.

"I . . ." She sniffed and wiped her nose. "I think

I've said all I can say to him." She looked apologetically at Tory. "I don't think he even hears it anymore."

The group was silent.

"I—I think I'm going to dump him." Martina exhaled, then smiled tremulously at Keenan.

"Yes!" Jan hissed.

Tory sighed, inexplicably sad.

"Good girl," Angelica added. "You've given him plenty of time. You don't want to find yourself turning forty and sitting in the same old situation, waiting on him to tell you how life's gonna be."

" . . . wait until it's too late . . ." The soft voice emerged after the encouraging sounds had dissipated.

It was, to everyone's surprise, Ruth Bitterman.

"What was that?" Keenan leaned toward her.

"Don't marry a man who ignores you," she said, a little louder. As the oldest, she was the gray sage of the battle. Scarred, defeated . . . and wise? "Trust me, it only gets worse."

Ruth's comment effectively ended the round table that day. No one ordered dessert, and Tory suspected that most of the women were wondering if they should go home and dump their boyfriends if only so that they didn't end up a ghost of a woman like Ruth Bitterman.

In fact, it was because she herself felt more justified about having broken up with Stewart that she

determined to try to talk to Keenan James alone
for a moment.

Keenan wanted to follow Vicky Smith from the
restaurant, but Jan caught him with some questions about the dog. Still, Keenan followed Vicky
with his eyes, wondering how far she'd get with
her businesslike—if jerky in her heels—stride before he could wriggle away from Jan.

He coaxed Jan toward the door as they talked.

From his vantage point, he couldn't help noticing Vicky's legs in the short skirt, long and slim
and leading like the road to ruin to a firm, rounded
ass. An ass, he thought, that moved in a way that
was more sultry than a New York City street de-
served. She held herself erect, as if she could make
herself taller than her slight figure was naturally,
and he wondered if some of her prickly attitude
came from the fact that she appeared as soft and
pliant as a fairy-tale princess on the outside. Sleeping Beauty just awakened, and looking startled.

Of course, then she opened her mouth.

He remembered something Fender had said about
her being whip smart and possibly putting off the
boyfriend with it.

Well, he'd gotten that right. She was a dynamo,
decisive and opinionated, who was altogether too
assured about offering advice to women in need.

Could she possibly be a shrink? It made sense. If Fender had sent her to check up on him, it would make sense to send someone with some expertise.

He needn't have worried about losing her due to Jan's delay. She was waiting for him outside the restaurant.

"Vicky," he said, surprised as she stepped toward him.

A warm September breeze blew her blond hair in sinuous, lapping waves, making it shimmer in the afternoon sun.

Vicky smiled at Jan and said good-bye, then moved toward Keenan. As she did, she tripped on the sidewalk and nearly toppled over on the high heels. He caught her wrist with one hand.

For a second he felt suspended; the delicate bones of her wrist, the soft skin and proximity of her slight body had him believing for just a moment that she was as ethereal and defenseless as she looked.

He shook himself, dropped her hand, and stepped back. "Sorry. I thought you were going to fall."

"I did too." She laughed nervously. Blood had flooded her face, turning her pale skin pink and heightening the gray of her eyes. She looked as vulnerable as a kitten. "Listen, I hope I didn't take over in there. I just . . . felt so bad for Martina."

He narrowed his eyes. No, this was not right. Inside she'd been a bulldozer, and out here she was turning belly-up. Something was definitely fishy.

"It's okay," he said warily.

"It's just," she continued, looking at the ground, "I wonder if you know just how dangerous a game it is you're playing."

Her eyes met his again, any whiff of shyness gone.

"These are women's *lives*," she added. "Not characters on some TV show."

Okay, that was an insult that stung. He had to hand it to her, she knew how to hit you where it hurt.

"Yeah, I figured that out right around the time they started speaking on their own," he said, putting his hands in his pockets. "But thanks for pointing it out just the same."

"It would be one thing if you had some training," she continued, either oblivious to or unconcerned about his reaction to her words, "but you're basing your advice on nothing but—but—"

"Let me help you out," he said, leaning in toward her, automatically noting her milky skin and the daintiness of her neck. "I'm basing my advice on sound psychological theories. Believe it or not, Miss Smith, I'm not as dumb as you may think. I've even read a book or two in my day."

"Let me guess. *Psychology for Dummies*?" Her tone was scathing.

"Hey, it's a good book." He grinned.

Her face darkened. "Forgive me for saying so, but it seems clear to me that Martina needs something more than sound-bite advice. I mean, I know we're all coming to the Just-Dump-Him Round Table because we've seen you on TV and all, but is that really the only advice you give? Oh wait, that and *Seal The Deal, Baby!*"

"For your information, the advice I gave Martina was based on the drive reduction theory, by a guy named Clark Hull. The longer she stays in that situation that is obviously enough for Rex, the lower his drive to change it becomes."

"Oh please. That is so basic." Vicky placed her hands on her slim hips. "The drive reduction theory only works when you're talking about cavemen having enough meat for the week. But when you're talking about modern life and needs and relationships, it's generally acknowledged that Abraham Maslow's motivational theory is much closer to the mark."

"Maslow?" he repeated. "You're bringing up Abraham Maslow?"

She shrugged, looking at him as if he were an imbecile. "Of course. He doesn't reduce things to merely primary and secondary drives. That doesn't work within the complexity of modern life. In his hierarchy of needs, love and belonging play a pivotal role."

He laughed. "You're giving guys way too much credit."

She continued, undaunted. "If Martina was to go

by Maslow, as most psychologists would advise, she would talk to Rex. Tell him about her needs, her hopes, and she would try to ascertain whether she contributes to his safety and security in the world. She would try to determine if he is feeling adequately self-actualized—"

"I hate to interrupt," Keenan said, "but that sounds like a lot of the bullshit women tell each other to excuse a guy for disregarding completely what they want. Where is Rex's concern about whether Martina is 'adequately self-actualized'?"

"If Martina rewards Rex with love and attention and consideration, his motivation will be tuned to her like a preset radio station," she said. "That's the expectancy theory, in case you haven't heard of it. I propose that perhaps she is too quick to punish him when he doesn't say or do things that match her ideas of the future."

"So you're blaming Martina for Rex's inertia?" he asked incredulously. "That's pretty cold. I think it's as simple as Rex not wanting to be a member of any club that would have someone like him as a member."

Vicky glared at him. "Oh *please*. Now you're citing Woody Allen?"

His lashes lowered slightly. So she did have some awareness of popular culture.

"Groucho Marx, actually," he countered. "Two can play the psycho-jargon game. It's the optimal level of arousal theory, as deciphered for the masses by Groucho and Woody Allen. We're driven to satisfy our needs, but not just at a basic level. We want to reach the highest level of satisfaction we can. So when it comes to marriage, Rex might be thinking he can still get Halle Berry."

She made a sound in the back of her throat. "You've got to be kidding. Now you're going to use psychology to justify Rex's egotism? You can't just toss theories around like marbles, Mr. James," she said heatedly. "Pick one and stick to it or all you're doing is playing psychological poker."

"Wow, marbles, poker, just what game is it that *you're* playing, Miss Smith? And why don't you tell me how it is you know so much about psychology?"

Chapter 9

She stopped as if caught in the safe with her hands on the dough.

Keenan didn't hold back a smile. If he was being evaluated he had a right to know. What did Fender think, that he was going to change what he was doing to suit some tricked-out shrink?

Vicky Smith cleared her throat and looked away, taming a lock of blowing hair behind one ear. "I read a lot of self-help books. I—I like the kind that draw on actual case studies and psychological theories. I think they offer the most concrete advice."

"Uh-huh." He crossed his arms over his chest and tilted his head. "It doesn't really follow, then, that you'd come to me, to something like the round table. I've made it clear I'm no doctor, and I'm sure Franklin Fender warned you you'd get no psychobabble from me."

Her eyes flashed up at him, and gone was the kitten. "'The drive reduction theory'?" she quoted. "'Homeostasis versus equilibrium restoration'? In your hands, the hands of a nonprofessional, what are those if not, as you say, psychobabble?"

"Tools," he said, fighting the urge to demand who she really was. If she were a man, he would have. What did that say about him? "You don't have to be a professional to read a book or two. I find it's best to know the babble even if I don't use it. Every once in a while it offers backup to those who question the validity of my points." He inclined his head toward her.

She flushed again. "Look, I'm sure you don't realize this, but those women in there . . . they're only trying to please *you*. I could see it clear as day with Martina. You told her to dump her longtime boyfriend and she's going to do it. For *you*. Not for herself or for the relationship or for any of the right reasons. You do realize that, don't you? Is that really what you want?"

He scoffed. "That's ridiculous. She's not doing it for me. She comes to me, to the round table, for just this kind of advice and I've never held back before. She knows that. Besides, no matter why she does it, it'll do her good. She needs to take some control—"

"But she's ceding her control to you!" Vicky exclaimed. "She's transferring her focal point of gratification from Rex to you. Instead of approval and validation from her significant other, she is getting it from you. You watch, next week she'll come in all proud as punch that she dumped this guy, and the *next* week—after she's realized that she's in it alone, that she's not all of a sudden coming home to the celebrity approval of Keenan James—she'll be a mess. Mark my words."

"Her 'focal point of gratification'?" He couldn't keep the incredulity from his voice. If she was telling the truth, she'd not only read a lot of self-help books, she'd digested and assimilated them into her DNA.

The breeze kicked up again, sending a plastic wrapper of some sort onto Vicky's leg. As she bent to brush it away, her hair swung down, exposing the pale nape of her neck.

He looked away, concentrated on the exhaust-stained back of a delivery truck across Fourteenth Street. He really needed to get laid if engaging in an argument with this barbed little woman turned him on.

Then again, she had been somewhat different at

the opening, hadn't she? Or had she just *looked* softer?

"Yes." She rubbed her hand against her skirt as the wrapper went on its way. "You need to take more care, be less . . . I don't know, charming with them."

He grinned. "Charming is in the eye of the beholder."

She blushed, and he felt mildly triumphant.

"I don't mean it in the good way," she said darkly. "Maybe it's instinctual for you. Maybe you don't know how to relate to women any other way. I don't know. All I know is, if you really want to help these women, you have to take yourself out of the equation."

He threw his hands out. "You know what? You're right. Maybe I should just phone it in. You know, 1–900–GET–REAL. Think that would be better?"

"I'm not kidding," she said with such deadly seriousness that he laughed.

"God forbid."

She huffed out a breath. "I can see you don't take this seriously. In that case, I won't offer any more opinions."

"I'd just like to know what makes you such an authority, Miss Smith. You've been to two meetings, claim to be qualified to tell me everything I'm doing wrong, and have decided that I'm not helping anyone?"

"You're doing some things right."

"Oh good. Thank you! So this isn't just an exercise in debunking the unconventional thing that's working." He laughed and shook his head. "I get the feeling you're one of those people who enjoy overturning the half-full glass."

"That's unfair."

"Maybe so." He took a deep breath and gazed down the street. New York bustled and rushed, cars belched exhaust, pedestrians pushed past one another, everything moved except the two of them. They were an island of opposition. Why did that bother him so much?

He turned back to her. "Do you want to know my opinion, *Miss Smith*? You came to this round table, at least in part, for the same reasons Martina did and you're intimidated by the advice you're getting."

Her nostrils flared. "That's *Dr.* Smith," she said, those straight brows drawing downward. "And I am *not* intimidated."

His eyes narrowed. "Doctor," he repeated. "Aha."

She blushed again. "I'm a—a dentist, remember?"

He chuckled, not believing her for a second. "That's right. But you know, for some reason I have a hard time picturing you in a white coat scraping plaque from the canines of businessmen." His eyes swept insolently down her body. "Tell me, doesn't that skirt get a little revealing in that situation?"

She recoiled, giving him a look that might have made him feel like a complete shit if she hadn't attacked him first. Tit for tat, psychologically speaking, he thought.

"I don't wear this skirt to work," she said tightly.

"Hm," he said, nodding. "Don't tell me you're just trying to please me too. Dressing up for lunch."

Her mouth dropped open in a silent gasp. "I resent that comment."

He tilted his head. "And I resent your accusation that I'm controlling the women I'm trying to help. I'm not doing this for any sort of ego gratification, *Doctor.* Believe me, I'm not getting a lot out of this myself. I'm only trying to help people. And if you doubt that, I have to wonder why you returned." He raised his brows. "Care to enlighten me on that score?"

"I—I didn't know—I didn't disagree with you, until this week."

"Okay, so you're telling me you agreed with me last week. When I told you that perhaps *you* were a little controlling?" Half a block down, a car honked, setting up a cacophony of others. He leaned toward her and added, finally feeling as if he had the upper hand, "A point that might have been a little noticeable this week too, if you'll forgive my saying so."

She leaned away from him and narrowed her eyes, looking more like a full-grown cat now. "I don't think I will forgive you, *Mr.* James. I find it fascinating that you accuse a woman who disagrees with you of being controlling. Is that based on your fear that she might wrest control from *you*?"

Keenan paused. Was that what he was doing? Did he resent her for offering conflicting advice to his "patient"? Had he possibly come to believe he was the all-knowing doctor he made a point of saying he wasn't? A statement that admittedly came out by rote lately, with little feeling for having to press the point home.

"*No*," he said strenuously. "No. You come to this group for my opinion and I give it. That you would argue with me is simply a sign that you're not ready for that opinion. The controlling part comes when you refuse to credit what I say as having any kind of validity. And you do it when I'm trying to advise another woman in the group."

There. That was it, he thought, nodding once.

She put her hands on her hips and regarded him steadily. "Isn't that what *group* therapy is all about? We learn from each other, I think you said today. But maybe you didn't mean *you*. Maybe you're threatened because you felt diminished in your role. If so, I'm sorry. We should simply agree to disagree." She paused, took a breath, and said more equably, "Listen, all I'm saying is, you should be careful that you're not just transferring your patients' urges to please from their boyfriends to you."

Fine, he thought. He should say it. *Good point. I'll take it into consideration. See you next week.* Then walk away, he told himself. But he didn't do it.

Instead he said, "Did Frank send you?"

"Who?" As the breeze blew her hair she turned partially away, guiding a handful of strands behind her ear. "I don't—"

"Franklin Fender," he said, taking a step sideways to keep her face in view. "Did he send you to check up on me?"

She lifted her head. "Yes, he sent me. But you knew that. I'm not checking up on you, I'm a friend of his wife's, of Katherine's."

"Kathleen." He smiled.

She paused. "Yes, sorry. I call her 'Kate,' so I forget." She swallowed. He watched her throat. "Listen, I have to go. I have . . . patients. A . . . root canal."

He raised his brows. "Yes, better get home and change."

She looked up at him. "Change?"

"You don't work in that skirt, right?"

She pressed her hands to her sides. "Right. But I . . . have clothes at the office."

"Uh-huh." He nodded, unable to keep the smirk from his face. She was lying, no question about it. The good thing was, he could not have been more confident that he would get it out of her eventually.

"Good-bye, Mr. James." She glanced at him quickly, then away, hesitated, then hastened off down the sidewalk.

"Good-bye, Dr. *Smith*," he said, his lip curling as he said it. Smith . . . He shook his head. How obvious.

There was no way she could do this book, Tory thought. The man was dangerous, a fraud, just as she'd suspected. Not only was he oblivious to it, but when she'd charitably decided to point it out to him—actually giving him an opportunity to correct his mistake—he'd turned on her. Turned on the very *idea* that he might be wrong.

It had been on the tip of her tongue to tell him about Jan and her fictional boyfriend. That would have shut him up, she was sure. But she couldn't betray the other women like that. Martina had told her in confidence, and she did not want to be the one who did not take such things seriously.

Still, the fact remained that she'd been right the first time. Keenan James's round tables were all about his ego and nothing about therapy. She ought to write an article on *that*. Heck, she could probably write a book on it. It just wasn't a book that anyone wanted.

She pressed her lips together and shook her head,

glancing at her watch. Now she was late for her afternoon sessions. That argument with Keenan had cost her time, plus she'd had to go home and change clothes. There was no way on earth she could have shown up at work in the getup she'd worn to the round table. They'd have thought she'd lost her mind.

Riding up to her office on the elevator, she felt a sheen of sweat form along her hairline. She wiped it away with two fingers. She needed to concentrate on her practice here, get better with the patients, because this book deal was not going to happen. There was no way she could justify touting the man's methods when they were so obviously self-gratifying. It would be a betrayal of everything she believed in.

So her success lay here, as difficult as that idea was to swallow. She just had to make the best of it.

She stepped off the elevator and headed for her office. Her secretary sat ramrod-straight behind her desk, stamping letters with the date they'd arrived.

"Weldman wants to see you," she said.

Tory stopped and pulled her organizer from her briefcase. Three doctors shared one assistant, so they were responsible for maintaining their own schedules. They just had to make sure the secretary had a copy.

"What time?" Tory flipped open the page to today and studied the list, sighing inwardly. She was discouraged by her two Monday clients. Neither of them seemed to be making any progress, and Tory had to fight a feeling of impatience with them, which was totally inappropriate. "I've got two clients, then a meeting and paperwork that really needs to be done before five. Though, honestly, my last patient really doesn't need to be coming so often anymore."

Not because he was doing so well, unfortunately, but because he was becoming too dependent on the appointments to make him feel better and wasn't doing enough work on his own. And he really ought to join a group instead of doing individual therapy.

She was about to make a note next to Barry Golden's name about moving him to every other week when her secretary stopped her with her next words.

"I've cleared your schedule."

Tory looked up. The woman's face was all business. "You've what?"

"I'm sorry," she said, her voice never losing its professional tone. "Weldman asked me to."

"When?" Tory demanded, shock making her voice hard. This had never happened before. How could she not have known about it? What was Weldman up to? Why wasn't it mentioned this morning?

"Friday," her secretary said. "While you were at

lunch. He came and asked me to clear your schedule for this afternoon."

"But *why?*" Tory's ire rose. "You don't just jerk patients around like that. They depend on their appointments. Some of these people are very volatile."

The woman's back straightened and her eyes went flinty. "*I* didn't jerk them around. Weldman did. And no, he didn't give me a reason. For some reason he doesn't think he needs to account for his actions to his secretary."

Tory took a step back. Of course it wasn't her fault, but it was unusual for her prim, professional assistant to speak to her that way just the same.

Maybe they knew about the round tables. Maybe they thought she should have asked before pursuing the possibility of writing a book.

Then the worst idea came to her: maybe they thought she was going to the round tables for actual *therapy*.

"I'm sorry," Tory said. "I didn't mean to snap at *you*. I'm just surprised. So when does Weldman want to see me?"

She knew the answer before the other woman even opened her mouth.

"Right now."

Tory swallowed hard. This was bad. This was not normal. Her client list had dwindled of late, and now her schedule was cleared and her boss wanted to see her right away.

Tory's cheeks burned and she got a horrible, queasy feeling in her stomach.

She was going to be fired.

∽❀∽

Tory stayed in her apartment for the rest of the week. When she spoke to Stewart, she didn't mention what had happened—that she'd been fired for spectacularly poor achievement in her job. Her *job*, which was to help people improve their lives and understanding of themselves. But she had failed, utterly, miserably. People were not improving under her care.

And she had known it. That was the worst part. She had *known* and she had kept at it, hoping *she'd* improve instead of thinking about what was best for those poor, unhappy people.

Tory was so ashamed of herself, she had barely left the bedroom for three days, had existed on popcorn and yogurt, and had summarily condemned herself for everything she had done since graduating college. She should have known in grad school that her path was not clinical psychology. She should have stuck to research, or experimental psychology. Or writing.

But no, those things had not offered enough money. Those things would not have allowed her to stay in New York, a city she loved, though she had not realized quite how much until it had oc-

curred to her, the last three days, that she'd probably have to leave it now that she had no way of
affording it.

She was just beginning to realize that the sheets
were covered with salt and her tee shirt stained
with purple Yoplait stains when someone knocked
on the door.

In the kitchen, by the sink where she had just
dropped six spoons excavated from amid the tan-
gle of her sheets, she froze. Who on earth could
that be? Certainly not Stewart. He never came here
under the best of circumstances. Why would he
come here on a Thursday afternoon?

"Tory? It's me, Claudia," her sister called through
the door. "I know you're in there because I just
heard you doing dishes."

Tory exhaled. Partly relieved and partly appalled. She and Claudia were not close, and telling
her popular, beautiful, successful sister that she'd
been fired was not something she was interested in
doing.

She opened the door.

Sure enough, Claudia looked terrific. She wore a
pencil-slim skirt with high-heeled boots and a short
leather jacket. Her long blond locks were brushed
back from her face, and she looked luminous in
just the right amount of makeup.

Tory instinctively put a hand to her head, wishing she'd washed her hair that morning. Then she

had the thought that she might be able to return some of the makeup she'd bought from Katya as she hadn't used any of it yet.

Claudia looked her up and down and shook her head. "You poor thing." In her arms was a brown grocery bag that crinkled as she passed Tory in the doorway.

"What do you mean?" Tory followed her into the little galley kitchen that jutted off the living room of her tiny one-bedroom apartment. "I—I wasn't feeling well, so I didn't go to work today."

Her fingers grasped the bottom of her tee shirt and pulled it down over her naked legs.

Claudia was unloading bananas and oranges and strawberries from the bag. "I just heard," she said sympathetically. "It's too awful. What *happened*?"

Tory's stomach began to curl. "What—what do you mean?"

"I mean . . ." Claudia took a cantaloupe the size of her head out of the seemingly bottomless bag. "Why did they fire you?"

Tory gasped. "They—why—how—?"

"I stopped by your office to take you to lunch, and they told me you didn't work there anymore. So I bought you some groceries." Claudia turned to look at her, concern in her eyes. "Your secretary was so nice, she told me all about it. How you came in one day and they'd cleared your schedule and you obviously didn't know anything about it and then you were gone. It's just awful! Are you okay?"

Claudia reached out and squeezed Tory's arm.

Tory took a step back. Then she turned and left the kitchen, walking on wooden legs to the bedroom and picking up her sweatpants from the floor.

Claudia followed.

"I can't believe my secretary told you all that," Tory said, dismayed because not only did her sister know the whole sordid story, but she'd also managed to make friends with a woman who'd been an ice princess to Tory for years.

She sat on the bed and threaded her feet into the legs of the sweatpants.

"She was very concerned about you." Claudia sat next to her on the bed. She smelled like Opium.

Tory scoffed and stood, pulling up her pants. "I'll bet. She was practically smirking when she told me Weldman had cleared my schedule."

"Really?" Claudia frowned. "I'm sure you misread her."

"I didn't misread her, Claudia," Tory said. "I worked there for almost three years and she was a bitch to me the whole time. I know what I'm talking about."

Claudia was silent a moment, just long enough for Tory to feel even worse than she had.

"I'm sorry," Tory said. "I—I guess I just wanted to be able to tell people, in my own way. I can't believe that wretched woman's telling the story to everyone." She sat back down on the bed.

Claudia patted her knee. "She didn't tell it to 'everyone.' She told it to your sister."

Tory hung her head. For some reason that was worse than telling everyone else. Her perfect sister, apple of their parents' eye. . .

"If it makes you feel any better," Claudia added, "she said everyone's been walking on eggshells ever since it happened. Nobody knew it was coming, and they're all afraid they're going to be next."

Tory's heart lifted slightly. "Really?"

For some reason she'd been sure everyone had known it was coming but her, and that once it had happened they were all relieved that she was gone. *Thank God that loser's not bringing down the office anymore.*

"Really. I think that's why she told me everything," Claudia said. "She seemed nervous too."

At that, Tory smiled. She hoped the woman did get fired. Serve her right for being so cold when it had happened to Tory.

But that wasn't fair. She was just being professional. And if what Claudia said was true, she probably *was* afraid she might be next. No wonder she'd been so touchy about not being informed what Weldman was up to when he'd told her to cancel Tory's afternoon appointments. She was out of the loop too.

"Oh God," Tory said, dropping her head into her hands. "I'm such an idiot."

"What are you talking about?" Claudia's hand began rubbing Tory's back, just as their mother's would have.

"I just—" Tears she'd been too numb to feel clogged her throat. "I think I know so much and I don't know *anything*. God, how can anybody stand me?"

"Tory," Claudia scolded softly. "What are you talking about? Everyone loves you."

Tory laughed through her tears. "That is so not true. I'm opinionated and cranky and defensive and—Claudia, you said it yourself, I don't even have any friends! What's *wrong* with me? Why am I like this? I'm supposed to know so much about human nature and I'm just . . . *wrong* all the time. And now I've joined that stupid round table and I spent Monday on my high horse telling Keenan James that *he* was an idiot and look at *me!* Fired from my job for incompetence. That very day! I went from lecturing Keenan James, a guy who's actually trying to help people, without even getting paid—"

She broke off, realizing anew the implications of her going into clinical practice because of the money. *She* was the opportunist, not Keenan James. *She* was the one forming opinions and guiding people for all the wrong reasons. Keenan James was a veritable Mother Teresa compared to her.

Though he was, part of her contended, still wrong. She shook her head.

"You do so have friends," Claudia said after a few minutes. "You have me. And you have Stewart. Don't go exaggerating, it'll only increase your misery."

"You're right." Tory sighed. "But I don't have to exaggerate. The truth is bad enough."

Claudia sighed too. "Tell me about it, Tor. Come on, do a little venting. I'm such an open book, but I never know what you're feeling."

Tory leaned back on the bed and began to tell Claudia all the ugly details, about how bad she was at her job, how desperate she had been to get out of it (ironically), how she wasn't sure what on earth to do with her life, now that she'd proven so bad at the one thing she was interested in.

Claudia lay down next to her, and they both looked at the ceiling.

"Well, what about that book deal? The one with Keenan James?" Claudia asked.

Tory let out a long breath. "I wasn't going to do it. But now . . ."

Claudia sat bolt upright. "You weren't going to do it?! Why not? What on earth are you thinking? This is your ticket, girl. You write a book with a celeb like him and you'll be able to write your own future."

Tory sat up slowly and shot her sister a wry glance. "Spoken like the true PR professional that you are."

"Hey, I'm good at what I do because I know a successful plan when I hear one. You're doing it, and that's that." Claudia stood up. "Now come on, get up. Take a shower and get dressed and let's you and I go out for dinner."

Tory looked down at her sweats, then around at the unmade bed, at the popcorn bags strewn about the floor, the television remote stuck between the pillows. "Oh I don't know. I was going to watch a movie. Besides, I can't afford it." She laughed helplessly.

"I'm paying. And it looks to me like you've watched way too much television this week. Come on, buck up. We're going out. I'm taking you to the trendiest place in Manhattan." Claudia turned her by the shoulders and swatted her on the butt. "Get moving."

Despite herself, Tory laughed, and trudged toward the shower.

The place was loud, dark, and teeming with people. Tory felt as if she were about to be crushed when Claudia pushed back through the crowd with a pink drink in a martini glass extended toward her.

"What is it?" Tory called over the crowd.

"A cosmopolitan," Claudia yelled back. She was moving to the beat of the music—or rather, to the beat. There didn't seem to be any actual music, and she looked perfectly at home. Claudia had always been a clubber and Simon reviled them, much as Tory herself did. This outing was probably as much for Claudia as it was for Tory.

"I can't believe how gorgeous you look in that outfit," Claudia said, leaning toward her. "If I'd seen it first I'd have bought it."

Tory wore the same thing she'd worn to the opening, and once again she felt like someone other than herself. Someone more comfortable in her skin. If it hadn't taken her half an hour to get the damn contacts in her eyes, she'd be tempted to put this outfit on every day. Wearing it with her clunky, scratched glasses, however, just wouldn't do.

"I have a source," she said, sipping the drink, wondering how Claudia would get along with Sasha. Sasha would probably curl up in her lap like a housecat, the way everyone did.

They'd eaten at a restaurant named Town, where they polished off a bottle of wine between the two of them, then, just when Tory thought the evening was over, Claudia instructed the cab to drop them at this place.

"What's the name of this place again?" Tory asked.

"Work." Claudia grinned. "I guess they wanted people to be able to tell their spouses they were at work without lying."

"Is that where you told Simon you were? At work?"

Claudia's face darkened. "I didn't tell Simon *anything*."

Tory's brows rose. "Trouble in paradise?"

Claudia rolled her eyes. "I don't want to talk about it. Suffice it to say, Simon is not the guy for me."

Though Claudia was still swaying with the music when she said it, Tory was shocked. "What do you mean? What happened?"

Claudia just shrugged and polished off her cosmopolitan. Tory had barely touched hers.

"I'll be right back," Claudia said, and turned toward the bar. "Can I get you another?" she asked over her shoulder.

Tory shook her head and held her full glass aloft.

She stood in the middle of the crowd, taking in the über-cool people around her. Men were dancing with men, women with women, women with men, and people by themselves. It was the least intimate place she'd ever been, and yet people were so close to each other, they could probably feel strangers' bodies gyrating against their own.

Just as she had the thought, someone's hand touched the small of her back, and she turned to get out of the way. Looking up into the stranger's face, she was shocked to see the pale blue eyes of Keenan James looking down on her.

His face immediately registered delight. "Vicky! Fancy meeting you here. I didn't take you for the club rat type."

His smile was genuine, as far as she could tell, and he looked handsome as homemade sin. Black shirt, black pants and shoes, and nothing else. No jewelry, no tacky belt buckle, just pure handsome man.

"I probably couldn't say the same." But she smiled, finding she really was kind of happy to see him. Despite being in this weird, otherworldly atmosphere, he seemed *normal*. Nice. And she felt like she owed him an apology.

She felt like she owed everyone in her life an apology.

"Are you kidding?" He shook his head. "I hate places like this. I was dragged here by a friend." He waved a hand vaguely in another direction. "What about you?"

She nodded. "Dragged."

He laughed, then looked her up and down. She remembered she wore the same outfit one of the only other times he'd seen her and blushed.

"You look beautiful," he said, no doubt reading her mind again.

She blushed harder. Thankfully it was too dark for him to notice. "It's new." She swept her hand down her dress. "I bought it for the opening last week and . . . I guess I like wearing it."

"It suits you. Can I get you a drink?"

She held up her cosmo, still mostly full, and shook her head.

He was about to head off to the bar, she was sure, when Claudia pushed back through the crowd to join them, two drinks in hand.

"Well hello!" she said, beaming her biggest, brightest smile, and on Claudia that was saying something.

This time Keenan's face registered something more than simple delight, Tory thought.

This time she could swear she saw *desire*.

Chapter 10

"I'm Claudia," the blond said, thrusting a drink at Vicky without looking at her. Vicky grabbed it awkwardly.

"Keenan," he said, taking her hand. She was pretty and bore a slight resemblance to Vicky. He wondered if they were related.

"I'm *so* glad to meet you!" Claudia said. "I've heard so much about you and I just want you to know I think the work you're doing is *so* important. It's so unlike a man to actually go out of his way to try to help women. To even listen to them. I think it's God's work you're doing, I really do."

Wide blue eyes, stared at him the way so many other women's did—half admiring, half inviting, and in this case, more than a little drunk.

"Hey, it keeps me off the street." He shot a glance toward Vicky. "And how much help it is seems to be debatable."

"No," Claudia insisted, tightening her grip on his hand. "It's *important*. You have to know that. What you're doing is an example to all men. Women all over the world probably wish their men were more like you. I know I do."

Keenan laughed and glanced again at Vicky, who was looking around for a place to put the other drink down.

"Here, let me take that off your hands," he said to her, touching her shoulder to get her attention.

She jumped and a little of the drink spilled over onto her hand. He took the glass from her and handed her back the napkin that had been folded under the base of it.

"Thanks," she said, looking serious. "Keenan, can I talk to you a minute?"

"Of course."

"Oh *yes*," Claudia said, leaning toward them both. Her drink tipped perilously in the direction of Vicky's cream-colored outfit. Keenan reached out a hand to tilt it upright as she continued. "You're *just* the man I need to talk to tonight."

Before either he or Vicky could say anything,

Claudia had taken him by the arm and was leading him away from the bar toward a spiral staircase that would take them to the balcony.

Vicky tugged at the other girl's arm and tried to stop her. "Claudia, no. We really have to go. Please, it's getting late."

"What are you worried about?" Claudia said over her shoulder. "It's not like you have to get up tomorrow." She laughed lightly.

Vicky looked as if she'd been struck.

Keenan sent her a questioning look, but Vicky's gaze had dropped to her side.

They made it to the balcony, where things were quieter, and Claudia beelined for a table where there was already one man sitting alone with a drink across from him, obviously for another person.

"You don't mind, do you?" she asked with a sweet smile and a gentle hand on his shoulder. "We really need these seats. They're for our VIP guest, Mr. Keenan James. I'm sure you've heard of him. Thank you so much for your cooperation."

Without waiting for his answer, she sat down and gestured toward the other two seats for Keenan and Vicky. The man looked up, saw Keenan, and recognition registered in his face.

"I'm so sorry," Keenan heard Vicky say.

But the man offered no objection, simply got up, grabbed his drinks, and met a woman coming out of the restroom.

"You and Vicky aren't sisters, by any chance, are you?" Keenan asked as they sat, looking at Vicky but addressing Claudia.

"Vicky!" Claudia burst out laughing.

Vicky leaned over and whispered something urgently in her ear, then turned to Keenan and said, "We get that all the time. Her real sister gets upset, so Claudia's in the habit of acting shocked that anyone would see a resemblance in us."

What an awful liar she was. Even worse than he was.

"I just can't believe we've run into you here," Vicky continued, leaning across the table toward him. "That's so strange. And you say you don't come here a lot?"

"No, never been here before tonight. I got an invitation in the mail and my, uh, friend"—he wondered what had happened to Nicole, who had happened to be at the apartment and seen the invite in his pile of mail—"said she'd been trying to get in here for weeks and couldn't do it. So I said I'd bring her."

"An *invitation*?" Vicky asked. "Did this place just open or something?"

Keenan shook his head. "I don't think so. It was sent by the company that does the public relations. I assumed they were trying to get more, uh, recognizable celebrities to come." He hated referring to himself as a celebrity. Most people didn't get that that side of his identity felt like someone else completely, so when he spoke of the celebrity Keenan James he did it with utter objectivity. It had nothing to do with ego. In fact, that persona felt like a suit of clothes he occasionally had to wear that was never comfortable.

"The company that does the public relations?" Vicky repeated, head turning slowly toward Claudia. "And what company would that be?"

"Here's what I wanted to talk to you about," Claudia interrupted, leaning toward Keenan and putting her hand on his forearm. "What do you think of a man who claims to be in love with a woman, who asks her to 'make him the happiest person in the world'"—this she said with great exaggeration—"by marrying him, who then turns around and says he won't marry her without a prenup?"

Vicky's mouth dropped open and Keenan wondered what, exactly, was going on here.

"I think that depends on a lot of variables," he said carefully.

"Keenan, I am so sorry," Vicky said, looking at him earnestly. "You don't have to do this. Claudia is just . . ." She shot her friend a dark look. "Fighting with her boyfriend."

"*Fiancé*," Claudia corrected in a hard voice. "For the moment." She looked back over at Keenan and smiled. "What variables?"

"I thought I'd find you here." The voice came from behind Vicky, and both girls swiveled toward a tall, thin man in a crewneck sweater and khakis.

Not the typical attire for this club, Keenan knew. He looked like a banker on his day off.

"What—how did you find me?" Claudia's voice was high and squeaky, not the throaty, honey-coated one she'd been using up to this point.

Keenan's brows rose. This was getting interesting. He leaned back in his chair and smiled at Vicky, who looked thunderstruck.

"You left edited 'invitations' to this shindig in the recycling," he said, squatting down beside her. "Claudia, come on. Let's talk about this some more. There's no need to make a federal case out of it. Now tell me where you've been staying and I'll go with you to get your stuff."

He glanced at Vicky, who turned her face away. "With your friend here?"

Claudia laughed insanely. "That's right, Simon. You are *sooo* perceptive. I've been staying with 'my friend here.'" She laughed again and poked Vicky in the arm.

Vicky leaned toward her and said something low, keeping her face averted from Crewneck.

Keenan felt as if he were watching an episode of *Mystery!*

"No I will *not* give him a chance. He's had his chance and he threw it away. All because he thinks I'm going to take all his *money*." Claudia turned to Simon. "Let me ask you this, Simon. Are you aware that the moment after we're married I will have the power to unplug you if you end up a vegetable in the hospital after some awful accident? So you're willing to trust me with your life, but you want a document saying I won't touch your money?"

Simon sighed, his face hiding all expression. "Claudia, please. You know how I hate it when you air our problems like this in front of strangers."

"They're not *strangers*, you moron," she said. "This is—OW!" She jumped and reached a hand under the table, suddenly glaring daggers at Vicky.

"Claudia, maybe you and Simon would like to take this to another table," Vicky said. "Look, one has opened up over there."

Simon looked at her gratefully. "Thank y—"

He stopped, looked shocked, then opened his mouth to say something more, but Vicky stood, taking Claudia by the arm and dragging her to a standing position.

"Come on, you two, talk it out over here." She dragged them across the balcony to an empty table near the emergency exit.

Keenan was intrigued. What had gotten Vicky so keyed up? Not that he'd ever seen her in any other state, but this seemed personal.

A moment later, she returned. "God, I hate it when she drinks. She'd stopped for a while. Simon doesn't like it, and I have to say I'm with him on that, at least." She shook her head.

"You two seem pretty tight." He sipped the sweet drink he'd taken off Vicky's hands earlier and grimaced.

"We're . . . like sisters," she said, a slight smile on her face. "I'm so sorry you had to be dragged into that, though. She's . . . she can be a little manipulative."

"Does she manipulate you?" he asked.

She laughed. "All the time."

Keenan couldn't help smiling. She laughed so rarely, it was nice to see it now. "Some counselors would say you should limit your exposure to her," he volunteered, unsure how she'd take unsolicited advice from him in this setting.

"I actually do," she said. "But she ambushed me this afternoon. I've had kind of a bad week."

"I'm sorry," he said, meaning it.

She shrugged. "It's okay. But Keenan, I am kind of glad I ran into you."

He grinned. "Are you now? That's a switch."

She smiled ruefully and looked at the table. Her fingers toyed with the napkin under the drink she'd barely touched. "I feel bad about . . . about the things I said on Monday. Well—not about the *things* I said, necessarily, but the way I said them. They were just thoughts of mine, but I didn't have to be such a know-it-all." She let out a heavy breath. "The truth is, I don't know much at all. I just have way too many opinions." She looked up through her lashes—an unexpectedly sexy look that he was sure she was completely unaware of—and gave a small smile.

He tilted his head, studied her pretty face a moment, and realized what it was he liked so much about her. "Vicky, to be perfectly honest, it's refreshing to have someone disagree with me."

Her eyes lit with something like hope. "Really? I wasn't just an obnoxious bitch?"

He laughed. "Well . . . that was refreshing too."

She dropped her lids.

He leaned across the table, put a hand on hers. She visibly jumped. "I was kidding," he said.

She met his eyes, in hers a very sage expression. "No you weren't. But that's okay. I . . . I'm turning over a new leaf. And honestly, I'd appreciate your candor too. You can tell me when I'm getting too . . . pushy."

"You got it." He glanced over his shoulder at Claudia and Simon. Claudia was crying now, but it wasn't stopping her from poking her boyfriend in the chest repeatedly with whatever points she was making.

"Hey, can I take you home? I've got the car service tonight," he said, glancing over his shoulder at Claudia. "And it looks like your friend might be a while."

Vicky beamed at him, and his skin warmed. "Thank you. I would *love* to go home."

He made a quick call on his cell phone, then rose to escort her toward the door. Tory waved to Claudia, who scowled at her, and then followed Keenan to the exit.

"What about the friend you came with?" she asked him over her shoulder as they exited. Her ears rang with echoes of the throbbing music, and her body fairly vibrated with it. Or was it not the music that had her so attuned?

"Nicole? She dumped me the moment we got in the door." He chuckled. "Don't worry. She can take care of herself."

A black car pulled up to the curb in front of them, and Keenan opened the back door. She felt like a celebrity, the way people in the line to get into the club stared at them. One of them yelled Keenan's name, but he ignored it and slid into the car after her.

She gave her address to the driver, then leaned her head back on the headrest and sighed as the tinted partition rose up between front seat and back.

What a week, she reflected. Between getting fired, lying in bed nonstop yet barely getting any sleep, then going out for a night on the town the likes of which she hadn't had since college—if then—Tory felt as if she were having an out-of-body experience. And now here she was in the back of a limousine with Keenan James.

She started to laugh, low at first, then louder, turning into giggles that threatened to overcome her.

She'd been fired. She'd been used by her sister—*again*—and here she was riding in a town car with a TV star. For once in her life she was exactly where *her sister* wanted to be.

"What's so funny?" Keenan asked.

Tory got hold of herself and turned her head on the seat toward him. "It's just—this is so weird. I can't believe I'm riding in this car with you, of all people."

He looked uncomfortable. "It's not something I would have predicted either."

"Well, that's a little different. It's not like I'm famous or anything. Quite the contrary, in fact."

He looked at her, and he seemed very close all of a sudden, in the back of this car. She'd never quite realized how intimate it was to sit in the backseat, in the dark, with someone you barely knew.

"You never seem to care that I'm famous," he said. "At least you never seem very impressed by it."

"Sorry." She smiled wryly. "I'm sure that disappoints you. It seems that disappointing people is something I've gotten pretty good at."

"No. I like it."

She picked up her head. "Really? Don't you like being famous?"

He shrugged, then seemed to think about it. "It has its upside. Lots of them, actually. But mostly it feels like a game I'm playing. Like I'm pretending to be someone else."

"I'd like to be someone else." She sighed. "But you probably have friends who knew you before you were famous. Don't they help?"

He thought a minute, looked out his side window, and said, "Actually no, I've lost touch with most people from my past. You know, you get into your job, work crazy hours, and you find yourself socializing mostly with the people you work with, or people in the same business as yours." He scratched the side of his face and looked at her askance. "In fact most of my friends are women, now that I think about it."

She snorted and laid her head back on the seat. "That doesn't surprise me."

She felt very comfortable in this car, shielded from the world, speeding through the city on silent wheels. For some reason she wished she could curl up and go to sleep in it, let it take her across the country so she could wake up and find herself in sunny California.

Keenan turned to her, a slight smile on his lips and those light eyes seeming to spark in the light of the passing streetlights. "See, now there's one of the downsides. People like you don't like me simply because I'm famous. They don't wait to get to know me at all before deciding I'm a jerk."

She met his eyes. He was quite handsome, it couldn't be denied, but the salient fact was, he was appealing on a personal level. When he talked to you, he looked at you, and when he was with you, his mind was right there with you.

Now here he was talking to her, sharing some of his thoughts. Maybe not the deepest ones, or the closely held secrets, but she could tell he was being honest.

"That may be true," she said finally, "but that's not why I don't like you. I think you're a jerk because I don't like what you're doing." She paused, then laughed. "Sorry, that didn't come out quite right."

He laughed with her. "No, no. It's okay. I pretty much knew that."

"I . . ." She hesitated, then decided what the hell. Her career was in the toilet, she was in a literally dead, dead-end relationship, and the man sitting next to her might be the only key within reach to any kind of future. "I actually do like you, Keenan. At least, I'm starting to. Tonight."

"Are you really?" He arched a brow in her direction, his tone undeniably pleased.

"Don't get overconfident, though," she added. "I'm only just making up my mind."

He pushed himself up on the seat, his hand brushing hers where it lay on the seat between them. She instantly sat up straighter too.

"Just so you know," he said, squeezing the hand he'd just touched, "I'm starting to like you too."

For some reason her mouth went dry and she had trouble swallowing. She extricated her hand from under his and said the first thing that came to her mind. "Oh come on, you always liked *me*."

He laughed, surprised, and she did too.

"A joke!" he crowed. "She made a joke!"

"I can make jokes," she said, mildly offended. It only confirmed what she'd realized earlier, however. Somewhere along the line she'd turned into a prune. A shriveled, defensive, *off*ensive, obnoxious downer.

"What about you, Vicky. You have lots of friends?" he asked gently.

She shook her head, thinking of Katya and Sasha, the two women she'd spent the most time with over the last few weeks. "Not really."

"You've got Claudia," he offered.

"As you might have noticed, that's not always a plus." She looked over at him. "I had no idea she'd pulled that stunt to meet you there tonight. If I had I would never have joined her."

"I'm a little surprised you did anyway. Like I said, you don't seem like the club type."

She sighed. "I'm not. I . . . got talked into it. I needed to do something different, and tonight was about as different as it gets for me."

The car pulled up in front of her brownstone, and Tory felt a twinge of regret that the ride wasn't longer. Something about the intimacy of riding in this car, talking so easily with a man who seemed actually interested in what she had to say, made her feel better than she had all week. Longer than that, even, if she cared to admit it.

"Thank you for the ride, Keenan," she said, scooting on the seat so that she faced him. She clutched her purse in her lap.

"You're welcome, Vicky," he said in that intimate tone he was so good at, and for a moment, his eyes held hers, there in the darkened back of the car.

She caught her breath. He seemed expectant; she *felt* expectant. Something hung in the air between them, and for some reason she didn't want to move until she found out what it was.

Slowly, he took her hand again and pressed her fingers to his lips. Warm, soft, Keenan James lips on her fingers, with those famous blue eyes looking up at her through those famous dark lashes.

Without realizing she was doing it, Tory leaned toward him, her fingers closing over his, and the next thing she knew, his lips had moved from her fingers to her mouth.

She fell into him, her hands holding on to his shirt, and felt his tongue probe her lips. She opened under the inquiry and their mouths were suddenly one, gently opening together, tongues exploring, Tory's heart tripping like a stone skipped across a pond.

He was warm, his body broad, his hands firm, and his lips—*oh!* his lips were divine. Skilled, soft, and yet firm. She and he moved as one, their movements instinctively in sync.

It was a kiss like no other she'd ever had. Satisfying a need that had been long buried. Always with Stewart she felt like she had to pay attention or she'd make a wrong move, teeth would hit or tongues would miss or lips would loosen too much.

But this . . . *this* was gentleness and promise all

in one. This had her entire body straining toward him, wanting . . . something. Something *more*. Nothing like with Stewart.

Stewart!

Tory pulled back, shocked at herself. Her heart beat so rapidly she felt light-headed. She opened her eyes and saw the face of a magazine ad, not her plain, safe Stewart. Her plain, safe *ex* Stewart.

She shook herself, feeling as strange as if the poster of David Cassidy she'd had on her childhood bedroom wall had come to life under her kisses.

Too late, she realized that the reason Keenan had sat there, so seemingly *expectant*, was because he was waiting for her to get out of the car. On *her* side. And she had been waiting for him to get out on his side because that was the way they'd gotten in. But the house was on *her* side. *Her side!*

She blushed to the roots of her hair and backed away quickly.

"I'm so sorry!" she exclaimed, grabbing her purse and sliding toward the door behind her. "I'm—please forgive me. Forget this ever happened. I don't know what . . ."

"Vicky—"

"No!" she cried, appalled all over again that she'd kissed a man who didn't even know her real name! She'd lied to him, made a fool of herself over him, and kissed him when he no doubt had *not* been expecting it. She had to get out of there as quickly as she could before he found out all that she was: an oblivious yet know-it-all, unemployed, evidently horny *liar*.

She opened the door, and even the dim overhead light in the car seemed too bright. She had never been so embarrassed.

She nearly leaped out of the backseat, stumbling on the curb and landing smack down on the sidewalk, grazing her palms.

"Vicky!" he said, moving toward the door to get out after her.

She scrambled to her feet. "I'm all right! I'm all right! *Please* stay there. I've got to go. Good-bye!"

She didn't even look at him, just ran up the stairs to the brownstone and yanked open the door to the foyer. She dug through her purse for her keys so frantically, she ripped the side of it, but she got them out and let herself into the stairwell before she heard any sound that indicated he had followed her.

She didn't stop running until she'd made it into her apartment. Then she leaned back against the door and panted, feeling like she might have a heart attack at any moment.

As her heartbeat slowed, she pressed a hand to her mouth, still tingling from his kiss.

She had kissed Keenan James. Her stomach flipped at the thought. What had she been thinking? What had *he* thought?

She closed her eyes and thought she might throw up. It probably happened to him all the time. He probably thought what he usually thought, something along the lines of *Not again*, or *If only it had been the other girl*.

Without turning on any lights, she tiptoed to the window and looked out onto the street. The town car was gone.

More importantly, Keenan James was gone, along with her sanity, her dignity and quite possibly her chance at a future in psychology books.

Chapter 11

Tory got up the next morning, picked up the portable phone, then sat with it on her lap for the better part of two hours.

Back and forth her mind went. She needed the money the book deal would bring in. But how could she work with Keenan, especially after what had happened last night?

On the other hand, it could mean a future in writing. But she didn't believe in what she'd be writing about.

Then again, okay, so she'd made a huge mistake

kissing Keenan. But why should she compound that mistake by giving up this opportunity?

In the end she decided that doing the book meant keeping her options open as long as possible. If things were untenable with Keenan, she could always quit the project later. Or be fired, again, by him or Fender or both, depending on what the contract required.

The one direction she wouldn't let her mind go—couldn't—was what the kiss actually *meant.* She knew that she'd fallen for his charm, his looks, and his polar oppositeness from Stewart. Not to mention his fame, which was what she hated most about the circumstance. (Did anyone really ever get over high school? she wondered. He was like the captain of the football team, popularity-wise.)

But she had no illusions that Keenan found her particularly attractive or that he was interested in any kind of romantic relationship with her. She was fairly certain he wouldn't even want the cowriting relationship. Though he'd kissed her back, it was probably automatic, and the more she thought about it, the more convinced she became that she had kissed him and not the other way around.

Finally, determining that this decision was at least not irrevocable, like turning down the deal would be, she dialed Franklin Fender's number. When he came on the line, she lost no time in telling him that she'd take the project. He was delighted, and peppered her with questions about what she thought of the round tables and their fearless leader.

Tory deflected as much as she could, then parried with a question of her own.

"Have you told Keenan there's to be a cowriter?" she asked. "I mean, I know you haven't told him about me specifically. I just wondered if he knew there was to be *some*one working on this with him."

"Er"—more paper moving crinkled over the line—"not yet. I have a meeting with him Monday morning. I'll let him know then."

She exhaled. "Okay, then. So I'll assume he knows at the Monday lunchtime round table."

"I'll call you if something comes up, but yes, go ahead and assume he knows."

"And you'll explain about me? About who I am and why I lied to him?" She hated how needy she sounded, how needy she *felt*. She didn't want to confess to Keenan that she'd kissed him under false pretenses. She almost couldn't bear the thought of him knowing her, *seeing* her, as Tory Hoffstra.

The thought immediately shamed her. She was turning into Claudia, manipulating people for her own ends, right down to putting on a false appearance with all that makeup and new clothes. She should have attended the round tables as she really was. He never would have kissed her then.

"I'll tell him it was all my idea," Fender said.

"Let's schedule a meet and greet for later next week. The three of us can hash out the project and iron out any details either of you might still be having difficulty with. Call my secretary Monday morning and have her work it into my schedule, all right?"

"Yes. Thank you, Mr. Fender."

"Thank *you*, Dr. Hoffstra. I look forward to working with you." He hung up.

"Don't thank me yet," she murmured as she hung up the phone.

"This is WTLK drive time!" the deejay crowed. "All talk, all the time."

Keenan thought that last could be the tagline for his life.

"I'm Matt Mitchell and we're back—live!—with Keenan James, writer for the blockbuster HBO series *Sex at Midnight*. You all remember that one, don't you? Took the world by storm five years ago and didn't let go until the final episode last May. Keenan, we're all wondering what's going on now with Dr. Rodman and his bevy of beauties. Any chance of a reunion movie?"

Keenan adjusted the headphones on his ears and leaned toward the microphone. "I'm open to it, but only if we can get all the original actors back."

"So you've got ideas? You know what comes next for these characters?"

"Oh yes. I know *exactly* what Dr. Rodman is up to now," Keenan said, referring to one of the main characters on *Sex at Midnight*. Perhaps he could relate a little too closely.

"I'll bet you do. Because—and this might come as a surprise to some of you listeners—rumor has it that after writing about a psychologist for five years you've actually taken the leap into being one yourself. What's that all about? Tell us about these round tables of yours."

Keenan launched into his spiel about the round tables, how they began casually enough and before he knew it they'd morphed into a regular gig. He made the point that he was *not* a doctor, as he always did, but that he was fascinated by the interplay between men and women and glad that he could help by offering an unvarnished male point of view.

"Now Keenan," Matt Mitchell said, his tone confidential, "in *Sex at Midnight* you wrote about a shrink who slept with half of his patients. Does life imitate art? And what is *up* with your love life? You're on every New York City list of most eligible bachelors."

Keenan chuckled. Talk about a bull's-eye question. Life was imitating art, and Keenan was the victim of both.

What were the ethics of his situation? Where was the line? *Was* there one? Vicky had already dumped her boyfriend, she was probably not a legitimate member of the round table, most likely being a plant of Fender's, so had he really done anything wrong last night? He didn't want to think so.

But then, he never wanted to think so.

"Considering that most of the women come to the round tables to talk about their boyfriends," Keenan said with a smile, "the opportunity rarely arises for art to imitate life, at least in my life."

If this were a television interview he'd have to think twice about issuing such a refutable lie. Refutable, at least, by one woman.

"*Most* of the women? *Rarely* arises? I gotta say you're leaving the door open a crack." Matt Mitchell laughed his big deejay laugh.

"I say most of the women because I do have one or two who come there to talk about their *girl*friends," Keenan said, knowing exactly what reaction that would get. Sometimes it was scary how well he played this game.

"Whoa-ho-*ho!*" the deejay sputtered, hitting some button on his dashboard to make a crashing-cymbal sound. "Tell me, what good does a male point of view do for a lesbian? Or are we dealing with bisexual issues here?"

Keenan chuckled at the predictability of the man's responses. It was one of the reasons he'd picked this show.

"No bisexuality," Keenan said, knowing that he'd hooked whatever audience might have wandered over that part of the radio dial at that moment, "not that I'm aware of. It's an attitude, I think, maybe more than a gender role. The yin and the yang, to get Buddhist about it. And that combination can occur in male-female, female-female, and I imagine even male-male relationships."

"Okay, let's not even *go* there." Matt Mitchell waved his hands as if he could be seen and guffawed again. "Back to the *women*. So, how many women you think you've—*ahem*—helped, huh, Keenan? I know these things are called the Just-Dump-Him Round Tables; where did that come from and how does that really help women? I gotta tell ya, it hasn't been helping me any." Laugh laugh laugh.

"Hey, I'm sorry about that," Keenan said. "I know I may be screwing things up for a lot of guys, but they've had it their way for a long time now. I'm thinking it's time for the girls. Maybe you should join us one day, Matt, and see what you're doing wrong."

"Me? At a table full of angry women? No thank you!"

Keenan laughed. "That name began as a joke, at first, as a play on the Algonquin Round Table. You know the famous circle of authors who met on a regular basis at the Algonquin to discuss everything from books to current affairs."

"Oh yeah, *that* round table." Matt rolled his eyes at Keenan. "We've all heard of that."

"So, since my advice to these women is often to

leave the men who are stringing them along—and this might be where you get into trouble, Matt— they began to be known as the Just-Dump-Him Round Tables."

"So you tell these women to dump their boy-friends, and they do? Well, here we are back to the table full of available women," Matt Mitchell said, hitting another button that made a wolf-whistle sound. "You're a good-looking guy, Keenan—"

"Why thank you, Matt," Keenan said, in a mock-seductive tone.

Matt donned an expression of horror, which made Keenan laugh.

"Oh good," Matt said, "he's kidding. Heh heh heh. But seriously, you're a good-looking guy. You're famous, successful, and more important-ly, as we've mentioned, *single*. Surely you've had women using these things as an opportunity to se-duce *you*."

Keenan's mind flashed to Vicky Smith, impulsive-ly leaning toward him and kissing him last night. Or did he kiss her? He *had* wanted to, he remem-bered that. For some strange reason that ride in the car had had him feeling oddly close to her, at-tracted to her. She seemed to be opening up, was more accessible than she ever had been before.

But what had really happened?

Suppose she *was* a plant by Fender, sent to in-vestigate him, would she tell the publisher what had happened? Had she, by chance, been sent to investigate that very thing? It wasn't the first time Keenan had been asked if the women ever came on to him, or if he used these round tables to get dates. After all, even if the women were there because of their boyfriends, they were there because they were *unhappy* with them.

"Matt, I can honestly say that I don't think I've ever been aware of actually being seduced," he said, searching for the right phrasing. "Seducing another, on the other hand . . ."

He let Matt Mitchell's boomy laugh fill the airwaves for a moment.

"No, I'm kidding," he added. "I've never seduced anyone from one of my round tables."

That was true, wasn't it?

"It's not my objective to use these women," he continued. "That would make me as bad as the guys they come to the round table to talk to me about. I'm doing this to help people. And having some guy put the moves on them while they're struggling with their current relationship would not be what I consider helpful."

"Well, that's darn big of you, Keenan. Let's take a break now, but we'll be back for more from Keenan James, writer of *Sex at Midnight* and keynote adviser at several weekly round tables for the lovelorn here in New York City. When we come back we'll open the phones."

Matt Mitchell hit the dash, whipped off his headgear, and winked at Keenan. "That was brilliant, man. I gotta go pee. Have some water and relax. You're doing great."

Keenan forced a smile and nodded, picking up his water glass.

She couldn't have done it on purpose, he thought, unable to get Vicky out of his head. Everything about her said she'd been just as startled by her actions as he'd been. Granted, he had kissed her hand, a classically seductive move that he'd truly thought would have no effect on her. But then . . . then she'd reacted. And *he'd* reacted.

And nobody was more surprised than he was when the kiss had nearly blown his socks off.

Matt Mitchell raced back into the room, zipping up his fly. He dove into the chair, which rolled right to the microphone, and slid on his headphones in a motion so practiced he'd obviously done it many times before. Keenan would never hear radio commercials the same way again.

"We're back!" Matt Mitchell sang. "With Keenan James, bachelor-at-large and psychological guru for lovesick women all over the city. Now to the phones. Whoa! Look at that! Lit up like a friggin' pinball machine! Ginger, who've we got?"

He tipped one finger in the direction of the producer, Ginger Myer, and she leaned into the microphone. "We've got Lucy on line three."

"Hello, Lucy, whaddya got for us?"

"Hi," a high female voice giggled. "I'm so excited to be talking to you, Keenan. You're really inspiring. I bought the *Straight Talk* DVD and I've made my boyfriend watch it with me twice."

Keenan laughed. "I'm sure he'd like to get on the other line and thank me for it, too."

"Well . . . we've been stuck for a while on the C-word."

"I hope you're talking about commitment," Keenan said, at which Matt roared a laugh.

"Yeah," Lucy said. "He says he's just not ready. But if he's not ready now, when will he be? We've been together three years and we've broken up twice because of this."

"Lucy, I'll give you the primer on my philosophy at the Just-Dump-Him Round Tables. 'Just Dump Him' isn't just a phrase, it's an acronym. J stands for jerks who don't deserve a second chance. D is for the fact that denial won't make you happy. And H is for hesitation means hang it up. I'm afraid your situation sounds like it fits at least two out of three categories."

"So I should . . . I should dump him?" she asked tremulously.

"You got it." Keenan smiled at Matt, who hit a button, and the sound of something crashing to the ground sounded.

"That's a dumpin' if I ever heard one," Matt crowed. "Thanks for calling, Lucy. Ginger, who else we got?"

Ginger purred into the microphone. "We've got

Harvey on line one with a question about psychology for Mr. James."

"Harve! What have you got for us?"

"Hello, Matt, thanks for having me on the show. I listen to you every day."

"Good to have you on. Always like to accommodate a loyal listener. What's your question for Keenan James?"

"I'm something of a student of psychology myself, Keenan," Harvey said. "Can I call you Keenan?"

Keenan leaned forward. "Sure. Call me whatever you want."

"Ha ha ha!" Matt boomed. "Brave words from a man who counsels women!"

The listener paused. Then said, "Thanks, Keenan. So, what I wanted to say was, I read a lot of books and subscribe to most of the mainstream psychology magazines and I'm wondering if you're aware of an article that appeared in the *New York Journal of Psychology*. It mentions you specifically as—and I'm quoting here—'an unschooled practitioner of a dangerous brand of pseudo mental health counseling.'"

Keenan rubbed a hand over his forehead and was glad once again that this was not a television interview. "Was that the one called 'No More Psychobabble'?"

"Yes, actually it is. And it was written by . . ." Flipping of pages resonated over the phone line. "Dr. Engelberta Hoffstra."

"Whoa!" Matt Mitchell interjected. "Engelberta Humperdinck—*who*? Heh heh heh."

"I actually did read that article," Keenan said. "I'll bet I'm one of the six people, including you, who did."

Matt Mitchell obligingly laughed, as did Harvey.

"But you see, that's just the point," Keenan said. "It's all well and good for people like Dr. Hoffstra to advocate psychoanalysis and cognitive therapy and whatever other fancy processes they have for unscrewing the human brain, but all they're doing is preaching their erudite theories to the academic choir. What I'm trying to do is bring mental health to the masses. *Psychology* to the masses. When it gets too highbrow it helps no one. Most of those articles are inaccessible, incomprehensible, and little more than psychological masturbation for doctoral candidates."

"Woo-hoo!" Matt Mitchell crowed. "The M-word!" A flick of a switch and the sound of a siren went off.

Keenan bit the inside of his cheek to keep from smirking. Sometimes you just had to give the people what they wanted.

"Hey Ginger," Matt called, though she was still right there looking at him, "see if we can't get this Humperdinck woman on the phone. Might be good to get her response, don't you think, Keenan?"

"Sure," Keenan said. "I've got nothing against hearing what Dr. Hoffstra has to say. But I'll bet you anything you won't get her. People who write articles like that don't want to talk to you and me, Matt. They want to talk to each other. More importantly, they want to *impress* each other."

"And a stick-up-the-ass academic wouldn't be impressed with a guy who had lunch with ten women every week?"

"I guess that would depend on whether or not he believed I was getting dates out of it."

Matt laughed loudly. "Who *wouldn't* be impressed if you were sleeping with all of 'em, that what you're saying?"

"I said no such thing," Keenan said, letting the smile be heard in his voice.

Matt boomed a laugh again. He was a laugh machine. "Ginger, we got Humperdinck?"

"You won't believe this, Matt," Ginger said, in her sensual radio voice. "Her office says she is no longer employed there. Think she was fired for the article?"

"Woo-hoo!" Matt crowed, hitting a button and getting the sound of applause. "Humperdinck goes *down*. And Keenan James is on his way *up*. We'll be back in just a minute to take more of your questions."

Tory went back to her "honest" form of dressing for that evening's event with Stewart. She had to get back to her old self. She had somehow forgotten who she was, dressing in those falsely flattering clothes, painting her face and letting someone like Claudia make her think she should be out doing things that were not in her normal repertoire for a reason.

That Claudia would be mad at her for abandoning her at the club paled in comparison to her humiliation with Keenan. And even her humiliation paled in comparison to the guilt she felt and would be smothered by when she saw Stewart.

Not that she owed him anything. They were, technically, broken up. But they hadn't exactly stopped seeing each other, maintaining the habit of getting together as they always had, and they occasionally discussed getting back together, though neither of them seemed in a hurry to make that decision.

She was to meet Stewart at his co-op—the same one where Keenan now lived, she was acutely aware—for drinks before going to the party hosted by the president of the symphony for the symphony's most important sponsors. There was no way Tory could get out of it; it was all Stewart had talked about for the last month. How he wanted to make an impression, talk to the symphony president about the upcoming CD and the possibility of Stewart including one of Bach's solo concertos for cello on it.

Tory was to be by his side for all of this, because Tory was his friend, his supporter, his confidence booster for the last eight years. Just because she had made a fool of herself over another man last night, did not give her the right to bail out on a night when Stewart needed her most. Quite the contrary, in fact.

She would tell him, of course. She had to tell him what happened, though not with whom and not before the party. Afterward. Yes, right afterward, she would tell, and he could do with the information what he wanted. If it meant he didn't want to consider reconciliation, then so be it. She wouldn't have to wrestle with that option anymore.

After spending half an hour trying to get her contact lenses in again—she was determined to get used to them, since her glasses were too scratched to wear in public—she got on the subway for Stewart's place, red-eyed and makeup-free. At five o'clock, she approached his building like a spy on a mission, ready to jump into the closest available doorway and hide her face if Keenan James were to appear. She virtually tiptoed past the man at the front desk and jumped when he said hello.

She pushed the button for the elevator and wrung her sweating palms together as she waited for it to arrive. What would she do if he was on it? She eyed the potted plant next to the elevator bay, but knew she could never make it over there in time to avoid seeing whoever was on the car.

The signal dinged and she jumped again, only to have a moment's panic when a tall man appeared from behind the doors. She took one step toward the plant, then, when her mind registered that it wasn't Keenan, she tried to step back, and got caught so off balance in the middle that she nearly fell over.

The man passed, with a quizzical look in her direction, and she stepped onto the elevator. This was ridiculous. She was acting like a crazy person. It was but further proof, however, that she absolutely could *not* tell Stewart whom it was she had kissed. Imagine if the two of them ran into him in the elevator sometime. It would be the height of awkwardness.

Not that it was any of Stewart's business, technically. Still, their bond of eight years required that she tell him if something like this happened. Didn't it? If only so that he could opt out of being her friend, if he wanted. She knew it would be hard for her if he told her he'd kissed someone else.

For some reason, though, while she was worried about hurting his feelings, she wasn't worried that he would stop seeing her. It had been so long since anything sexual had passed between them that she couldn't fathom jealousy, or even concern, on Stewart's part.

She walked down the long hallway to Stewart's door, knocked twice, and let herself in as usual.

"Oh, Tory, good! Come quick," Stewart said, more animated than she'd seen him in some time. He waved her over with big circular hand motions. "Come on, come on, quick."

He moved to the stereo tuner on the bookshelves and turned up the volume.

Matt Mitchell's drive time radio show was on. Keenan James's voice filled the room.

"Why thank you, Matt."

"Oh good," Matt said, laughing. "He's kidding. But seriously, you're a good-looking guy. You're famous, successful, and more importantly, as we've mentioned, *single*. Surely you've had women using these things as an opportunity to seduce *you*."

Tory's mouth went dry.

"Matt, I can honestly say that I don't think I've ever been aware of actually being seduced," he said soberly. Then after a pause added, "Seducing another, on the other hand . . ."

Tory gasped, and felt instantly sick to her stomach. He *had* seduced her! He'd talked to her and kissed her hand and made *eyes* at her in the back of that damn town car. He'd known exactly what he was doing, and she'd fallen right into it!

She pressed her palms to her hot cheeks.

Stewart looked at her. "What's wrong with you?"

"Shh!" She stared at the radio, unable to either walk away or turn it off. Something in her had to hear what else he had to say.

" . . . never seduced anyone from one of my round tables."

Oh yeah, *right*, she thought. He *had* to say that, and it was clear to her that he was being blatantly insincere. She could hear it in his voice, a tone he was making no attempt to disguise.

"It's not my objective to use these women," he continued.

She snorted. "Unbelievable."

"I guess you were right about him," Stewart said. "Wasn't that your suspicion all along?"

"You're damn right it was," she said darkly. "And now we know. I cannot believe he's on the *radio* saying this stuff. Doesn't he at least have the sense to keep his unscrupulousness to himself?"

"I guess you can't do the book now," Stewart said sadly.

Tory felt another cannonball land in her stomach.

She'd already committed to the book. She'd had no other choice. How else was she to make a living? She'd been fired for poor job performance, it wasn't as if she were going to be able to waltz back out and get another job in a psychology practice. She didn't even want to. She could open her own, but what clients would she have? She couldn't think of one from the group she'd had at Weldman's who would abandon his practice for hers.

And she wouldn't blame them. She was a terrible therapist.

The book was all she had, and she'd already committed to it. But now . . . how could she write a book with a man who had not only *used* her but who admitted to it openly on the radio?

Her mind spun, the rest of the program a blur, until Stewart's voice hooted, "Did you hear that?!"

"It's all well and good," Keenan was saying, "for people like Dr. Hoffstra to advocate psychoanalysis and cognitive therapy and whatever other fancy processes they have for unscrewing the human brain, but all they're doing is preaching their erudite theories to the academic choir . . ."

"Is he talking about *me*?"

"Yes!" Stewart exulted and turned amazed eyes upon her. "He's talking about *you*, can you believe it? And your article on psychobabble. I guess he *does* know who you are!"

" . . . psychological masturbation for doctoral candidates."

"That *bastard*," she said, throwing her purse on the couch.

"Wow," was all Stewart said.

Tory listened as the horrible deejay—to whom she would never listen again—called her "Humperdinck" and threatened to get her on the phone. Her eyes flew to her purse, wherein lay her cell phone. There wasn't any way they could get that number, was there?

The program went on, one word worse than the next, until she heard the woman on the show say, "You won't believe this, Matt."

And then her horrible secret was out.

"Her office says she is no longer employed there. Think she was fired for the article?"

Stewart turned flabbergasted eyes on Tory and she looked at him helplessly.

"You *quit your job*?" he demanded.

She tilted her head uncomfortably to the side. She didn't want to lie to him, but she just could not get the word "fired" out from between her lips. He'd be as horrified as she was.

"I . . . uh . . ." She picked at the button of her suit jacket, feeling like a trapped animal. "I decided to do the book."

Chapter 12

"Keenan!" Fiona wailed. "That bloody dog has made off with my blush brush again!"

Keenan stumbled as he pried one shoe onto his foot and hopped across the carpet toward the living room. "Barbra Streisand!" he called. "Come back here."

He found her in the living room, rolling on the carpet, legs in the air, a look of unqualified glee on her hairy face.

"Barbra Streisand!" he said again.

She flipped upright and looked at him as if something wonderful was about to happen. Behind her, Keenan could see Fiona's makeup brush. The dog had been rolling on it.

He bent to pick up the brush, but could not resist Barbra's tail thumping and scratched the dog behind the ears.

"It's a good thing you're cute," he muttered.

The dog jumped up and trotted back into the bedroom behind him.

"Can't you put her back in her cage?" Fiona eyed the dog warily as it ambled toward her.

"I could," Keenan said, sitting on the edge of the bed to tie his shoe. "But she's already in it so much, I feel guilty putting her away when I'm home."

Fiona grumbled and leaned toward the mirror on the vanity as Barbra Streisand squeezed between Fiona and the wall to lie down on the floor at Fiona's feet.

"Now that's better," Fiona said, lining her eyes with a tiny brush, "you can keep my feet warm."

Keenan picked up his tie from beside him, flipped up his collar, and put the tie around his neck, watching Fiona apply her makeup. It was like watching an artist at work. Beside her on the bathroom vanity lay a veritable surgeon's tray of tools, arrayed on a towel that draped over the counter like an operating curtain.

He liked the way Fiona looked without makeup, he thought. She looked younger, fresher. Not that she wasn't a knockout when she was all "tarted up," as she would say. It was just, it seemed like she was putting on a mask to deal with the public, instead of facing them as herself.

But it wasn't any of his business, he reflected. They had decided months ago that they were better off as friends. She would stay with him when she was in town, but it was rare that anything sexual went on between them anymore.

As Keenan watched Fiona, both the towel and tools beside her began to move, all at once, sliding slowly toward the edge of the counter. Fiona shifted on the stool and it stopped. Must have been sitting on a corner of it, he thought, but a moment later the towel started to move again.

It took Keenan too long to realize what was behind the motion. From underneath the vanity the dog had gotten hold of the towel and was gently pulling it toward the floor. He had just shot to his feet when the whole thing went tumbling down.

Fiona shrieked. Pots of makeup showered the bathroom floor—fuchsias and tans, blushes and blacks—all sprayed into Jackson Pollock–like chaos on the ceramic tile.

At the ensuing human commotion, Barbra Streisand shot out from beside Fiona's stool, towel still in her mouth, and raced across the bedroom, disappearing out the door.

"Louis, we're going to be late," Tory said, standing by the front door in her suit, purse clutched under one arm, holding the key at the ready to lock the door.

She could not get Keenan James's words out of her head. She wished she'd never gone to that stupid round table, never talked to Franklin Fender, never decided to write a book.

But then, if she hadn't, she'd just be unemployed right now, instead of employed as a writer with a man whose philosophies and ethics she wholeheartedly disapproved of.

Stewart looked at her through the front hall mirror without turning around, the ends of his tie in his hands. "What did you call me?"

"Stewart," she said, startled. She scanned back through her memory.

"No you didn't. You called me 'Louis.'"

"Oh." She breathed a wry laugh. That's what she got for even *thinking* about the round table.

"Who's *Louis*?" he demanded. His eyes were uncharacteristically intent on her. His thinning blond hair was brushed meticulously back, looking baby soft on his pale skin.

Could he possibly be jealous? The thought made her feel sicker than she already did. Fine time for him to start paying attention, just when she had to tell him that she had kissed another man. The worst part was, he would never suspect it. It would come out of the blue. She hated thinking about what a shock it would be.

Maybe she didn't have to tell him, she thought. After all, it wasn't as if it was going to happen again.

"He's you," she said, moving toward him and squeezing his arm with one hand. "It's what I call you at the round tables. You remember, I told you I had to make up a boyfriend to talk about. So I made up a you I call Louis."

"And you talk about me?" He turned to her fully. "What do you say? I hope it's nothing inappropriate. I do have a reputation to think of, you know."

"That's why I call you Louis. Come on, Stewart, I told you about all of this." She waved a hand and turned away. She didn't want him to see her face. "And I don't say a whole lot that's true, so don't worry about that. I just make stuff up so my reasons for being there seem obvious." She glanced back over her shoulder to see if Stewart was still looking at her.

It was all true, she told herself firmly. She had told Stewart about the group and what she was doing there, and while she had said some things that were true, it was only because she didn't want to forget her lies. Besides, she'd actually exaggerated their sex life; she couldn't imagine any man would be unhappy about that.

Stewart's gaze turned inward, a look he frequently wore. "Hunh," he said, and faced the mirror again.

Tory exhaled quietly. They were on their way to the Upper East Side—a building where Stewart had always *wanted* to live but couldn't afford to—where Cameron Lessing, president of the symphony, was hosting a party for symphony members and their choicest supporters. It was to be an "intimate" gathering of two hundred people, and Stewart, as usual, was making sure he was dressed well enough to be mistaken for a resident of the tony building.

Tory hated parties like this. Mostly she hated hearing Stewart use his big fake laugh with the money people and hearing herself issue dull platitudes of appreciation and support to the symphonic powers-that-be. For a moment she wished she could have visited Katya and worn some of her new clothes. She would have fit in much better with the crowd they were about to see.

But those outfits had already gotten her into enough trouble.

Stewart finally got his tie exactly right and they left, moving silently down the long hall to the elevators. Once in, Tory asked hesitantly, "Does it bother you that I talk about a false relationship in the group?"

"Hm?" He turned his head slightly in her direction. "Not if you're making stuff up. Why would I care about that?"

"Because I do sort of base him on you," she admitted. "Just to keep what I say straight. But it's for a good cause."

"Good cause?" he repeated, watching the numbers above the doors as the elevator moved downward. Twelve . . . eleven . . . ten. . . .

Stewart lived on the fourteenth floor, which was really the thirteenth, but the building skipped the thirteenth in numbering the stories. Such a large concession to superstition had always irritated her.

She breathed a sigh of relief with every floor that passed without stopping. Less chance of seeing Keenan that way.

"Yes, for the book." She looked at the side of his face, getting that disoriented feeling she sometimes got that she had been in their relationship alone. Or he had been. Writing a book was a goal she'd been working toward for six years; it was hard to believe he'd forget it.

"Oh right. Of course, the book," he repeated. After a beat of continuing to focus on the floor numbers, he turned a distracted smile to her, raised one arm, and squeezed her around the shoulders. "Good for you."

Tory let silence descend again and tried not to get

neurotic about running into Keenan. For a second she felt light-headed and realized she'd been holding her breath. This couldn't go on, she thought, her having to move through this building like a swimmer under water until she got to a place where Keenan James couldn't see her.

Her cheeks warmed as she remembered the look in his eyes just before he'd kissed her. He'd been listening so closely to her, looking at her so appreciatively. Paying attention.

When was the last time Stewart had paid attention to her like that?

"Oh my God," she breathed, pushing her hands up over her face to the smooth crown of her head, her drawn-back hair snug in its traditional bun. She was doing just what Martina was doing. Thinking that the transitory attention of a charismatic man meant something. Nobody maintained that *heat* that Keenan James projected over a span of eight years, especially not after they'd broken up. She herself probably never looked at Stewart that way anymore either.

She turned to him, put a hand on his arm, and said, "Stewart."

He looked at her and she leaned forward, going up on her toes to kiss him. Just to reassure herself that what they'd had was real. But just as she got close—his face showing incomprehension, even mild impatience—the elevator doors opened.

Stewart moved forward, Tory came down hard

on her flats, and they moved out of the elevator together.

"What's going on with you?" he asked, looking at her uneasily as they crossed the marble floor.

"Nothing," she sighed, eyes skittering around the lobby and blessedly finding no one.

They went out into the cool night air for a cab.

Cameron Lessing's apartment—if you could call the palatial, high-ceilinged, five-bedroom residence an apartment—was hot and teeming with people, all of them richly and immaculately dressed. It wasn't black tie, thank God. Tory hated those. She had one cocktail dress, with a high neck that scratched her skin and made the evening an exercise in not satisfying the itch, and she refused to buy another just for the occasional fund-raiser.

No, this evening was a suit night, and Tory had on her bone-colored suit with her black flats. Her one concession to the evening was the clutch purse. She knew she couldn't very well get away with the giant leather briefcase she usually carried.

As they sought out Mr. Lessing in the crowd, Tory passed her gaze around the room in the vain hope that someone interesting might be there. Who that might be, she couldn't imagine, but she needed to distract herself from the mental aerobics she'd been doing since kissing Keenan James, then hearing him on the radio talking about doing it all the time. Not only that, but she needed to stop the incessant chanting of her mind that she'd been a fool, a dupe, a victim of celebrity just like all those other women she'd always secretly derided.

Unfortunately the only interesting conversation she'd ever had at one of these things had been with the wife of the first violinist, who'd been clinically depressed at the time and unaware of it. Tory had actually gotten her into therapy with a colleague. But what did it say about her—Tory Hoffstra—that her most gratifying party conversation had been with a mentally ill guest?

"Cameron!" Stewart thundered, making Tory jump to attention. "Good to see you. The place is looking marvelous. Did you redecorate?"

"As a matter of fact we did," Cameron said, looking pleased.

Tory gaped at Stewart. He never, ever noticed what she wore or if she got her hair cut, but he'd remembered Cameron Lessing's *decor*?

"Heather decided that blue was too . . . facile," Lessing continued. "So we had it done over in cream and beige, though that's not what the decorators called it. What was it? They had to keep correcting me, you know . . ." He looked toward the ceiling, perhaps hoping the memory of it hovered in the subtle recessed lighting.

"Elephant Ivory and Riviera Sand," his wife, Heather, supplied as she joined their little group, looping her arm through her husband's. Heather had huge hair that tumbled over her shoulders, and wore dangling chandelier earrings that contained many, no doubt real diamonds. "He's such a *man*," she confided smugly to Tory.

"Yes," Tory said, blanking on how to make conversation out of the comment.

"Cameron, Heather, you remember my girl-friend," Stewart said with an enormously artificial smile at them and then her.

"Yes, of course, Terry." Cameron smiled briefly in her direction.

When Stewart said nothing to correct him—had he noticed?—Tory said firmly, "It's Tory, Cameron. Dr. Tory Hoffstra. We've met several times before."

Beside her, Stewart stiffened, but she'd gotten Cameron Lessing's attention and felt marginally less invisible in the glittering crowd.

He gave her a straight, concentrated look and said, "I'm so sorry. Dr. Tory Hoffstra, of course. It was a slip of the tongue." He smiled, looking bemused at her assertiveness. "It certainly won't happen again."

She inclined her head graciously, and felt momentarily proud for standing up for herself. Just because she eschewed the false pretenses of fancy clothes and jewelry didn't mean she had to relegate herself to being as ignorable as the wallpaper.

She was just about to add something smart about his color choices in the room when Heather burst out, "Oh my God, he's *here*. I can't believe he came. You must excuse me."

Without looking at any of them, she slid her arm out from her husband's and brushed past Tory as if she were in a trance and the Pied Piper was calling.

"Hm, important guest?" Stewart muttered, frowning at Cameron.

But Cameron was looking toward the door as well.

"Oh, you know," Cameron said, craning his neck. "She loves the celebrities, people in the public eye. I'd better go join her." And without waiting for a response he left too.

Tory and Stewart looked at each other.

"*I'm* in the public eye," Stewart said.

Tory turned toward the door and tried to see through the crowd, but she was shorter than most people and could see only the crush of bodies immediately surrounding them. Once again she wished for one of the outfits she wore to the round table—or at least the spiked heels.

As the group moved into the room a gap opened, and through it Tory saw the straight dark hair and lightning-quick smile of Keenan James.

Her breath left her.

Beside him stood a woman who seemed eight feet tall, with perfect skin, dark Sophia Loren eyes, a shimmering dress of silver that seemed to drip off her like water, and a smile that appeared at once effortless and erotic.

Tory clutched her purse in suddenly damp hands, looked down at her suit—remembering that this was the one Sasha had called a "bag"—and turned on her flat heel. "I—I need to go."

"Go?" Stewart repeated, appalled. "We're not leaving."

"To the, uh, restroom." She looked frantically around for a break in the crowd, and some indication of where that room might be.

"Hey, isn't that that guy?" Stewart said, eyes on the group at the door. "Wait, that's him. That's Keenan James! Tory! You don't need to be embarrassed. Just *talk* to him about what he said on the radio—"

Tory didn't wait to enumerate all the reasons she *should* be embarrassed to face Keenan James, not to mention why she shouldn't let him see her *here*, like the fact that she was anonymous in the group, or that he thought the real her was an idiot, because the biggest reason for her at this moment was that she was dressed in a bag suit and looked like the quintessential academic that he'd scorned in his radio interview.

She shoved through the crowd, spilling one man's drink, stepping on another's foot, and kept on pushing until she was sure she was invisible to Stewart and everyone behind him.

She made it to a table full of hors d'oeuvres in the corner of the room and shrank up against a marble statue of a naked armless woman. It was supposed to be classical, she supposed, but the look of sensual ecstasy on the stone face was distinctly modern.

She pushed a crab puff into her mouth and chewed vigorously, her eyes feverishly watching the crowd, caught between wanting to seem like a normal partygoer to those around her and wanting to flee like an endangered species.

She couldn't let him see her. Couldn't have a conversation with him. Couldn't let Stewart talk to him, not if he thought he'd be doing her a favor to make them talk about the radio show. And she certainly couldn't let anyone introduce her to him. He would think *she* was the unethical one when it was *he* who was kissing people who came to him for help! Theoretically.

She popped another crab puff into her mouth, as if possibly he wouldn't recognize her with her cheeks bulging like a hamster's. She grabbed a plate and filled it with the puffs. A waiter cruised by with a tray carrying glasses of wine, and she nearly tackled him. She chose red because the bulb of the glass was bigger. If she kept it in front of her face, perhaps he wouldn't notice her. Then she could pass out from too much alcohol and roll right under the sofa. No one would recognize her there.

It didn't take her long to realize that sucking down crab puffs and wine was a strategy she couldn't maintain for long. She searched the room. While it was mobbed with people, there was nothing else short of the drapes that appeared suitable for hiding behind. No large plants, no tall furniture she could get behind, no half-hidden window seats. As she scrutinized an armchair with a high back, and calculated how to evict its elderly occupant, Stewart pushed through the crowd. When he saw her, his face darkened.

"Here you are! I've been looking all over. You're behaving like a child, Tory. Just talk to the man. So he said a few bad things about your article; straighten him out." He took her arm, attempting to guide her forward. "It's incredible how people are fawning all over him. If you talk to him quickly, while Cameron and Heather are still hanging on his every word, it'll look good for both of us. Come on."

"Stewart, I *told* you, I'm supposed to be anonymous in his group. If I reveal myself to him now he'll just think I'm a liar, and that won't do either one of us any good." She pulled back on his arm.

He stopped. "Oh yes, right. Damn. I'd forgotten you were trying to be anonymous. But doesn't he have to find out who you are when you work on this book? I think now's the time, Tory. This is an opportunity."

For whom? she wanted to ask.

"Stewart, I haven't even found the restroom yet." She pulled herself free.

Stewart raised a brow at the plate full of crab

puffs in her hand. "Apparently not. It looks like you got rather distracted." He frowned. "Don't let Cameron see how you've cleaned out his hors d'oeuvres or he'll consider you a liability for the next party."

She heard a laugh coming from a group nearby, saw the bodies near her moving aside with whispers and furtive glances, then spotted Keenan James's hair above the heads of others. He was coming toward them. Well, toward the bar, more likely. She spun, turning her back toward him, and bumped into an older man who wore—of all things—a kilt.

The man turned to her, bushy gray brows descending over hawklike eyes. "I beg your pardon," he said, his tone conveying that the contact was emphatically not his fault.

"Crab puff?" she asked, holding the plate out.

"Oh." His face cleared. "Thank you very much. Dear?" He turned to a white-haired woman with lipstick on her teeth. "Crab puff?"

Behind her, Tory heard Stewart's hale-fellow-well-met voice. "Hello there! Excuse me, Mr. James! We met a couple of months ago. I'm on the board of the co-op? There's someone over here I'd like you to meet . . ."

Tory shoved the plate toward the white-haired woman. "Here, have them all."

"Oh. Thank you," the woman said, grabbing the plate before it fell to the floor.

Tory pushed past them through the crowd until she saw a woman emerging from a hallway, snapping shut the clasp of her purse.

The restroom, Tory thought with relief, and ran for the opening.

She made it down the hall, into the room, slammed the door, and leaned back on the granite countertop, breathing hard. She couldn't keep this up; she had to leave. Even if Stewart maintained her cover, she couldn't avoid Keenan James all night. The apartment wasn't *that* big. And once he saw her, he couldn't start calling her Vicky without people noticing, could he?

Actually maybe he could. Even Cameron Lessing, one of the few people here she'd met on more than one occasion, never remembered her name, so why not go by Vicky for the evening? She took a gulp of her wine, then put the glass on the counter, thinking.

Someone knocked on the door. "Anybody in there?" an accented female voice inquired. The doorknob rattled.

"Just a second," Tory called, heart beating frantically. She flushed the toilet.

"Oh. Sorry." The voice faded.

No, she couldn't risk it. She only had to stay anonymous another few days, and Fender would explain the whole thing to Keenan. In the meantime, she had to get out of here. She could tell

Stewart she was sick! Of course. They'd taken a cab here. She didn't need him to leave. If she told him she was liable to embarrass him in front of everyone, he'd let her go without a second thought.

She faced the sink, turned on the water, and washed her hands for the benefit of the woman outside the door. As she did, she looked at herself in the mirror. Her eyes were wide and frantic in her pale face. The suit, as her eyes grazed downward, really did look like a bag, she thought.

Why oh why did she have to come tonight? Why did *he* have to come? This was her world, in a way. Or it had been.

What a stupid position to find herself in, she thought, hiding in a bathroom from a man she'd accidentally kissed with whom she was going to be working on a book about crappy pop psychology that she didn't even believe in.

When she could put it off no longer, she opened the door. Waiting in the hallway was the eight-foot-tall woman who'd arrived with Keenan James.

"Sorry I took so long," Tory said, craning her head to look up at the woman's face. Okay, so she wasn't eight feet tall. Maybe six. And her high yet somehow delicate shoes no doubt had a lot to do with that.

"That's all right," the woman said in an enviable British accent. "I do hate to rush people, but I had two martinis before I got here." She smiled

brilliantly and—Tory had to admit—warmly.
Tory pictured the Amazon beauty and Keenan
James standing elegantly by a fireplace, toasting
their magnificence with stylish martini glasses,
before heading to the stodgy world of the symphony.

Tory smiled back and edged out of the doorway.
The woman entered the bathroom. For a moment,
Tory leaned against the hall wall, trying to think
of a way to talk to Stewart without running into
Keenan, until someone else came down the pas-
sageway. It occurred to Tory that she could go the
opposite way down the hall, maybe hide out in a
bedroom. But with her luck she'd be discovered
and thought to be burgling the place.

She'd just have to hope Stewart was finished talking to Keenan about how they lived in the same
building and should get to know each other—she
was sure he'd consider that helpful to her—so she
could tell him she was leaving.

She crept out of the hallway, her eyes peeled for
Stewart and her nerves steeled for Keenan James.
As she edged past the enormous marble hearth—
wherein a veritable bonfire raged; no *wonder* it was
so damn hot in here—she caught sight of Stewart.
He was talking to the man in the kilt.

She breathed a sigh of relief. Stewart turned to
her, his eyes lighting and a smile spreading across
his face.

"There you are," he said. He and the kilt man moved the few steps toward where she stood by the fireplace. Beside them, her heart sank as she saw Keenan James, talking with Cameron Lessing. She dropped her gaze, as if not seeing him would cause him not to see her, then glanced up discreetly through her lashes.

The kilted man reached her first. "Excuse me, miss," he said in an offhand tone. "I wonder if you might fetch us some more of those crab puffs." He turned back to Keenan. "They really are the most divine things, you must try one."

Keenan's eyes grazed her and moved back to the kilted man.

Tory gaped at him, then nearly laughed. He hadn't recognized her! And why would he? She wasn't painted up like a circus performer.

A second of jubilation was all she was to have, however.

"Have you met Stewart's girlfriend?" Cameron asked, looking at her as if remembering her was something he should be praised for.

Tory stiffened.

Keenan's eyes snapped back to hers, then swept her up and down as if she'd rolled in the fireplace grate.

"Vicky?" he said, disbelief in his tone.

"Actually it's Tory," Cameron elaborated, looking at her proudly. Then added, echoing her earlier pronouncement and enunciating all too clearly, "Dr. Tory Hoffstra."

Stewart looked at her and shrugged, then turned back to Keenan. "You might know her better as Engelberta. Dr. Engelberta Hoffstra. The one who wrote the article you talked about today on the radio. Wonderful interview, by the way. I heard the entire thing. I think it's fascinating, what you're doing. Absolutely fascinating."

Stewart blathered on while Tory's eyes met Keenan's. As she watched, a tornado of emotions swirling in her chest, his eyes grew flinty.

"So," he said, over Stewart's sycophantic rant, "you *were* a plant."

Chapter 13

At that moment, Heather Lessing rejoined them, sparing Tory the awkwardness of having to answer Keenan's appalling statement.

"I've had to open up another coatroom because that stupid woman said the first one was full," she hissed to Cameron. "Full? I asked her. How could it be full, it's a sixteen-by-twelve-foot room! She said the coats were falling off the bed onto the floor . . ."

"Oh, pardon me, dear," the kilted man said to Tory, his eyes accusing, as if she'd lied to him, "I thought you were one of the servers."

Tory was sorry to realize she'd left her wine in the bathroom. Not that befuddling her brain was likely to get her out of this mess, but still. It might help her pretend she wasn't actually here.

Cameron shushed his wife and looked at Keenan. "So you already know Tory?" Cameron glanced at Tory with interest.

Stewart puffed up. "They've actually—"

"We just recently met," she said, wondering if there was any chance she could pull Keenan aside and try to explain. Then again, *he* owed *her* an explanation too, didn't he? "How are you, Keenan? I'm surprised to see you here, of all places."

Keenan's face was assessing, looking at her as if she'd revealed another head. He kept looking from her face to her suit, all the way down to her feet and back again.

"I came with a friend who loves the symphony," Keenan said as his eyes raked her.

"Yes, the lovely Fiona," Cameron said, looking about them. "Where is Fiona? I haven't told her about the spring program yet. I think she's going to be very excited."

Keenan looked easily over their heads. "She just went to the restroom. I'm sure she'll be back in a minute."

Tory looked from Keenan to Stewart, thinking they were like ice cream and beans. Next to Keenan's tall, toned angles, poor Stewart looked clumsy and round. Keenan's sharp blue eyes were laserlike compared to Stewart's milk-soft brown ones. Worst of all, Keenan's smile was quick and captivating, seeming to reveal even more the forced nature of Stewart's.

Of course neither of them was smiling now.

The bottom line, however, was that though ice cream was sweet and delicious, beans were better for her. Besides, she knew that Stewart's falseness came from a deep insecurity, not the surfeit of confidence that the overly gifted Keenan James enjoyed.

"The lovely Fiona" appeared at Keenan's elbow a second later as if conjured, and Tory recognized the woman from the bathroom. "I've brought you a glass of wine, Kee; I don't think they've got any beer."

"Beer?" Cameron repeated. "Of course we've got beer. Just one minute." He flagged down a server who was, Tory hoped the kilted man noted, dressed in no way like she was. "We need a beer here. What would you like, Keenan? We have microbrews, imports, domestics, you name it."

Keenan smiled easily at the server, a young man who gawked at him like he was the lead singer of a rock group. "Whatever you lay your hands on first."

"Yes, sir, Mr. James, sir." The server nodded. "And can I just say, I loved *Sex at Midnight*."

"Thank you." Keenan looked at him appreciatively, for all the world as if the kid's opinion mattered.

"The beer?" Cameron said tightly to the blushing boy. "And take this glass with you," he added, ever so solicitous of Fiona's two-fisted state.

"I'll take that," Tory said, reaching out.

Cameron's eyes grazed her. "Of course, Tory." He handed the glass of white to her.

Tory kicked herself again for making such a point of her name to him. That's what she got for standing up for herself. She'd been outed in the most awkward way possible.

"Fiona," Keenan said, "this is Tory . . . I'm sorry, what was the last name again?" Those blue eyes pinned her where she stood.

Tory looked straight back and said coldly, "Humperdinck."

Stewart laughed uncomfortably and gripped her arm with one hand, looking around the group. "She's kidding, of course. Her last name—as Cameron has already mentioned," he added significantly to Tory, "is Hoffstra. Dr. *Hoffstra*. She's quite well-known in psychological circles."

Tory turned to Stewart. "Keenan, you know Stewart Reasoner from your co-op, don't you? Did you know he also plays first cello for the NYCS? He's brilliant." She beamed Stewart a smile. "Tell them about the solo suites of Bach's you've been working on. He's the next Ma, if you ask me."

Stewart flushed and looked at Cameron. "Of course that's for the powers-that-be to determine.

And the audience, of course. But thank you, dear. Tory's very loyal."

"Is she?" Keenan raised his brows at her and tilted his head.

"The next Ma," Cameron said. "High praise indeed."

"Keenan." Tory turned to him with as cool an expression as she could muster. "Could I talk to you for just a moment? I have a question about . . ." She glanced around the group. "About what you're doing." *What* the hell *you're doing*, was what she wanted to say.

He eyed her steadily. "My weekly round tables, do you mean?"

She felt a blush creep up her neck. "Yes, exactly."

"Are you thinking you'd like to join one of them?" he asked equably. Toying with her, she knew.

The blush was complete now, up her cheeks to her hairline. "Of course not." She laughed breathlessly. "I wanted to ask you about them from a *professional* standpoint."

"Ah, from a *professional* standpoint," he repeated. "I think that's an excellent idea."

"Shall we step over here?" She motioned toward the hallway where the restroom was. Surely there was another room down that hall they could borrow for a moment. "I don't want to bore everyone here with the details." She gave him a tight smile.

"Nonsense!" Cameron said. "I know I, for one,

would be intrigued by a conversation about Keenan's profession. And yours too, of course, Dr. Hoffstra."

Tory wished she could kick him, but instead she tried to give him a gracious smile. "I do agree, Cameron, that Keenan's profession *is* fascinating, dealing as it does with television and making up stories and all that. But I wanted to discuss with him further a conversation we started last week about the differences between Maslow's hierarchy of needs and Hull's theory of motivation." She shifted her eyes to Keenan. "Shall we?"

His mouth had quirked up on one side, and he gazed at her with something close to amusement.

She turned on her heel and edged through the crowd toward the hallway, hoping he was following. She clutched her wineglass in one hand, the stem slick in her palm, and wished she hadn't eaten so many crab puffs. Her stomach was tied in such a knot, it would be a wonder if she didn't get sick.

By the time they reached the hall, Keenan had decided that the only tack to take in the situation would be to face the problem head-on. If she'd been a plant of Fender's, sent to check out his methods, then that kiss they'd shared had been a disaster. It did, however, explain why she had leaned over to kiss him, something that had surprised him despite its being something a number of other women had done in his past. He simply had never expected it from her, never thought he'd be able to crack that hard shell she wore around herself. But she'd been different that night at the club. Vulnerable.

When they reached a door in the hall she paused before it, and he automatically reached around her to open it. She startled and glared at him.

"Thank you," she muttered, and stepped into the darkened room.

From where he stood it was obvious this was where the hostess had taken the coats, as a large pile of something lay on a bed in the corner. He reached over to a lamp on a table and clicked it once. The room, with gilded wallpaper and heavy dark furniture, glowed richly in the dim wattage.

"So let me guess," Keenan began, keeping his tone level. "You were a plant by Fender, sent to check up on me, and you think you've exposed some dark underside to my mission. You're going to report back to him that I am not what I claim and should not be allowed to write that book. Or worse. As you freely admitted, your friend lured me to the club the other night so that you could stage a scene where you kissed me and had a photographer nearby recording the incident as a way of debunking what I'm trying to do. Or—"

"Remind me to talk to you about delusional disorders and their relationship to schizophrenia," she interrupted.

He laughed. "*I'm* schizophrenic, Dr./Ms. Hoffstra/Smith?"

She pressed her lips together and looked briefly away.

"All right," he added. "Why don't you explain? And start with that outfit you've got on. Did you think you could disguise yourself from me by wearing clothes three sizes too big?"

She looked down at herself, and her hands clenched by her side. He felt bad for his words when he noted the color in her cheeks. Or was that just a trick of the lighting?

Hard to say who or what was playing tricks on whom these days.

"*This* isn't the disguise," she said, those wide gray eyes looking back up at him. They appeared at once scared and rebellious. The angry kitten again. "The disguise is the makeup and the fancy clothes I wore to the round table," she said, sweeping her hand up around her face and down her body. She didn't look at him. "This . . . *this* is the real me. The real, plain, unglamorous me."

He shook his head. "It all looks the same to me. At least the part I can see around that suit. If nothing else," he added, "I'd know those eyes anywhere."

Those eyes shot up to his. "You are just full of lines, aren't you? Is this how you get around your problems? Flirt your way out of them? I'm trying to be serious."

He folded his arms across his chest. "Have I *got* a problem?"

"I'll say you do," she said, her voice trembling. She glanced away from him again, gesticulating with her words. "You—you as much as admitted to seducing people in that radio interview you did. You might as well have stated right out, 'I'm using you' to all those women in your groups, because I'm sure *I'm* not the first one you've kissed." She met his gaze again. "Nor do I kid myself I'll be the last. Don't you think that's unethical? Don't you see how dangerous that kind of thing is?"

He moved his hands to his pockets and leaned toward her a little. "I'll let you in on a little secret: I was kidding." He leaned back and tilted his head, his expression serious. "I've never seduced anyone from those round tables."

"Haven't you?" Her eyes met his defiantly again.

He raised his brows. "Have I? Are you saying I seduced you, Vic—ah, Tory, was it? I may have to call you Victoria for a while."

She flushed. "We—we *kissed*!"

"We did."

They looked at each other mutinously a moment.

"Are you saying that I kissed you?" he asked gently.

Her gazed dropped and she turned halfway away. She moved to the bed and put one hand on the wooden footboard.

"I—I don't know. I . . . wasn't sure, afterward. I thought it was . . . me. But at the time I wondered . . ." She put a hand over her face, and for a second he feared she was crying. Her narrow shoulders bent, and something inside him reached out to her.

She was tortured by the event, he realized. Tortured by one simple, little kiss.

He moved toward her and touched her shoulder. When she didn't move, he turned her to him. "You're more worried about your behavior than mine, aren't you? It's not my ethics you're questioning . . . is it?"

She exhaled slowly. "I . . . it's . . ."

"Here," he said softly, looking into her miserable, upturned eyes. "You can tell Fender that I kissed you."

With that he leaned down and touched her lips with his.

For a moment, all of time seemed to halt, suspended for the breadth of the kiss, his lips gentle upon her soft, surprised mouth. Then all hell broke loose. Or all heaven.

Tory's lips opened under his and her arms went round his neck. He pulled her toward him with both hands on her rib cage and allowed himself to fall into the kiss. It was as shocking as it had been the first time. Electric, sizzling. His body felt energized as desire flared to life beneath her touch.

He moved his arms around her and pulled her body along the length of his. She was like a dynamo, like something unleashed from years of imprisonment. He felt it emanating from her in waves: *passion*.

And his rose up to meet it.

Her hair was corn silk under his hands, her lips soft as butter, and her pretty, pale face like that of some tragic figure from a Renaissance painting. He pushed her toward the wall and she leaned back against it, her hands moving up to cup his face.

His hand grabbed the bottom of her suit jacket and probed beneath it. His fingers found a silky camisole underneath. She gasped against his mouth but he shushed her. This was like nothing he'd ever felt, two bodies so simultaneously, so unexpectedly igniting. She moved under his hands, under his mouth, her legs brushing his.

He pulled against the silky fabric of the camisole until his fingers found flesh. He slid his palms up her sides, then cupped her breasts. She was delectable, small but firm and perfectly shaped. He wanted to take her and throw her on the bed, take off the awful, cloaking clothes she wore and gaze on the pale perfection of her body.

"Keenan, no," she whispered, but her mouth found his again and kissed him furiously. Her body arched into his, and her arms held him too tight for him to believe her words.

"No, what?" he whispered back, letting his lips trail down to her neck while one hand pulled the fabric of her skirt up to her hip. She wore thigh-high stockings, he felt, and her skin was smooth above the elastic. He nearly groaned with pleasure as his hand found the apex of her thighs and the heat there. He held her through the cotton panties.

"Oh my God," she gulped.

He slipped a finger inside the fabric and felt the extent of her desire.

Outside the closed door the party swirled obliviously—talking, eating, music—but inside this room, this dim, quiet room, it was just the two of them. Just the two of them and this uncontrollable urge.

He moved his thumb upward and found the spot that made her writhe. She inhaled sharply and threw her head back against the wall. He did not let up. One of her legs rose to wind around his, and he moved his other hand to the fly of his pants.

"Keenan," she whispered, her hand coming down onto his, "we shouldn't. Someone might . . ."

But her hand strayed to his pants, then unzipped his fly and moved inside to the throbbing organ within. Her hand encircled him and he laid his forehead against hers, exhaling slowly. "Vic—toria," he laughed slightly, "please."

She moved her hand up along his length and he thought he might ruin the whole deal for them both. Never had he been aroused to the point of nearly coming before performing the act. He clenched his teeth and moved his fingers over her heat again.

She pulled him toward her and he lifted her slightly. He helped her guide him to her center, and just as he thought he might explode, he pushed into her tight, slick, honeyed heat.

"Oh God," she gasped, both legs circling his waist. "Keenan . . ."

He braced her against the wall and thrust, once, twice, three times. She bent her head into him and cried out into his shoulder, climaxing almost immediately but muffling the sound as best she could.

He couldn't stop then. Pushing into her again and again. She threw her head back and arched, making it easier for him to move. He held her buttocks, thrusting into her, her back against the wall, skirt around her waist, his pants around his ankles.

He came with a burst of light behind his closed eyes, his nerves vibrating all across his body and his heart threatening to pump right out of his chest. He held her close, his face in her hair, inhaling the sweet clean scent of her, absorbing the soft, pliant strength of her.

They stayed that way for several long minutes before she slid her legs down, her feet touching back on the floor.

She didn't look at him as she pushed her skirt down over her hips.

He bent, pulled up his pants and zipped them, then reached a hand out to push the hair back from her face. "Tory?" he asked quietly. "Are you all right?"

He saw her lips curve as she straightened her clothing but she didn't look up. "I-I'm not sure I can trust my knees."

He chuckled and pulled her to him, wrapping

his arms around her. "My God, that was . . . amazing."

He felt her head tilt upward. "Was it?"

He leaned back and looked down at her, mouth quirked into a smile. "Didn't you think so?"

She gazed up at him, in her eyes an expression he could not read. Troubled yet soft. "I . . ." she began. "There's something—" She stopped. Then she swallowed, lowered her head, and pulled out of his embrace. "I have to go."

With that she took swift steps toward the door, opened it, and disappeared through it.

Tory pressed the buzzer for apartment number four and heard a static-obscured voice ask who was there.

"It's Tor—Vicky Smith, from the round table?" she said, leaning close to the intercom. Around her a cold October wind blew, and she pushed her hands into her coat pockets.

The front door buzzed and she pulled it open. As she walked up the four flights to Angelica's loft, she understood why the woman was so slim. Just carrying a bag of groceries up those steep, old stairs would burn whatever calories the bag contained.

Angelica waited for her at the top of the stairs, in her arms a brown dog that looked at her voraciously. "Vicky, I'm delighted to see you. Surprised, but delighted."

Tory stopped dead, eyeing the dog nervously. It had pointed ears and large eyes. "Is that a pit bull?"

Angelica burst out laughing. "It's a Chihuahua. His name is Pav, short for Pavlov."

Tory tried to smile. "I'm sorry, I'm just a little nervous around dogs."

Angelica looked from the dog to where Tory stood by the top of the stairs and smiled gently. "What if I just hang on to him? I won't put him down, I promise. And if that still bothers you I'll put him in the bedroom."

Tory liked the way everything Angelica said was delivered slowly, with great deliberation, as if she'd thought about her words and really meant them. In her arms, the dog trembled, as if anxious to jump down and start gnawing on Tory's leg bone.

She took a deep breath, acutely aware of the fact that she was stopping by unannounced, and so unwilling to put Angelica out any further by making her put her dog away.

"Of course, that'll be fine." She forced herself to take a step forward and address the animal. "Hello, doggy," she said, looking into its face. She started to reach out, to pat his head, but drew back.

"Let's just take things one step at a time," Angelica said. "You can work up to petting him.'

Tory smiled, relieved. "I'm so sorry to bother you at home on the weekend."

Angelica waved a hand. "Pah! Weekends." She

laughed. "Ever since I quit my day job a couple years ago, I haven't known a weekend from a weekday. Sometimes the only way I figure out it's Saturday is because the restaurants are all crowded."

Tory smiled, figuring she was heading into the same territory herself, now that she was unemployed. "Must be nice."

"It is," Angelica agreed, motioning her into the apartment. "Except that you start to dislike weekends after a while, when everyone in the world is out doing what you want to do and taking up space."

Tory entered the loft and caught her breath. The place was incredible, with huge potted plants—trees almost—and long, sheer drapes hanging from the industrial-size windows. Oriental rugs and deep, cushy furniture were arranged in a conversation circle near a cast-iron fireplace built into one brick wall. This was separated by a Japanese shoji screen from a dining area with a long, solid wood table. Beyond that was the studio, with easels and workbenches and tools, all bathed in glorious light. But as enormous as the place felt, it was divided so that each area held its own appeal, had its own atmosphere.

Tory wished she lived there.

"This place is . . ." she began, but didn't know the adjective to use. Huge. Eclectic. Welcoming.

"A mess," Angelica finished for her. "But that's what you get."

Tory blushed. "I'm so sorry. I would have called first, but I couldn't find your number. It was only because you'd mentioned where you lived at the opening that I was able to find you."

"I'm glad you did. And I meant that's what you get for visiting at all." Angelica laid a hand on her shoulder and guided her toward the puffy couch, still clutching the dog. "I wouldn't have cleaned even if you'd called, I'm sorry to say. It's just not in me."

Tory smiled. *Just not in me.* She wished she accepted herself like that. She wished she even *knew* herself like that.

"Can I get you some tea?" Angelica asked.

Tory deliberated. She wasn't sure how to even begin the conversation she wanted to have; a further delay could only help.

"That would be great." She smiled her relief. At least Angelica didn't seem put off by her sudden appearance.

Angelica moved off to an area separated from the main room by a wall that did not reach the ceiling. In fact, none of the walls in the place did, she noted, the ceiling being all exposed ducts and vents and fans and whatnot, painted black.

She wondered where Angelica's partner was, and hoped she wasn't at home or likely to interrupt.

"Here we go." Angelica flowed back into the room in her palazzo pants and knee-length vest. The sleeves of her filmy shirt were belled at the ends. She looked elegant and artsy, better than Tory did on her best days, and Angelica was just relaxing at home.

Tory looked down at her jeans and sweater. How pedestrian.

"You're probably wondering what on earth I'm doing here," Tory said, picking up one of the steaming cups from the tray Angelica had laid on the table in front of the couch.

Angelica sat at the opposite end of the sofa, tucked her feet up under her, letting the dog curl onto her lap, and looked benignly at Tory. "I was hoping it was a social visit. We did talk about getting together, didn't we? I hope nothing's wrong."

"No, no," Tory said vaguely. "Well, I'm a little troubled. About myself. And I just . . ." She looked into Angelica's deep, amber eyes. "I didn't have anyone else to talk to about it."

How pathetic was that? she thought, hoping Angelica didn't think the same.

"Then I'm delighted you thought of me." She smiled calmly.

Everything about Angelica was calm, Tory noticed yet again. She found herself breathing easier just being here. Even with the animal crouching on the woman's lap.

"God, I wish I could live here," Tory said, looking around.

Angelica laughed. "Maybe we ought to get to know each other a little better, first."

Tory blushed bright red and closed her eyes tight. "No, no, I'm sorry, I didn't mean it that way!"

Then—thinking Angelica might believe she meant it romantically, then with her emphatic denial think she was homophobic—she blushed even deeper.

"I mean, I only—I just find it so appealing here."

"I know what you meant," Angelica said, leaning over to lay a cool hand on one of Tory's. The dog shrank back against her body. "Relax, Vicky. What can I help you with?"

Tory exhaled. "First, my name isn't Vicky. Or well, it is. It's Victoria. But I go by Tory, normally."

Angelica nodded. "I'm not surprised. I thought you seemed particularly concerned with maintaining your anonymity in the group."

"It's not just that," Tory said, then, after a bracing breath, added. "I wanted to tell you the truth, what I'm really doing at the round table." Without waiting for a response for fear of chickening out, she went on to explain about her false presence in the group. She started with her clothes and makeup transformation, and went from there, speaking quickly, not looking at Angelica, and hoping at the end of it all that she wouldn't be asked to leave.

She didn't mention that she had committed to cowrite the book with Keenan—that, she decided, shouldn't be revealed until Keenan himself knew it—but she confessed to being there to check out what he was doing, and in the meantime lying about most everything to the other women.

"Well, not everything," Tory said, in conclusion. "The stuff about my relationship was true. Mostly." She hung her head miserably.

"Tory, dear, you must stop punishing yourself. You did what you had to do. You were trying to be objective, to be responsible. I would have much less respect for you if you'd just decided to do the book based on Keenan's name, instead of trying to find out if what he was doing was legitimate. I think what you did was *admirable*."

Tory took another sip of her tea and stared into the fire. It was gas, she noted, but looked very real. Angelica must have been quite a successful painter.

"That's kind of you. And I guess maybe you're right about that part." Tory dipped her head toward her cup and let her hair hang down by the side of her face, shielding her. "But that's not what I'm *really* ashamed of. I, ever since joining the group, I've been like another person. Doing things I never would have done before."

Starting with developing a ridiculous kind of crush on *Keenan*. But while she wanted to talk about what happened, his identity would have to be dragged from her while under some particularly grueling form of torture.

"Like what?" Angelica probed gently.

"Okay, last night I went to a party with Stewart— oh, uh, that's Louis. It was a symphony fund-raiser and I've been to dozens of them over the years. But last night somebody was there. Somebody I've been sort of . . . reluctantly attracted to the past few weeks."

"Why reluctantly?"

She ran a finger around the rim of her teacup. "Well, he's not my type, really. And I think he might be . . . insincere. But it's mostly that he's kind of exciting, in a way. I think I've fallen into that old trap of wanting the bad boy." She scoffed lightly. "And I thought I'd outgrown that after high school."

"Mm." Angelica shook her head. "There's something about that that none of us outgrows."

Tory's eyes flashed up to Angelica's. There was a story there, she thought. "Well, I kind of followed through on the attraction at the party."

"What do you mean, followed through? With Stewart there?"

Tory ran a hand over her eyes, then up through her hair. "Yes! God, I still can hardly believe it. I—I—I can't even get the words out." She laughed incredulously, then looked sideways at Angelica. "And I hope it's okay to tell you this, but the way we're so open in the group . . ."

"Tory, you couldn't tell me anything that would shock me," Angelica said. "Trust me."

Tory wasn't so sure about that. She swallowed, looked back at her teacup, and blurted, "I had sex with this man in the coatroom at the party."

Angelica was silent. Silent for a long time. Tory finally looked up at her.

She was smiling. Not looking at Tory but smiling to herself as she leaned over and put her empty teacup on the coffee table.

"Angelica?" Tory said tentatively.

"Yes?" She looked quietly over at Tory.

"Are you . . . appalled at me?"

Angelica smiled. "No, I'm not appalled," she said finally. "But I am a little surprised. That's all, just a little. But if you want to know the truth, it sounds healthy to me."

"Healthy?" Tory repeated. "To have sex with one man while you're at a party with another? To have sex with someone in a public place, not even mentioning the fact that I've never even been on a date with this man. I'm—I'm appalled at myself. I don't even know who I am anymore."

"It sounds to me like you're finally finding out who you are. By throwing out what you considered to be the 'real' you, you're finding out who you want to be. You said you liked the clothes, and the way the makeup made you feel—"

"Yes, but I think that was just because it was so *different* from the real me. I felt safe, completely hidden."

"Or maybe you felt safe because you were completely yourself."

Tory was stunned by the statement. Not because it was unexpected so much as because it rang some inner bell of truth. Could it be? Was she really the type to wear makeup and have sex in a coatroom? And what did that say about her? Was she not as intelligent and unpretentious as she liked to think?

"And might I remind you," Angelica said, "that you and Stewart have broken up. You broke up because of this very reason, the lack of passion. What are the chances that you and Stewart were going to have sex at that party, hm?"

The very idea made a gasp of laughter burst from Tory. "The chance of Stewart and me having sex *anywhere* was pretty much nil."

"Well, then," Angelica said, "I think you did the right thing."

Tory placed her cup on the coffee table and felt something loosen inside of her, some pent-up, wound-up, knotted-up center of her coming apart. She felt like she could take a deep breath for the first time in weeks. She was right to have come here.

"You remind me," Angelica said, "of a woman in Keenan's Wednesday group. She's an accountant who always wanted to be an actress, but she was painfully shy. Keenan built up her self-esteem to the point where she was brave enough to audition for a part in her community theater. She got the part and was so good at it that a man in the audience came back to meet her after one of the performances. And he's perfect for her. They're together to this day, a year later. You see, she too had to disguise herself before she could *become* herself. Just like you."

Tory hated to think that falling for Keenan

James—a man who would never look to someone like her for an actual relationship—was who she really was. But she didn't mind discovering that she actually had some passion herself. It was something she had long wondered about, whether her problems with Stewart sprang from him or from her.

"Wait," Tory said, after completing her own thought process. "You go to another of Keenan's round tables, in addition to the Monday one?"

Angelica smiled faintly. "I go to all of them."

This roused a dozen questions in Tory's mind, none of which she could ask. What kind of problems could Angelica be facing that she decided to seek Keenan's "therapy" eight times a month?

But despite all she'd just revealed herself, she didn't feel she could ask. Angelica would have to volunteer some information first, demonstrate that she wished to talk, before Tory would probe.

"Wow," was all she said, and when Angelica said nothing further, Tory rose to her feet. "I guess I should go. But Angelica, I can't thank you enough for your help today. I feel better than I have in weeks. Really."

Angelica gave her a gracious smile, rose and squeezed her hand. "That's what friends are for."

Tory smiled. Friends. She had a girlfriend. And it was unbelievably comforting. In fact, she'd gotten so comfortable that she hadn't even remembered the dog was in the room until they stood up and Angelica cradled it in one arm again.

"Good-bye, Pav," she said. Then she added hesitantly to Angelica, "If *you* ever need someone to talk to . . ."

Angelica held the door for her. "You'll be the first one I call."

Tory Hoffstra left the loft looking like the weight of the world had just been lifted off her shoulders.

Angelica smiled smugly to herself as she closed the door, then cleared the teacups off the coffee table.

She hadn't lost her touch, she reflected. Lord, but this was getting interesting. A *coatroom at a party* . . . Keenan hadn't told her that part.

Chapter 14

"Come on in, Keenan," Angelica said, placing Pavlov on the floor to play with Barbra Streisand. "Can I get you a drink?"

Keenan unhooked his dog's leash and watched her tear off through the huge apartment after Angelica's tiny dog.

"Sure, what have you got?"

"I have it all, darling," she said with a throaty laugh.

"I'll take a vodka tonic, then." He smiled at her but ran a hand up and through his hair. It was damp from the drizzle outside. "It's a bitch of a night."

"Just the way I like them," Angelica said, pouring his drink and a Drambuie for herself.

She handed him the vodka tonic and they moved to the couch. Keenan sat on one end, Angelica on the other. She had lit the fire, and a soothing warmth came from the grate.

He reflected on the fact that he was more relaxed around Angelica than around just about anyone else he knew. Part of it was her personality, of course. She was tranquillity personified. The other, however, was because he knew she wanted nothing from him. She was a woman, but she was not interested in him in any way, and never would be. But it wasn't like being with a man either—there was no competition, no one-upmanship.

He took a swallow and felt his insides uncoil. He'd been in a knot since Friday night, when Vicky/Tory Smith/Hoffstra had rocked his world and sent his mind reeling.

"So what did you want to see me about?" he asked.

Angelica raised her hands over her head and readjusted what looked like Chinese chopsticks in her elaborate braids.

"I had a visitor yesterday," she said beguilingly. "Someone you'll be even more surprised to hear about than I was."

He lifted his brows. "Not Jan, I hope? I did speak

to her, thank you very much. Now I'm without a dog sitter."

She smiled. "Actually, it was another of your conquests, Kee." She took a sip of her drink and eyed him over the rim. "Really, darling, a *coat closet*?"

Keenan managed to maintain his composure but only by taking a walloping big gulp of his drink. He managed a laugh. "She told you about it?"

Angelica was shaking her head. "You sure know how to treat a girl."

"Hey, it took me by surprise too."

"I could base all kinds of analyses on the fact that it was a private yet public environment, in a room filled with garments meant to protect our bodies from hostile elements . . ."

He smiled sincerely then. "Settle down, Doctor. You were hired to judge what I do at the round tables, not whenever it strikes your fancy."

"Point taken."

"So she came to talk to you?" He tried to imagine it, Vick—er—Tory opening up to someone. "What did she say?"

Angelica used a swizzle stick to stir her drink with one manicured hand. "Actually, I feel I shouldn't divulge exactly *what* she said, only that she came to see me. And she didn't actually tell me it was you either."

He nodded his head thoughtfully. "Did you tell her who you are? What you, uh, do? For me, that is?"

She shook her head. "No, it really wasn't relevant. Besides, I can't believe it would be a huge revelation that you had a psychiatrist—"

"Former," he added, with a grin.

"Yes of course. A *former* psychiatrist . . . My, it feels good to say that. Anyway, I think it would put her mind at ease if she knew you took what you were doing seriously enough to check up on yourself."

He laughed and swirled the ice in his drink. "No it wouldn't. It would only add fuel to her conviction that I'm a charlatan. She'd become convinced that I know it myself and had you there as liability insurance. Trust me on that, Angelica. The woman is searching for ways to prove I'm not doing any good."

"So prove to her you are."

"I'm trying." He held out a hand helplessly. "But it doesn't help when you go telling her that Jan is secretly in love with me and only in the group for that reason. Not to mention that I take advantage of her by having her take care of my dog."

"I didn't tell her," Angelica said. "Martina did. That's how I found out. But still. You should have seen that coming."

He shrugged. "I thought she was just nuts about dogs."

"Keenan, when are you going to get it through your head that you're a very attractive man." She smiled as she said, it and he knew she was teasing him, but he felt frustration engulf him.

"Yeah, I get that. Women find me attractive. But do you know how sick I am of tiptoeing around people on the off chance that I'll lead someone on without knowing it? Okay, okay." He held up one hand as if she'd protested. "I know it's a terrible thing to complain about and I'm lucky and all that crap, but God *damn* I'm sick of finding out a friend is not a friend because they want something more."

"As opposed to Miss Smith. Or Dr. Hoffstra." Angelica tilted her head.

He smiled wryly. "I admit, that's part of her appeal. She doesn't like me."

"Well . . ."

His eyes flashed to hers. "Does she?"

Pavlov came racing across the room and took a flying leap into Angelica's lap. Incredibly, this did not upset her drink; she merely raised it high as the tiny dog curled up in her lap.

Behind her, like the Tasmanian devil, Keenan's dog careened across the slippery floor, bounced hip-first into the wall opposite them, then—Fred Flintstone–like—paddled madly against the hardwood until her feet caught and she shot toward Keenan.

He had his arm out, bent at the elbow, and caught the dog in the chest in a practiced move that bounced her back onto her butt in a sitting position.

Angelica laughed. "Nice training."

He shook his head as he grabbed the dog by the collar and pushed her into a lying down position beside him on the floor. "I don't know who's training who." He looked sternly at the dog and adopted the most alpha voice he had. "*Stay.*"

He sat back and exhaled, looking at Pavlov in Angelica's lap. "Why couldn't Mom have gotten a Chihuahua?"

"How is your mother?" Her voice was compassionate.

He shrugged and felt a familiar weight in his gut. "About the same. Still asking about Brady every time I go there."

"He has no plans to come back?"

"He's thinking about it." Keenan rubbed his fingers over his eyes. "You'd think for a pilot it would be a piece of cake to come visit his own damn mother once in a while."

Angelica angled her head against the back of the sofa and looked at him kindly. "You're doing all you can. You are not responsible for the relationship between Brady and your mother."

"I know." He sighed. Then he turned to her with a bemused smile. "You didn't answer my question. Does Vi—ah—Tory Hoffstra *not* dislike me?"

Angelica's hand stroked the back of her dog. The Chihuahua kept his huge round eyes focused on Keenan, his ears trembling slightly. "I don't want to say anything specific. But Keenan, I feel I must point out that she's much more vulnerable than your typical coatroom conquests."

"*I'd* like to point out that I have never before had a coatroom conquest," he said.

"You know what I'm saying." She looked at him seriously. "Don't toy with her."

He ran his hand through his hair again and stood, moving toward the fire. Barbra Streisand raised her head to watch him, but at a threatening look from him did not get up.

"What about her toying with me? Hm?" He turned to look at Angelica. "She kissed me in the car that night. And that whole thing at the party started when *she* pulled *me* into that room."

Angelica's brows rose. "To kiss you?"

He looked back at the fire. "To talk. To explain about who she was."

"Ah."

"But believe me when I say that she was not resistant to . . . all that ensued." He shifted so his back was to the fire and sipped his drink.

"I do believe you," she said. "That's why I think you need to be careful with her."

Keenan thought about that a moment, eyeing Angelica suspiciously. "Because she was not resistant?"

She inclined her head briefly.

"Are you saying," he asked slowly, "that she might have *feelings* for me? Like, something other than aversion?"

This could be interesting, he thought. This could be *very* interesting.

Angelica gave him a half smile and merely met his eyes, saying nothing.

"Because I have not gotten that impression," he added.

Angelica merely raised her brows, as if to say, *That's your problem.*

He studied her, wishing he could read her mind, just for a moment, just to see exactly what it was she knew, exactly what it was Tory Hoffstra had told her.

He nodded his head slowly.

Yes, this was *very* interesting.

It was like heading to the gallows, Tory thought, this trip up the elevator to Franklin Fender's office. The meeting with the three of them was set for Thursday at five, and she presumed that Keenan had been apprised of her identity and the purpose of her surreptitious presence at his round table.

She had been too cowardly to go back to the round table lunch that Monday. After his meeting with Fender, Keenan knew all about her and would probably think that she had lied to him yet again.

But even aside from all of that, she didn't think she could look him in the eye after what they'd done Friday evening. She was so *ashamed.* Despite all the things Angelica had said about it being healthy, Tory thought it would have been healthier if she didn't have to actually see the man in question again, and in such difficult circumstances.

Since it was likely Keenan did that sort of thing all the time, he probably hadn't thought twice about it. She had turned herself into nothing but another notch on his belt, and the fact that she had done it to herself was what bothered her most about it. Sure, sure, that was a cliché, but still. He was a player, a celebrity, a gorgeous man who had women all over him. And she . . . she was just a plain Jane who'd shot briefly into the stars, only to burn up on reentry into her own atmosphere.

Her self-respect would only have remained intact if she could honestly say it had only been about sex. But the fact was, he had been kind to her, attentive, and he'd *seemed* as moved as she was by their physical contact. All those things had had her thinking, at least at the moment, that the act had meant something more, was part of something *emotional*.

She was a fool.

The only way to handle the situation, she'd decided, was to act as if she did it all the time too. Or at least act as if it was an exciting night, but one that conferred no obligations and created no expectations of anything further.

It was, she decided, the least humiliating course of action.

Tory stopped at Fender's secretary's desk and

waited while she buzzed the editor. Though Tory had disapproved of herself for doing it, she had dressed in one of the outfits Sasha had picked out for her—the longer pencil skirt, rather than the short—and had used just a little of Katya's make-up. Just to make her look less wan. She didn't want Keenan thinking she was pining over him. After all, if there had been any reason at all for hope that the disastrous evening at Cameron Lessing's would lead to something more, it had evaporated during the week when she had heard nothing from Keenan.

Not that she had hoped for anything.

Not that she had thought for a second what it would be like to be *involved* with Keenan James.

No, she didn't want that.

The secretary rose and smiled at her. "Right this way, Dr. Hoffstra."

It was strange; people seemed to be nicer to her when she wore the makeup and clothes. Or they at least seemed to notice her, whereas before she was treated as someone who could not possibly be important.

She entered the office, her eyes seeking out Franklin Fender, but her entire being immediately aware of the tall figure standing in front of the windows.

"Dr. Hoffstra, welcome," Fender said, rising from behind his desk and rounding it to come shake her hand. His eyes looked her over in a way that telegraphed surprise.

Tory felt annoyed. For God's sake, it was just some new clothes and a little makeup. It wasn't as if she'd dyed her hair and worn a bunny suit.

"You know Keenan, of course." He motioned toward the man in front of the windows, and Tory inclined her head in his direction without looking at him.

"Of course, hello."

"Doctor."

How could one word convey so much? The very sound of his voice sent a shiver down her spine, while his tone conveyed skepticism, sarcasm, dismay, and anger.

Tory did not believe she was making this up.

Fender cleared his throat and gestured toward one of the chairs in front of the desk. Tory sat.

"It appears that we, uh," Fender began, "have a little problem."

Tory raised her brows and clenched her hands in her lap. "Oh?" She looked only at Fender.

"Yes, Keenan has informed me that he, ah, he objects to the idea of a cowriter."

Tory exhaled slowly. "With all due respect, sir, didn't you anticipate this?"

Fender looked at her sharply. "His objection, Doctor, is to the writer, not the 'co.'"

Tory's face heated. Steeling herself, she glanced over at Keenan, silhouetted against the window, his expression hidden from her. She could only make out his posture: arms folded across his chest, one leg crossing the other at the ankle, left shoulder against the glass.

"May I ask why?" She kept her voice level and patted herself on the back for the Herculean effort. Then it occurred to her that Keenan was exactly the sort of person to *say* why, complete with details of the . . . encounter on Friday night.

Fender's phone buzzed and she could swear he looked relieved. Maybe Keenan had already told him.

She knew she was relieved.

Fender picked up the receiver, said several mono-syllabic words into it, and ended with, "I'll be right there." He hung up. "Excuse me a moment, will you? Maybe you two can work this out between you while I'm gone. In any case, I'll be back in a few minutes."

Neither Tory nor Keenan said anything as Fender left the office. Even in her worst imaginings of this meeting, she had not anticipated being left alone in the room with him. Images of that night in the coatroom burst into her mind like scenes from *Caligula*.

"It seems you're just full of surprises." Again that voice sent shivers up her spine.

She bent her head. Then, realizing how sub-missive it probably looked, raised it and looked straight ahead.

"You knew I was sent by Fender."

"Not for the reasons you gave," he said.

She gripped her hands together in her lap. "I wasn't at liberty to reveal all until Mr. Fender had spoken to you."

He chuckled softly. "You weren't at liberty to reveal all?"

She flushed and closed her eyes briefly.

"I have to tell you," he continued, "I wasn't surprised you turned out to be someone else. I'd had suspicions all along, you know. You were too . . . up-tight to be someone who was really seeking help."

"*Uptight?*" she repeated, uptightly.

He laughed once. "Honey, you embody the word."

She turned in her seat and looked at him squarely, squinting against the light behind him to try to see his face. "I'm *sorry* if I infiltrated your turf, Keenan, but there is no need to start calling me names. You're threatened by me, I understand that. It's natural."

"Threatened by you? Maybe that's 'natural' for others," he said, shaking his head, "but I am not like others. Listen, you can out-therapist me, and God knows you can spout theories like you grew them all in your garden and nurtured them with your own abundant fertilizer, but I am *not* threatened. Nor did I ask to be analyzed. And I'm pretty sure I don't want to share my project with someone who has merely jumped on the bandwagon—not to mention a few other things—to further her own career."

"*You* didn't ask, but Fender—"

"Gave you permission to come into the group and abuse the trust of everyone there? Is that what you consider good therapy? You lied to me—lied to all of us—and you were condescending and superior and in general just a wellspring of animosity in an otherwise healthy, productive group. What good could possibly have come of that? How could that help you assess what I was doing?"

She twisted in her seat and glared at him. "You knew all this the other night, Keenan, and you didn't seem so mad about it then."

The moment she said the words she regretted them. Above all things, she had wanted to avoid mentioning Friday night, had thought surely if it came up at all *he* would be the one to do it and she could take her cues from whatever it was he'd said.

But now she'd done it. She'd stepped right into it, big time.

She spun back in her seat and leaned back, arms crossed tightly across her chest.

"Ah, the other night." She could hear the smile in his voice. "First of all, the other night I didn't know you were doing your best to horn in on my book deal. If I had, maybe what happened might not have happened."

"Why?" she asked, doing her best to sound nonchalant. "I don't see how what happened between us should change anything. In fact, we don't even need to talk about it. It happened. It's over. Let's move on. *Now* can you accept me as the cowriter?"

"Forgive me, Tory, but I don't think it's as simple as that. I know you're the real therapist and all, but after an event like that do you really think we can put it behind us and just work together? Impartially. *Impassively?*"

Tory's palms started to sweat. She needed this job, and he was absolutely right that she'd jumped on it to further her own career. But that wasn't the only reason.

"Contrary to what you might think, Keenan, I am impassive about you in every respect. Besides, I think you need me to help you with this book," she said, and heard a scoff.

He moved away from the window and into her field of vision. Her stomach twisted at the sight of him. He was dressed in a dark blue shirt, a slightly lighter tie in the same hue, and dress pants, and he looked good enough to eat.

Those clear blue eyes, however, were uncompromising, nailing her where she sat. "And what, exactly, do I need you *for?*"

Was it just her, or did he mean that to sound kind of sexual?

"You need me to keep you from ruining women's lives," she said firmly, right into that handsome, confident face.

"Wow," he said, raising a brow and smiling in a way that made her think he wasn't really amused.

He put his hands in his pockets, falsely casual. "Is that what I was doing?"

She uncrossed her arms and gripped the arms of the chair. "Yes. You were telling them what to do. You weren't offering opinions or helping them see what was really in their hearts, you were challenging them to do what *you* wanted."

"That's not true," he said. "Can I remind you that you only came to two meetings? How can you claim to know everything about what I'm doing?"

"I saw enough." She pressed her lips together.

"I disagree. I give opinions, Tory. Surely you've heard of that. It's what some people do instead of making intractable pronouncements about what they think is true. I don't tell anybody they *have* to do anything. You must have noticed the dynamic. I encourage people to disagree with me if they want. But you—"

"*I* disagreed with you. I was the *only one* who disagreed. Everyone else was so busy kissing your—"

"You want to know what I think, *Doctor*?" he interrupted. "I think you're so disgusted with yourself for what happened between us the other night that you're determined to discredit me and everything I stand for. I think, to put it in your own language, you have some sexual repression issues to deal with."

She flushed hot. He thought she was sexually repressed? After the wildest sex she'd ever had with a man?

"Oh that's convenient," she said, her voice thick.

"Which brings me to my original point." Keenan looked at her squarely for a long moment. "How can you cowrite a book you don't believe in, with a man you have, at least in your own mind, discredited?"

She hesitated a long moment, stomach churning. How could she have had sex with someone who would use it against her this way? What on earth was wrong with her? She should *run* back to Stewart, and fast.

"That's a complicated question," she said.

He smiled wryly. "Then answer this one. Maybe it'll be easier. How"—he stepped closer to her again, lowering his voice—"are we supposed to work together when we both know what can happen between us?"

She swallowed and maintained eye contact. "You tell me."

"You'd like me to tell you how it'll be?" he asked. "With pleasure."

"That's not what I meant. I don't expect you to make the rules. I only expect you to respect me, and I'm wondering if you can do it."

He closed his eyes and shook his head. "Dr. Hoffstra, please." He looked at her again, sitting there in her sexy skirt and her tight little bun, her legs crossed as if they had never ventured up and around his hips. Who did she think she was fooling? Anybody with eyes could see what smoldered inside that petite little body. "You think there might be some question of self-control?"

She smiled. "You said it, not I."

"What are we now, in seventh grade?" he asked. "There's no shame in it, Doctor. So you found a man desirable and you acted on it. *It's natural,*" he quoted with a broad smile.

She wanted to smack him, she really did. But that would require touching him, and she didn't think she could do that again without getting into more trouble. How that could be, she had no idea. She was furious with him, and yet if he touched her the way he had the other night—stroking her face, pushing her hair behind her ear—she would fall right into him.

"I meant that *you're* the one who's uncontrollable," she said. "If you'll recall, there were two of us in that room, and I was *not* the one who . . . initiated things."

"Ah, back to the schoolroom. As if it matters who started it."

"I believe it does."

"All right. I admit it. I started it. But we both finished it, did we not?"

She opened her mouth, then closed it. Opened it again, then snapped it shut and nodded curtly.

He smiled. "Good. I hope that wasn't painful."

"What is your point?"

"My point is, we have both breached what might be considered the ethical line in our respective situations."

"I agree. However, as the supposed 'therapist' in the dynamic, you were more culpable than I."

"Were you still thinking of me as the therapist? How flattering. Because at that point, *Doctor*, I believe we were colleagues, considering you had just been outed as a therapist yourself."

"We are *not* colleagues," she muttered. "Co-workers, maybe."

He shook his head, chuckling. "The question remains, after all that, do you really think you can write a book with me?"

She scoffed. "Are you saying I might have a hard time resisting you?"

He grinned wider. "Now that's interesting. Perhaps we should analyze your response. Why would you assume I meant that you might have a hard time resisting me?"

As he'd hoped, that rendered her speechless, and flooded her face with color.

He stepped toward her and took her chin gently between his forefinger and thumb, tipping her face so that she looked up at him. Her skin was soft.

"Because I have to tell you, Engelberta," he added slyly, "that kind of modesty can be a real turn-on."

She sat rigid as he chucked her lightly on the chin, then turned and moved toward the door. She came to life when he opened it.

"You're leaving?" she asked, standing, hands clenched by her sides. If he left, her chances of writing a book were finished.

"I'm going to look for Fender."

"What are you going to tell him?"

He turned back. "I'm going to tell him I'll do the book."

She held her breath. "With me?"

He inclined his head. "With you."

She exhaled in relief, shoulders slumping slightly. "Are you going to tell him—?" she halted. "Are you going to explain about the, uh . . ."

"The complication?" he mock-whispered.

She straightened.

"Why, do you think I should?" he asked.

She tried to affect an unconcerned air and sat back down in the chair. "Do whatever you want."

He lifted a brow. "I always do."

Chapter 15

"I cannot believe you just *left* me in that bar," Claudia said, sliding into the booth at Carl's Diner.

Tory had finally called her to see how she and Simon were doing—and to take her medicine, as she thought of it, after leaving her at Work a couple of weeks ago—and Claudia had said she couldn't talk then but would meet her for breakfast the following morning.

"I left you with your fiancé," Tory pointed out, sliding onto the red vinyl of the opposite bench.

She put her purse beside her and unbuttoned her jacket. She had gone back to see Sasha to buy some more casual clothes, even though she couldn't really afford it yet, and today wore a camel-colored cashmere sweater with a pair of deliciously soft dark brown pants. Her hair was loose, and she wore a little of Katya's makeup as well.

It was amazing how much more powerful she felt sitting with Claudia, not being the invisible dowdy sister.

"You left me so that you could be alone with Keenan James. After *I* was the one who did all the work to get him there!" As she said this, Claudia leaned forward and poked a decisive finger into the table.

"Claudia, if I wanted to be alone with Keenan," Tory said, picking up the menu and opening it, "I wouldn't have to lure him to a nightclub to do it. I see him every week. And I'm going to be seeing him even more often now that we're going to start working on the book."

Claudia's eyes narrowed. "And look at you." She thrust a hand out in Tory's direction. "You're all dolled up again. I've got to tell you, Tory, you've changed. I never thought I'd see the day when you, of all people, changed yourself to suit a man."

Tory clenched her teeth. "I have not changed to suit a man. I just got some nicer clothes."

Claudia picked up her menu and continued knowingly. "But I think I should warn you not to get your hopes up. Men like Keenan James are not easy to catch, and you're not very experienced when it comes to dating. Guys like him need some artifice, some game playing. Not a lot, just something to titillate their desires. And no matter how many nice new sweaters you buy, you're just not the titillating type."

Tory studied the menu. "Gosh, I'm tempted to order the bull but it seems you're already so full of it, Claudia, they're probably out."

Tory looked up to see Claudia staring at her, mouth dropped open. Then Claudia snorted and laid her head on the table, laughing.

Tory's mouth twitched, then she started laughing too.

Claudia raised her head, still smiling. "My God, Tory, what *have* you been doing to yourself? That was a pretty good comeback."

"A little personal therapy, I guess," Tory said, if sex and stress could be considered therapy. But as Angelica had said, it came in many different forms. Soon she'd be getting manicures and rivaling Claudia for closet power.

"Well, it's working." Claudia looked her over. "That really is a nice sweater."

"Saks," Tory said. "I'm a Saks girl these days. Even if it is going to run me into the poorhouse."

The waitress arrived and took their orders, prompting both of them to chuckle again with thoughts of ordering bull.

"So, seriously, Claudia." Tory leaned her arms on

the table. "What's going on with you and Simon?"

Claudia sighed. "I don't know. I just don't know what to think of this whole prenup thing. It feels so . . . just *wrong* to marry someone who doesn't trust me."

"Maybe it's not about *you*," Tory offered, realizing this might be a tough concept for Claudia. "Divorce is a force of its own, regardless of who's involved. The lawyers stir things up between the couple so they can rack up the bills going back and forth with the arguments. A prenup these days is more defense against the system than against each other, I think."

Claudia looked thoughtful. "Hm. I've never thought of it that way."

"Believe me, I've talked to enough people who've been through a divorce in my practice to know it takes two reasonable people and makes them insane."

Claudia smiled. "Are you allowed to call your patients 'insane'?"

"They're not my patients anymore." Tory shrugged.

"But what about the fact that he's already thinking divorce?" Claudia asked plaintively. "Isn't there something wrong with that? I mean, we're not even married yet. We're still supposed to be consumed with *love*. How can he be thinking about it not working?"

Tory sighed. "Claudia, you're not sixteen years old anymore. Neither of you are. You'd have to live in a cave not to know that marriage is a risky proposition, and everyone in the world thinks theirs is going to be the one that lasts. Look at you, you're already breaking up over the first difficult problem you've faced."

"Now it's *my* fault?" Claudia said. Nothing got Claudia's back up like being blamed for something. "No, I'm sorry, but I don't buy that. We broke up because of Simon's fundamental lack of belief in me. That's not just some 'difficult problem.'"

"Yes it is. That's what makes it difficult." Tory laid her menu down on the table. "Look, answer me this: are you interested in Simon's money? Seriously. Don't you make enough yourself?"

Claudia thought a moment. "If he cheats on me, I'm taking him to the fucking *cleaner's*," she said finally. "But otherwise . . . no, I guess I don't care about his money."

"Then sign the prenup. Big deal. It'll protect you as well as him."

"I don't know . . ." Claudia chewed her bottom lip. "I want a guy who loves me unconditionally. Who'd give me anything to make me happy. Is that ridiculous?"

Tory looked at her sympathetically. It must be tough for women who grew up believing all the fairy tales. It was as if Claudia was just now learning the truth about Santa Claus, and the one who supposedly loved her most was the one disillusioning her. She understood the dilemma, for both of them.

"It's not ridiculous," Tory answered slowly. "But are you willing to do the same for him?"

"I am!" Claudia said earnestly. "He's the first man I've been with whose happiness really *does* matter to me, to be honest."

"Then sign the prenup. *For him*. As a declaration of your love."

Claudia frowned. "God, I hate it when you do that. Turn things around against me. I know that logic doesn't make sense somehow, but I'm going to have to think about it."

They perused their menus again. When the busboy brought them water they each picked up their glasses and took a sip.

"So what's going on with you and Stewart?" Claudia asked, placing her glass back on the table. "I thought you guys would have gotten married long before I did. You've been together forever."

Tory made a face, trying to decide if she should tell Claudia the truth. The next thing she knew her parents would know, then they'd be calling with questions that Tory wasn't sure she was ready to answer yet. She started slowly, "Stewart and I have . . ."

"You didn't break up!" Claudia looked scandalized. "Tell me—was it his nasal voice? That would have driven me crazy *years* ago."

"We're just on a break," Tory said, trying to

backpedal. She hated when Claudia got on her anti-Stewart kick. "We'd both gotten pretty apathetic about the relationship, so we're stepping back for a while."

"You're kidding. When did this happen?"

Tory's eyes skidded away from her sister's intense interest. "A few months ago. It's no big deal. It's hardly any different. We still see each other."

"No big deal? This is huge. And it's great, Tory. Really! You can do so much better. Especially now that you've—" Her eyes widened. "Ah, now I understand the new look."

"No, no. The new look is just coincidental." Tory toyed with her fork.

"Yeah, right." Claudia looked skeptical. "And yet it's just in time for Keenan James."

Try as she might, Tory could not stop the blush that crept up her neck to her face.

Claudia inhaled sharply and leaned forward. "I *knew* it! You *do* like him. Admit it."

"Claudia, come on. This isn't elementary school. Keenan and I are working together. That's all." She looked around the diner, hoping their food was coming, but she couldn't find their waitress.

"Oh honey." Claudia reached across the table and gripped Tory's fist where it lay holding the fork. "Don't do it. Men like him are trouble. He'll just break your heart."

Tory leaned back in the booth. "He's not going to break my heart! We're only working together."

Claudia sat back too. "Yes, but I can see by your face that you're in love with him."

"Good God, I am *not* in love with him." Tory's voice rose with the words. "What, have you been watching soap operas lately or something?"

"That is *so* irresponsible," Claudia said.

"*What?*"

"Of him! He should know the effect he has on women, and he's been leading you on. I saw how he treated you that night at the club, like you were some kind of close confidant. Of course someone with little experience in the dating arena would misunderstand that kind of friendliness. He should be taken to task for it. I feel like calling him up."

"Claudia, have you lost your mind? Keenan and I are—are coworkers. So he was friendly with me!" God, if only she *knew*. "I'm a grown woman. I can handle it."

Claudia looked at her pityingly. "That's what they all say."

Tory had a lot to think about as she headed to Saks after breakfast. She'd decided she needed some more lip glosses, different colors, now that she was wearing makeup every day. Plus she wanted to see how Katya was doing. She hoped Katya had been able to convince her boyfriend to go see one of the therapists Tory had recommended.

She decided to walk through the park on her way

to the store. It wasn't exactly on her way, but it was such a beautiful day a little nature would do her good, she decided. Something about talking to Claudia always made her feel unsettled.

It wasn't that she felt insulted by Claudia's remarks about her naïveté when it came to Keenan; she was mostly afraid that Claudia was right. She was in way over her head and in danger of being hurt. She probably would have been better off if Keenan had refused to work with her. Instead, he'd turned on a dime and agreed to do the book. Why? she wondered. *Was* he being irresponsible? Was he leading her on?

She was crossing through a copse of trees when she heard a voice not far away, crooning. At least it sounded like a crooning voice. Maybe someone was moaning, the victim of a mugging perhaps.

She stepped off the path toward the sound, then thought of the urban legend about the crying baby on the doorstep and wondered if she was walking into a trap. Apparently people did stuff like that, lured you to your door—or into the woods—with an unusual sound, then attacked you.

She paused. Did she really need to know what was going on in the trees?

The voice grew louder. " . . . *are the luckiest people* . . ."

Someone was singing.

Her brows rose. She knew that song. It was by Barbra Streisand. Had thinking about Keenan actually conjured someone singing Barbra Streisand? It was even a man's voice.

" . . . *iiiiin the woooooorld* . . ."

Whoever it was was getting into it now. She smiled to herself and leaned against a tree.

" . . . *with one person* . . ."

She inhaled sharply.

" . . . *one very special person* . . ."

The voice sounded familiar. Could she be imagining it?

She crept forward until she could see beyond the brush. The breeze in the trees muffled her steps, and as she peered around a particularly wide trunk, she saw—sure enough—Keenan James crouched in the weeds, singing. A few yards away Barbra Streisand—the dog, not the singer—gazed back at Keenan, enthralled, head cocked.

She couldn't help it. She laughed out loud.

Keenan's head whipped around. The dog caught sight of her, then leaped forward. Tory shrieked.

Fortunately, Keenan was between her and the dog, and as the animal streaked by he grabbed her by the fur.

Barbra gave a yelp that sounded a lot like Tory's, before Keenan got his hands on the collar. Tory fell back against a tree, making a sound somewhere between a laugh and a wail, her heart thundering in her chest.

"Thanks for your help," he said dryly, snapping a leash on the dog. He wasn't looking at Tory.

"Were you *singing* to your dog?" she gasped. The dog restrained, Tory's amusement bounced right back.

"Sit, Barbra. Sit, SIT!" he commanded, finally pushing the dog's butt onto the ground with one hand. "It's the only way she'll come sometimes."

Tory couldn't believe what she was seeing— Keenan James was actually *blushing.* And he still would not look at her, making some pretense of getting the dog's hair out from under her collar.

"Didn't work today, though, did it," he muttered, gently jerking the dog's leash. Barbra glanced up at him, tongue lolling. "Stupid mutt."

Tory tried to keep herself from letting loose another guffaw. "Maybe she's sick of that song."

Finally his eyes flashed up to hers. "*Everybody* is sick of that song."

"Maybe you should try 'What's New Pussycat?'" She gave him an innocent look.

"Did you just happen to come along at this opportune moment?" he asked. "Or were you looking for me?"

He looked good, she had to admit, dressed in jeans and a sweater, like the quintessential camper from a clothing catalog. The dog was a little incongruous— she should have been bigger, maybe with a dead duck in her mouth—but otherwise the two of them looked perfectly at home in the woods.

"No, no," she said, straightening and hefting her purse back up onto her shoulder. "I just got lucky.

Is there going to be an encore, or have the house-lights gone up?"

She could see a smile playing about his lips. "Dr. Hoffstra, you're getting to be quite the comedienne."

It was Tory's turn to blush. "Hey, when the material's there . . ." She gestured toward him and the dog.

"Yes, well. Maybe it's good we ran into each other," he said, clearing his throat and looking away from her again. "We can schedule our first meeting to work on the book."

"Uh, sure."

He took it from there, all business. They arranged a time to meet, he made a few suggestions about how to begin, she said she'd think about it too, and he took off with the dog.

Tory turned as he left and watched him go, thinking how much she liked him when he was unsure of himself.

Tory walked into Saks lost in a reverie about the encounter. Keenan had actually seemed embarrassed to be caught by her. Well, who wouldn't be? He was singing to his dog in the woods, for God's sake. Still, she'd never seen him like that, almost nervous. Because of her!

"Tory!"

She glanced up to see Katya waving to her from

behind her counter. Her face fairly glowed as her smile beamed out.

"Katya, how are you?" she asked, coming closer.

"I am wonderful! And you?"

Tory beamed back. How could she not? Katya exuded energy and happiness, as opposed to last time when she was nothing but tired and discouraged.

"I'm very well. You look wonderful; are things going better with your boyfriend?" Tory asked, feeling sure that was the case. Nothing else could bring a smile that big to a woman's face. She hoped the counseling had gotten them back on track.

"Pah! That loser," Sasha's voice carried from behind Tory, just before she joined them. "Katya has *new* boyfriend now."

Tory turned back to Katya. "Is that true? What happened?"

Katya looked a little abashed. "Things, you know, they didn't go so well at the therapy." She shrugged, held her hands out helplessly. "So I told Yuri I am through with him. Finished!"

"She finally took my advice," Sasha said darkly. "Yuri was bad stuff. Is good to just dump him. Like the guy on TV says. He don't treat you right, just dump him."

"Oh." Tory felt her insides shrink within her. Just dump him. And it had worked, obviously. Katya was happier than she'd ever seen her.

Keenan was right again.

Tory swallowed, suddenly overwhelmed by how

little credit she'd given him for helping people. His heart was in the right place. As, it seemed, his advice was. More often than hers, lately.

"Yes, I am afraid," Katya said, "is true. I dumped him and then I met Sten." She sighed happily. "Sten is wonderful."

"Sten is good man." Sasha nodded approvingly, a satisfied smile on her face. "Sten is perfect for Kat. You can see, yes? He makes her happy."

"Does he, Katya? I'm so glad," Tory said, meaning it, but feeling as if she'd recommended arsenic when honey was all that was needed.

"Oh yes. He is wonderful. I hope someday you meet him." Katya's eyes veritably *sparkled*, for pity's sake.

"So what about *you*," Sasha demanded, "you are here for winter clothes, yes? Fall is going, must have cute things for winter. Then you find good man like Sten."

"Oh I hope you do!" Katya enthused. "You should be as happy as I am."

"Uh." Tory looked from one sister to the other. Sasha expectant, Katya excited. "Yes, right. I must have cute things for winter."

❧

Keenan looked around the apartment one last time, unwilling to analyze why he was being so attentive to how clean the place was just because Tory Hoffstra was coming over.

All he knew was, she seemed intent on thinking badly of him, and he had no desire to provide any fuel for that fire. Dust on the coffee table? *You have no right to give advice to women.* Dishes in the sink? *Who do you think you are, telling people how to run their lives?* Dirt on the floor? *You obviously don't know a thing about how regular people, let alone women, live.*

He'd purchased what Jan called a "marrow bone" from the butcher to keep the dog happy in her crate. He would put her in there shortly after Tory arrived, after first making her sit and stay while Tory petted her. This, at least, was what the book he'd gotten on dog training had said to do, so the dog didn't get neurotic about visitors.

Shortly after one o'clock, someone knocked on the door. Barbra leaped to her feet and sprang for the door like a deer in a spring meadow. She gave a few happy barks and looked back at him.

"Okay, that's enough. *Come,* Barbra Streisand," he said, grabbing the dog by the collar. "Good dog. Now *sit.* Good, Barbra." He made her sit, then scratched her behind the ears.

He was working on getting the dog to respond to something other than her full name. He hoped he'd been embarrassed for the last time after creating a sensation last week among the people in Central Park when he'd had to run through the park yell-ing *Barbra Streisand!* because the dog had gotten away from him.

He opened the door.

Tory Hoffstra stood in the hall with her briefcase held in front of her like a shield, and an expression of terror on her face.

He tried to smile, as the dog wrestled against his restraining hand. "Sorry, I'm trying to train her. Would you mind petting her while she's sitting? Then I'll put her away in the crate."

"You—you want me to touch her?" she asked, not moving from the hall.

"Yeah. Just a quick pat on the head, or scratch under the chin will do. I just want to reward her for being so"—Barbra stood up and he yanked her back into a sitting position—"good."

Tory moved forward slowly, one hand stretched as far away from herself as possible, and kept the briefcase between the dog and her body. It occurred to him that she was afraid, but since she was moving toward the dog, he decided not to interrupt.

She put her hand gingerly on top of the dog's head, and fast as a frog's tongue, Barbra swiped her on the wrist with a swift, wet lick.

Tory gasped and drew back as if stung by a cattle prod.

"Okay!" Keenan said, ignoring the dynamic. "Good girl, Barbra. Thank you very much, Tory."

He shot an appreciative smile over his shoulder as he dragged the dog away from the door toward the crate in his bedroom. "I'll be right back."

He hoped by the time he got back Tory would be inside the apartment. Once in the spare bedroom he pushed Barbra into the crate and took the marrow bone from the bookshelf next to it, where he'd placed it at the ready. He was gratified to see the dog take the thing with alacrity and lie down to start working on it. He watched her a moment, happy that she was ignoring him. Maybe it wasn't mean to keep her in here while he had company.

Back out in the living room, Tory was standing, briefcase still in hand, looking around. He smiled to himself, glad he'd cleaned up even though the maid had been there just two days before.

"Sorry about that." He motioned Tory toward the couch. "I'm obviously not a natural at dog training, but I'm working on it."

She gave him a tight smile as she sat on the couch, her eyes wide and uncertain. "You seem to be doing all right at it."

It was that defenseless look she had, he decided, that disarmed him so often. Something about her screamed *vulnerable*, even though when she spoke she seemed more than capable of taking care of herself.

"I don't know about that." He clapped his hands together in front of him. "So. What can I get for you? Something to drink before we start?"

She shook her head and bent to open her brief-case, her hair swinging forward to mask the side of her face. "I made some notes last night for an outline. Just some chapter headings we might consider. And I'm hoping you don't want to stick with that silly *Seal The Deal, Baby* thing."

She looked up, pushed the locks behind one ear, and held out a piece of paper toward him.

He wished it weren't the middle of the afternoon. He could really use a drink. Something about her was actually making him *nervous*.

"We can talk about that." He leaned forward and took the paper from her, remembering as he looked at her pale fingers how that hand had felt gripping him, guiding him, urging him—

He focused on the writing. *Adolescence and Attraction, Maturity and Companionship, Commitment. . .*

"Uh, yeah, these are good," he said, slowly sitting down across from her. "But maybe we could jazz the wording up a little. For example, maybe something like, I don't know, *Boys Boys Boys* for the teenage years." He looked up at her.

Though he could swear she had been looking at him, she looked down at the pad of paper in her lap when his eyes rose to hers.

"Sure," she said, and drew a blue circle on one corner of the paper to get the pen going. "I guess we could do that."

"Look, this is ridiculous," he said, standing up.

"We're sitting here like a couple of teenagers ourselves, not looking at each other, while both of us know what's standing between us. Let's just talk about it and get it out in the open."

Those wide eyes flashed up to him, looking vulnerable all over again. "Okay." She took a deep breath. "I'm sorry I had to lie to you about the book. I really did want to know what you were doing before committing to it, and that's why I went to the round table anonymously. I had no idea it would become so . . . personal."

Keenan nearly laughed, but stopped himself in time. "So, you're tense because you think I might still be upset about the book deal?"

She looked back down at the paper. "Is there something else?"

He put his hands on his hips and tilted his head. "Don't do that. Don't be disingenuous, Tory. Directness looks much better on you."

Her brow darkened. "I'm not interested in what looks better on me, Keenan. Why don't *you* try being direct? What are *you* trying to get at?"

"The coatroom?" he said, throwing his arms out and turning around. He ran a hand through his hair and turned back to her. "You and me and our mutual attraction. Don't you think *that's* what's hanging between us right now?"

She folded her hands in her lap. "I guess I thought we'd decided to forget about that."

He laughed. "And have you?"

"Well I was *trying*, until you brought it up again."
She raised and lowered her hands in her lap in exasperation.

"Come on," he chided, moving around the chair
to the couch where she sat. "Tell me you don't
think about it. Tell me it doesn't stick in your mind
until you think it might drive you crazy. Tell me
you don't wonder why on earth you're attracted in
that way *to me*."

He sat down facing her on the other end of the
couch.

She stiffened and blushed. He loved that she
blushed.

"Are you saying you don't know why it happened with me?" She looked down at the uphol-
stery between them.

He frowned, frustrated. "Well, sure. Do you
know why it happened?"

She looked up at the ceiling and swallowed. "I
know I'm not a model, or an actress, or one of
those gorgeous girls you go out with—"

"Tory." He grabbed her hand. "I meant, we don't
get along. We see eye-to-eye on nothing. We've done
nothing but argue since the moment we laid eyes on
each other. *That's* why I don't understand it. Not
because you're not gorgeous." He hesitated, hearing the way those words played in his head, then
laughed once and added quietly, "You *are* gorgeous,
Tory. Maybe the fact that you don't know it is part
of the reason we ended up in that coatroom."

She managed to blush even redder and extricated her hand from his. "That's nice of you to say, but I know I'm not your type. Not for . . ." She looked up at him wryly. "Anything else. And . . . okay, to be honest, my problem is I've never done anything like that before, and I'm just not sure how to move on. Especially when I have to keep seeing you."

He leaned back. "Talking about it helps, though. Don't you think?"

He saw a tiny smile light her face. "I guess. Though I have to admit to feeling a little . . . awkward about it."

"Naturally." He paused. "So let's just say it outright. I'm attracted to you, and you're attracted to me, all right? Whether or not it makes any sense."

She looked at him warily, as if he might be inviting her into a trap.

He grinned. "Now when have I ever given you cause to mistrust me so completely?"

She laughed. "When you showed me a side of myself I had no idea existed."

He exhaled slowly and softened his grin into a genuine smile. "Right back at you."

She looked over at him and they shared a moment, he thought, of revelation. They'd brought something out in each other. That wasn't bad, was it? He'd showed her her wild side and she'd shown him. . .

He shifted in the seat, uncomfortable with his own question.

He'd *felt* for her that night. Not pity, not commiseration, not even empathy. He'd seen her in distress and he'd felt *her*. Felt her pain in his own heart.

He stood up abruptly. "So, okay. Let's leave it at that, then, all right? Unless you have something else you want to say." He moved away from the sofa toward the chair where he'd originally sat.

"No, no. That's enough for me," she said, with a nervous laugh.

"Okay." He sat back down, picked up her paper and a pad of his own. "So, chapter one, the teenage years."

She directed her attention to her pad. "Right."

To Keenan's surprise, they were actually able to work for some time without incident. At times he was even able to forget that there was tension in the room. They were basically mapping out what each chapter would contain, talking points, section headers, and basic ideas. She would propose saying something and he would translate it into plain English. Or he would make a statement that she could relate to a psychological theory. They didn't even hit many snags or disagreements until it came to the chapter on commitment.

"I'm telling you, there is no such thing as fear of commitment," he said, leaning back in his chair. "It's a myth."

"Spoken like a man with major commitment issues."

"Why do you say that?"

"Because look at you! You date a slew of gorgeous women, never for longer than a few months—which could lead one to believe that as soon as they get close, you go running—and you're, what, closing in on thirty-five? What was the last long-term relationship you had?" She leaned back on the couch and looked at him like the counselor she was. Inquisitive, impassive, superior.

"I'm thirty-four. And maybe I just haven't met the right woman yet. Besides, you were in a long-term relationship and it didn't get you any closer to marriage, did it?"

She opened her mouth to speak, then closed it, looking startled. The therapist who had her own situation turned against her. It wasn't likely that had happened to her before.

"You know what? Never mind. Let's not make this personal," he said, letting her off the hook. "There are lots of ways to go about looking for the right person. But the fact remains that if a guy wants you, he'll commit. Fear of commitment is a crock."

"Oh please. What about all those guys in long-term relationships who just can't seem to bring themselves to marry?"

Keenan shrugged. "They don't want to. They don't want to get married, or they don't want to get married to *that woman*."

Tory dropped her pen on her pad and massaged her fingers, frowning at him. "Then why don't they break up with the woman? If they're so sure of what they want or don't want, why do they hang out for years at a time, with the lame excuse that they're just not ready?"

"Because they're chickenshit."

Tory laughed, and Keenan smiled with the sound. When she was not nervous or angry or combative, she was adorable.

"As long as we're in the barnyard," she replied, "I can say without hesitation that that's bullshit."

Keenan laughed, and the two looked at each other with mutual mirth, until Tory realized what she was doing and looked away.

"No, I really think we need a section on men's fear of commitment," she stated. "There are no two ways about it. They may have reasons for it, like a disturbance in their attachments as a child, or they may just see how well 'I'm not ready' works for their friends in that situation. But they definitely have complexes about attaching themselves in a marital situation."

"Tory, Tory, Tory," he said, shaking his head. "A man would rather cut off his own ear than break up with a woman. That's why you never hear about ultimatums from men. Even if they're the ones who want to get married and their girlfriends are dragging their feet—which happens, I've heard." He grinned. "They will not say, 'Marry me or I'm leaving.' They'll hang around forever. Same with men who don't want to get married. They'll never say,

'Shut up about marriage or I'm leaving.' They'll just turn into boyfriends who are so deficient or awful in some way that *you'll* break up with *them*."

Tory's brows drew together. "That's not true."

"Oh yes. It is," he said. "The mistake that women make is confusing presence with commitment. They figure if the guy's still around, they're just afraid of marriage, not afraid of marriage to them. It's like that scene in *When Harry Met Sally*; you saw that movie, didn't you?"

"Uh, I've heard of it."

He laughed. "You've never seen *When Harry Met Sally*? Jesus, no wonder you're so out of touch. I'm renting it and you're watching it before we write the first chapter."

She rolled her eyes.

"In that movie," he continued, "there's a scene where Meg Ryan's boyfriend, who she broke up with because he said he didn't want to get married, gets engaged. And she realizes that it wasn't that he didn't want to marry, as he'd always said, it was that he didn't want to marry *her*."

Tory was silent for a long moment, giving Keenan time to remember that, if she'd been telling at least some truth in the round table, she might have been in a similar situation.

"Excuse me a minute," she said, standing and moving toward the hall off the living room. "The restroom . . . ?"

"The end of the hall," he said, mentally kicking

himself. But dammit, how did you talk about relationships without getting into an area that someone had experienced? If they were going to do this, they had to take themselves out of the equation.

On the other hand, if she'd been in his round table a little longer, wouldn't he have told her the same thing?

Of course he would have. He'd done nothing wrong.

He twisted in his seat and looked toward the hall. No movement.

Why should he care that she was reacting this way? She'd had to hear the truth and he'd told it. He did it all the time. Women cried, but he always felt it was better that they knew. What was different now?

The little voice in the back of his mind he'd been trying to ignore for days piped up too loud to disregard: *Because you're emotionally involved*.

He was emotionally involved. He felt for Tory Hoffstra. No, he *had feelings* for Tory Hoffstra.

No, he was *falling in love. . .*

He closed his eyes and heard the bathroom door open.

He stood up, and when he turned around she emerged from the hall, surprised to see him on his feet.

"Listen, that's probably enough for today," he said, putting his hands in his pockets.

"Okay." She nodded.

He wasn't sure but she looked okay. No obvious sign of tears or visible upset.

"Can I just say," he started, studying her, "that Stewart is a fool?"

Those gray eyes widened. "What?"

He moved toward her and took her hands.

"Listen, I'm sorry if I said something that made you feel bad. But if what you said in the round table is true, and Stewart is the idiot who was dragging his feet, then I have to tell you you can do a whole lot better than that."

She frowned and tried to pull her hands back. "Stewart is a good man—"

"No." He gripped her hands tighter, but not so tight that she couldn't have gotten loose, if she'd really wanted. "Don't defend him. Don't do that to yourself."

She did look like she might cry then, and it tore at his heart.

Unsure of what else to do, he pulled her toward him, intending to hug her. But either she raised her head, or he lowered his, because without forming another thought, he was kissing her.

Chapter 16

Tory's heart leaped as he bent to kiss her. Her body, without consulting her mind, pressed immediately forward into Keenan's.

Who could think about Stewart when Keenan was in the room? When he'd brought up men not wanting to marry the women they were with, all she could think was, if she let herself feel for Keenan, she was heading straight into another situation with a noncommittal man.

What kind of fool would do that? Willfully, knowingly jump from the frying pan into the fire? At least with Stewart she'd felt secure. He would never cheat on her, and he would never leave her.

But Keenan . . . a man who could have whatever he wanted, *whomever* he wanted, whenever he wanted. . .

All that flew straight out the window, however, when he touched her. Something about his lips, his hands, his hard, tall, compelling body enveloped her in a haze of wanting that could not be refused.

Her mind said, *No!* but her body said, *Just this once, just for a minute, just until. . .*

Until his hands touched her skin, moving her sweater up from her jeans and laying his palms against her bare back. She let her head fall sideways as his mouth strayed to her neck, and he ran his tongue along a spot just under her ear, causing shivers of pleasure to rocket up her spine.

She thought about stopping him, about saying they mustn't do this, but she couldn't think of any reason why except that it would be difficult later. And that was already a problem.

She moved her hands to his head and held it, her fingers woven into the soft, dark waves. Who would have thought a man so thoroughly masculine would have such soft hair?

He moved his lips to kiss her again, and she opened her eyes briefly to find him looking at her.

The look in his eyes was pure heat. If that pale blue could have glowed, she would have sworn it was doing so now.

"I think I owe you a bed," he said, his voice husky.

If she'd had any doubts, that slight rasp in his throat would have convinced her. It made her think of early mornings and shared coffee, Sunday newspapers and breakfast. It made her feel close to him, though they'd never shared any of those things and probably never would.

When she didn't object, he took her hand and led her toward the bedroom.

She glanced quickly around the room when they entered—black and white framed photos on the wall, espresso-colored dressers, modern lamps, and in the middle a king-size bed.

Tory suddenly felt awkward. She was standing in a designer room, with a designer man, about to have sex. This wasn't her. This wasn't her life. She'd never wake up here and get up to make coffee, retrieve the paper from the front door, cook breakfast.

Keenan turned and looked at her, his eyes seeming to read every thought that crossed her brain. But instead of speaking he reached up, took her face in his hands, and kissed her long, slow, and deep. Kissed her until her knees went weak and her worries melted into a molten pool of desire deep in her belly.

"You are so beautiful," he whispered, drawing her close and holding her as if he simply wanted her close, was not just eager to have sex.

She laughed weakly, deprecatingly, and lowered her head, her forehead on his chest.

"Tory," he said.

She looked up and he grinned, then he swung her around so she landed on the bed.

She let out a shriek, then couldn't help laughing as he pinned her where she lay.

"No second thoughts," he commanded, holding her wrists to the bed and kissing her soundly. "No self-sabotage," he added, laying a big one right on her neck. "And no looking at me like I'm a stranger." He nailed her with a sober look.

She smiled. "I know you, Keenan James," she said, low.

After a second, he laughed. "Why doesn't that reassure me?"

Despite his smile, the look on his face was so, so . . . almost *sad*, that she felt a sudden surge of emotion for him. He was handsome, he was famous, he must get tired of people being with him because of those reasons. But now here she was thinking twice about being with him because of those very same things. He couldn't win. And he seemed to recognize that.

"Keenan," she said, forcing herself to look straight into his eyes, to see him as the person he was, without all the trappings. She put her hands on either side of his face and brought it down for a gentle kiss. "You're an amazing man," she said, meaning it.

He looked almost grateful. His eyes softened, his

mouth relaxed into a slight smile, and she could have sworn he was about to say something.

Instead he lowered his head to hers and kissed her again.

Heat shot up between them immediately. She moved her hands to his chest and began unbuttoning his shirt. He pulled her sweater over her head and unhooked her bra in less time than it took her to do it herself. They sat up and pushed out of the rest of their clothing. Then they came together naked, kneeling on the bed.

The touch of his skin on hers set her alight. He was warm and strong, but as her hand clasped his hardness he let out a sound from deep in his throat, and she felt as if she was as powerful and in control as he'd been moments before.

She lay back on the bed, drawing him toward her, and he lowered his mouth to her breast. The sensation took her breath away. He suckled one while his other hand did marvelous, tweaking things to the other, creating a conflagration inside her that had her arching up toward him. Never had she felt so purely sensual, as if he knew secrets about her body that she had not suspected existed. Stimulate this area and that area went ballistic. Touch her here and the rest of her arced toward him. She moved her hands to his hips and pulled them toward hers.

She wanted him, wanted him so badly she didn't

care what came next, could not think about a moment beyond the one that was coming, when he would slide inside her and make her feel whole.

"Wait," he whispered, and pulled himself away. She felt the bed depress as he moved away and heard a drawer open next to it. A second later she heard the tearing of foil, and she knew he had gotten a condom.

He kept them next to the bed.

Well, where else would he keep them? Engelberta asked, but the moment had Tory suddenly feeling the presence of other women. Dozens of them.

He came back, lay down beside her, and ran his fingers around one nipple. She closed her eyes with the sensation.

"Tory," he said softly, "I'm sorry about the other night. I . . . wasn't prepared. I just want you to know that I'm, uh, clean." He laughed awkwardly. "Tested, you know. And I hope I didn't put you at risk of . . ."

She opened her eyes and he was looking at her, brows raised, as if he didn't want to complete the sentence.

She couldn't help it, she started to laugh. Amusement bubbled up inside her so quickly that for a moment she almost couldn't speak. "For someone," she began, marshalling her laughter, "who has no trouble bringing up—okay, *obliquely*— STDs just before making love with a woman . . ." She cracked up again.

"What?" he said, his tone injured but his expression bemused.

"You can't say the word 'pregnant' out loud?" she asked, trying to contain her giggles.

He snorted as he started to laugh, and that made her laugh even harder. Tears squeezed from her eyes.

He levered himself on top of her and said, "That's enough out of you. Are you going to answer the question or not?"

She grinned up at him. "Not until you ask it."

He dropped his head back and rolled his eyes. "I didn't put you at risk of becoming *pregnant*"—he overenunciated the word—"did I?"

Still smiling, she said, "No, but thank you for asking. I've been on birth control pills for years to keep my cycles regular." She angled her head and gazed into his eyes. "And I've also been tested, so if you want to get rid of that shower cap I'm all for it."

With a laugh, he snapped off the condom and kissed her. She opened her mouth to his kiss, and spread her legs for his manhood, whereupon he slid easily into her and, just as she had imagined, she felt whole.

It took only a moment for Keenan to realize that she was gone. The light around the edges of the blinds was dim, so he knew it was early, but the emptiness in the bed beside him was glaring.

He had done this to people, was his second thought. He had left women in the middle of the night, believing they'd agreed the evening was just about sex, and perhaps subjected them to this hollowness, this insane, juvenile *questioning* about whether the emotions he felt soaring between them last night were real or a figment of his imagination.

It didn't matter that he might deserve this, though. He was *not* going to accept it.

He sat up in bed, ran his hands along the sides of his head, scratched his scalp to wake himself up, then swung his legs over the side of the bed.

He walked stiffly to the walk-in closet—last night had been a workout, with passions rising between them time and again—and thought about how much they had laughed as they'd made love. They'd been like a couple of puppies, wrestling and playing. He'd never experienced that before, the verbal jousting and shared sense of humor while touching and feeling and getting turned on like he'd never been turned on before.

He grabbed his sweatpants and headed for the hall. He could already hear Barbra stirring in her crate. Realizing he had to take her outside—dammit—he headed back to the closet to get his sweatshirt. He really needed to hire a dog walker for the morning shift. But then he could just picture someone showing up at six A.M. when Tory might actually have *stayed* the whole night. She was definitely the type to feel awkward about that. Besides, he already had someone coming in the afternoons to feed and walk Barbra. Soon she wouldn't be his dog at all.

Barbra was standing up and wiggling her whole body when he entered the spare bedroom. Taking her leash from the top of the crate, he opened the gate, clipped the leash on, and walked her out of the room. She was a furball of energy. While she had gotten the idea that forward motion, a.k.a. pulling on the leash, was forbidden, she had decided that vertical motion was okay, and she was actually bouncing up and down on all fours as they moved toward the living room.

They were halfway to the door when Keenan spotted the piece of paper on the dining room table. He stopped, gazed at it from a distance for a long moment, then moved to pick it up.

Keenan,

As wonderful as last night was, I think we both know this can't continue to happen. It's a dead end for both of us and we really need to focus on our work. We can talk about this if you want, but I'd really appreciate your respect in this area.

Yours,
Tory

Well, he'd never done that to a woman, he thought, sitting down hard on one of the dining room chairs. Barbra bounced over to him and laid her front paws on his thigh. He pushed her gently off, and she opted for simply laying her chin on his leg, her tail wagging back and forth on the floor like a propeller.

I'd really appreciate your respect. That was the killer. It precluded him from saying anything. It precluded him from convincing her how good they could be. It precluded him from begging.

He stood and headed for the door, noting that even Barbra's steps were not as bouncy as before.

Tory was the biggest fool on the planet. She had left Keenan's building early, for fear of what the two of them would find upon waking up in the same bed. Surprise? Dismay? Wouldn't someone like Keenan not expect her to stay the whole night? Would he wonder what on earth he'd been thinking when he woke up next to someone who was emphatically not a supermodel? Especially not first thing in the morning.

After all, it was one thing to have spontaneous sex with someone; it was another to wake up and try to make conversation with that person the next day.

In the back of her mind, there was also the fact

that if she left at seven, or eight, or nine, when people were up and about, there was the chance that she would run into Stewart. How would she explain that? Not that she owed him any explanation, but still.

She stopped at a bagel place on the way home and picked up a coffee and a bagel with cream cheese, thinking the whole time about how her legs felt tired and energized at the same time, how her body was both chafed and glowing, how her heart felt full despite the ache she'd found in it this morning.

But she didn't want to go home. Didn't want to return to her tired little apartment with its claustrophobia-inducing walls and closet full of former-Tory rags. She didn't like who she'd been, but she didn't know who she was now.

Last night had been amazing. A connection she'd never had before with any other man. Okay, so she'd been with only two other men—Stewart and a boy in college with whom she'd had an immature relationship—but the combination of laughter and conversation and sensuality and passion . . . she had felt such *trust* for him last night. Such comfort.

Where had that all gone this morning?

She took a bite out of her bagel and it caught in her throat. She chewed more, fearing she might burst into tears with the mouthful of dough, and forced it down her throat. Tears stung the backs of her eyes, and she had to work to keep her mouth from turning downward. She tossed the rest of the bagel in a nearby garbage can.

She was walking slowly down the street, sipping her coffee and contemplating taking her broken heart by Tiffany's, like Holly Golightly in *Breakfast at Tiffany's*, when her phone rang.

Her heart leaped. Maybe it was Keenan. Maybe he'd been disappointed that she was gone. Maybe he too wanted the newspaper/coffee/breakfast morning that she had fantasized about. Maybe he'd say something like, *What were you thinking leaving like that? Last night was a revelation! I'm in love with you, Tory!*

But though she knew that was a ridiculous hope, she was still disappointed to see Claudia's name on the screen. She opened the phone and put it to her ear.

"You *really* helped me out last week," her sister began without preamble.

"What?" Tory said, and was horrified to hear the break in her voice. She was going to start crying. Thank God she was only on the phone. She put a hand over her eyes and leaned back against the wall of a nearby building.

"Tory?"

She cleared her throat, but her voice still came out an octave too high, "It's me."

"Are you all right?" Claudia asked. "Where are you? I called you at home but you weren't there."

"I'm . . ." She put all her effort into making her voice sound normal. "I'm at a bagel place. Why?"

"Your voice sounds all, like, weird."

Tory couldn't answer. Tears had trickled out of her eyelids and she was only barely holding on to her self-control.

"Are you still there?" Claudia asked.

"Yes," Tory squeaked.

"You're crying!" Claudia exclaimed. "And it's only seven o'clock in the morning. What on earth could have happened already?"

Tory shook her head.

"Okay, where are you? I'm coming to meet you," Claudia announced.

Though it was a surprise even to herself, Tory felt relieved. She needed to talk this out. Needed to get this guy out of her system and reinforce that she'd done the right thing. She couldn't have stayed in that situation, not knowing how badly it was bound to end. Because the longer she stayed, the more she felt for Keenan, and she simply refused to have her heart broken by a celebrity.

"Oh, I probably won't still be here by the time you can get here," Tory said brokenly. "It's rush hour and you're all the way out in Brooklyn and I couldn't even eat the bagel . . ."

"Where are *you*?"

"I'm at West Eighty-sixth Street, just off the park."

"The Upper West Side? Good Lord. Okay, meet

me at the castle. I'll be there in twenty minutes."

Tory was too fatigued by her own emotions to object.

Forty minutes later, Claudia found her at the castle in Central Park. She was sitting on one of the top benches, looking out over Turtle Pond.

"Wow, it's a beautiful morning, isn't it?" Claudia asked. She was dressed like a figure skater in a white knit hat, mittens, and scarf, with a heavy white sweater. Her long blond hair spilled out in curls from underneath the hat. She looked like Suzy Chapstick.

Tory looked up at her cynically. "Whatever you say."

"What in the world happened to you?" Claudia asked, sitting down next to her. "You *have* been crying. See, that's one of the downsides to make-up." She reached a hand out and smudged something off Tory's right cheek. Claudia smiled sadly. "This is about Keenan James, isn't it."

Tory covered her eyes and lowered her head, her elbow resting on her knee. "Yes. God. You were right. You were right about all of it. He's too much for me, but I've—I've gotten involved with him anyway. I'm such a *fool*."

"Tory, you're not a fool. God, the man's not a celebrity for nothing. He's gorgeous. And he's smart, and funny, and accessible."

Tory sniffed. "Thanks, that helps. I was worried I wasn't remembering all of his good points."

Claudia laughed. "So what happened? Did you sleep with him?"

Tory nodded miserably.

She leaned in close. "And how *was* it?"

Tory lifted her head slightly and shot her a look.

"Okay, sorry, not time for that yet. So, was this last night?"

"Yes," Tory said, sighing. "And the night of that symphony party." She decided not to add the details of that. Claudia would never get back to the subject at hand.

"Twice?" Claudia asked. "You slept with him on two different occasions?"

Tory nodded.

"Well, that's *huge*, Tor. I mean, I'd understand your concern if you'd just slept with him last night and he ditched you early this morning. But he slept with you twice. He wasn't trying to avoid you or didn't say something after the first time like, we're working together so we shouldn't let this happen again. Or something else like that. Because that would be a *clear* sign that he was only in it for the sex."

Tory lifted her head, frowning. "But . . . I ditched *him* early this morning. And I left a note about how we're working together, so we shouldn't do it again."

Claudia stared at her. "Are you crazy? I thought you'd fallen for him. Isn't that why you're crying?"

"Yes, but Claudia, I know exactly what's coming. Don't *you*? Keenan James is never going to fall for *me*. So I guess I just wanted to beat him to the punch or something."

"That's the most immature thing I've ever heard you say." Claudia's face bore a look of utter disapproval. "How do you know he doesn't have feelings for you? Feelings you just trampled, by the way, with your *note*. Jesus, I can't believe you left him a *note*, for God's sake. Can you imagine what we'd be saying about him if he'd done that to you?"

Tory hadn't thought of it that way. She'd pulled a stunt right out of the book of classic one-night stands. Okay, two-night stands. She'd blown him off.

"All right. So it was not very . . . graceful. But the fact is, there's no way Keenan James would want a relationship with me. I was just protecting myself."

"Uh-huh." Claudia looked at her skeptically.

"It's true. He dates supermodels and actresses. Beautiful women. Women who don't argue with him all the time."

Claudia shook her head. "You know, for a shrink you sure don't know much about men. He hasn't had a long-term relationship in, like, *ever*, as far as I can tell from the tabloids. And I do read them religiously, as you know. Maybe he doesn't *like* dating famous women. Maybe he's tired of those kinds of women. Maybe he *likes* that you argue with him."

"That's ridiculous. Nobody gets tired of beautiful women, except other women."

"I said 'famous women,' Tory," Claudia said

soberly. "Because you yourself *are* a beautiful woman."

Tory scoffed. "You're just saying that because you're my sister."

"That's right," Claudia said. "You're *my* sister—and aren't *I* beautiful?"

Tory glanced over to see Claudia grinning. "You got all the good genes."

"That's not true. Ever since you've been dressing up a little nicer, and doing your hair and your face, you've looked a lot like me. Even Simon said so, and you know he doesn't notice anything, normally."

Despite herself, Tory felt a tiny spark of belief light her heart. Maybe she wasn't the ugly duckling of the family anymore. Maybe she'd just made herself that way so she wouldn't have to compete with Claudia. And now . . . now that she'd discovered she wasn't content with her dowdy role, well, maybe she wasn't quite as plain as she'd made herself out to be.

"Besides," Claudia added, "you're way smart, you're funny when you want to be, and you don't take any shit from people. That's attractive, Tory. And I bet that's *really* attractive to him. You know how people are always kowtowing to stars."

She laughed slightly. "I definitely don't kowtow."

"I'd be shocked if you did," Claudia said. "Besides, what about all that stuff you're always spouting about *talking* to one another. Telling someone your feelings. You were all down on Keenan because he talked about dumping people without giving them a chance, and that's exactly what you've just done!"

"Oh my God." Tory's head spun. Claudia was right. "And Keenan . . ."

"Is the one hanging in there!" Claudia crowed. "You are so busted, Tory. Your position and Keenan's are a lot closer than you've been willing to admit."

"I can't believe it," Tory murmured. It was all well and good for her to be the theorist with the broad view, but when you were fighting in the front lines, the scenery changed.

They sat in companionable silence for several minutes before Tory, pulling herself together, said, "So what were you saying on the phone when you called? I helped you?"

Claudia stood up. "Come on, let's go get some coffee." She pulled Tory up by the arm. "I was saying that you helped me with Simon."

"Did you talk to him about the prenup?" Tory asked. "Are you guys back together?"

They made their way down the castle steps and out into the park.

"I did." Claudia tugged at one of her mittens. "And we are. See, I started thinking about what you said about prenups being because of the system, not because of me, and how that made much more sense with what I know about Simon's character. I mean, he'd give me anything I wanted, I think that's why his stubbornness on this was so shocking."

"The man does know how to be stubborn," Tory agreed.

"Yes!" Claudia enthused. Tory looked over at her, startled. "But you see I also realized that the fact that he wasn't caving on the issue was one of the things I'm most attracted to about him: he's got a *spine*. He's not like all those other guys I dated who were half afraid of me. Simon will do anything for me, except be a doormat. And I *love* that about him. Hey, maybe that's what Keenan likes so much about you!"

Claudia elbowed Tory as they walked, and Tory swerved, thinking, *Maybe she's right*. It was so clear in Claudia's case that that was exactly what she needed from a man.

"Anyway," Claudia continued, "so I made signing the prenup all about my love for him, made it this big gesture, just like you said. Plus," she added cheerfully, "now he owes me."

Chapter 17

"Tory, thank God you're here."

It wasn't exactly what she'd been expecting Keenan to say, but she'd take it. It was a lot *better* than she'd been expecting. He thanked God she was there! Surely that meant something good. Despite the fact that he hadn't called, or responded to her note in any way. Not that it exactly invited response.

The only trouble was, Keenan said the words, then turned immediately away from her and strode back into the apartment. She stood confused for a moment in the doorway, then followed him in.

He turned when they were both in the dining room, having picked up a leather leash from the table. From the back hall Tory could hear what sounded like someone with a hammer pounding erratically on something hollow.

"I am so sorry to do this to you," he said, "you have no idea."

Tory's stomach dropped. Keenan's face was dead serious, wearing an expression she'd never seen before.

"I just got a call from the nursing home." His voice thickened but he continued firmly. "It's my mother. Something's happened. She lost consciousness and they're not sure if it's a stroke or something related to this cold she's had. Colds, you know, they can turn into pneumonia so quick, otherwise I would never ask you—"

"Keenan, it's okay," she said, taking a step toward him in concern. "You have to go to her, of course. But don't try to anticipate what's wrong until you have all the facts. You'll only upset yourself. It could be something simpler."

He huffed out a deep breath, rubbed a hand over his eyes. "Thank you. I know. Listen, I hate to leave you with this—"

"Please," she protested. "I understand. Go, go! We can work another time."

He swallowed and looked at her steadily. "It's not just that. It's . . . it's Barbra. She's . . ." He rolled his eyes and laughed once, mirthlessly. "I gave her

this bone, a marrow bone, and it's the kind of bone
with a hole in the center, shaped kind of like a tall
donut—"

"Keenan, does this have a point? Don't worry
about her, and don't worry about me. You should
get going." She moved toward him again, as if to
take his arm and guide him to the door, but something stopped her from touching him.

He took a deep breath. "Here's the thing. She's
got it stuck on her lower jaw. The bone. And I can't
get it off. She's in there beating herself up in the
crate trying to get rid of it. There's a little blood on
her—the hair around her face, and I'm not sure . .
. Anyway, I need you to take her to the vet. Could
you do that for me? It's only five blocks." He took
the last step to reach her and grabbed both of her
hands, looking into her eyes so deeply her stomach
flipped. "Tory, I know you're afraid of dogs, but
you have to believe me. This dog will *never* hurt
you. I swear it. Hell, she couldn't bite you now
even if—"

"Keenan, *go*," she said firmly. There was no decision to make here. He had to go and she had to
help him. "I'll take her, don't worry."

He closed his eyes briefly. "Thank you," he said
simply, but never had the words sounded so sincere to her. "Here's the name and address of the
vet. They know you're coming," he added, pushing a business card and the leash into her hands
and moving swiftly toward the door. Once there,

he paused for a second, his hand on the knob, and looked back at her. "Tory . . ."

She clutched the card and the leash in both hands. "Yes?"

He hesitated, then shook his head, never mind. "Thank you."

And he was gone.

Tory stood stock-still in the center of the dining room, looking at the door through which he'd just disappeared. Behind her, the hammering noise continued, and slowly it dawned on her that *that* must be Barbra, in her cage, trying to get the bone off her jaw.

Tory turned and headed slowly toward the hallway, following the noise to a closed door. She put one hand on the knob and turned it, then pushed the door open.

It was another bedroom and it housed a treadmill, an elliptical machine, a television, and a green plastic cage with a metal grate for a door. Inside stood the dog, momentarily still at Tory's arrival.

She looked at Tory pathetically, a clean, white, circular bone around her lower jaw, as if someone had played ringtoss and looped it over her chin.

Silence reigned only for a second, though, because Barbra, not sensing immediate help, began throwing her head from side to side, and dragging the bone against the metal grate door.

Great, Tory thought, *now she's armed.*

She looked at the crate. How was she supposed

to get that wild animal out of the box *and* put her leash on *and* get her to go the direction they needed to go? She'd have to block the front of the crate the moment she opened it, so she could hook the leash on the dog's collar. But that would require actual contact with the animal.

She took a step closer, her palms sweating and her heart racing. She thought for a moment she might be sick. But it was true, the way the bone was over her chin, she might not be able to bite.

On the other hand, she still had teeth on the *upper* part of her mouth, and if she got something like, say, Tory's hand between—

This is unproductive, Tory thought. She should take her own advice, the same she'd just given Keenan, and try not to anticipate too much. He said the dog wouldn't bite her, so she had to trust the dog wouldn't bite her.

She took a deep breath and bent to look at the door to the cage. It looked like a simple mechanism, just squeeze the handle and open it. Barbra had stopped once again and was looking at her as if to say, *Yes, just squeeze the damn handle, you idiot, and open it!*

Drool dripped down the dog's chin, wetting her beard and the bone and the floor of the cage.

Tory found the hook for the leash, put it at the ready in her right hand, and squeezed open the door. At the same time she stood, stepping right in front of the opening the moment the gate swung free. The dog rushed forward and tried to squeeze between her legs.

For a moment, Tory thought she would faint. But she couldn't. If she did, she'd only wake up in this room with the dog loose and possibly gnawing on her head.

She reached down without looking, grabbed a handful of hair, and was startled at how soft it was. Not like fur at all. It felt like baby hair. She glanced down, found the dog looking up at her, her eyes pathetic and her tail wagging so hard it struck the inside of the cage.

Tory's heart went out to her. She looked, Tory could swear, *grateful.*

She reached up to the dog's neck, found the collar, and spun it as the dog put her head against Tory's thighs, for all the world as if cooperating with the operation. She snapped the leash on and stepped back.

Barbra literally bounced out of the crate, whining and wiggling, heading for the door.

Tory followed. She could make this quick. Maybe if they ran, the dog would forget Tory was behind her.

Barbra knew exactly where they were going. All Tory had to do was follow. She decided not to lock Keenan's door, as she'd have to come back to drop her off again, and she didn't have a key. Or maybe, she thought hopefully, the vet would hang on to the dog and Keenan could just pick her up later.

No such luck. After she'd run the five blocks to Dr. Clayton's office, the receptionist said they didn't "board" dogs, and the only way Tory could leave the animal was if she was having surgery.

"Well, I don't know," Tory said, looking down at Barbra's pitiful face. "They might do something surgical. I don't know how they're going to fix this."

The receptionist stood up in order to look over the counter at the dog, and burst out laughing.

Barbra hung her head and scooted behind Tory, pressing up against her legs. Tory felt something blossom inside her at the dog's trust, some buried maternal-type instinct.

"Hey," Tory objected, fixing the receptionist with a chastising glare. "She's embarrassed enough as it is."

The receptionist squelched her laughter and sat down again. "Just have a seat in the waiting room," she said, unable to repress a smile, "the doctor will be right with you."

They went to sit down in the waiting area. Barbra was fairly docile now. She'd no doubt exhausted herself with her exertions to get the bone off her face. Not to mention the five-block run to the vet.

Tory sat on one of the wooden chairs and Barbra dropped like a bag of monkey wrenches to the floor in front of her, right on top of Tory's shoes. The bone clacked loudly on the tile floor as the dog laid her head down.

An older man with a cat in a carrier looked over

at them. The cat mewled and Barbra lifted her head, drool dripping off the end of the bone.

"What are you in for?" the man asked, staring at Barbra.

Tory raised her eyebrows. What were they *in* for? The dog had a *bone* stuck on the end of her face, what did he think they were in for?

She took a calming breath and said, "Rabies vaccine."

His pale brown eyes shot up to hers and she looked back at him calmly, daring him to say something else.

Barbra put her head back down, the bone clacking once again on the floor.

An hour and a half later, and one bone lighter, Tory and Barbra left the vet, both of them wearing an extra spring in their step now that the crisis was over.

Tory couldn't believe how simple it was. The vet had some kind of tool that essentially just snipped the bone in half. Of course it helped that they had a couple of vet techs to hold Barbra while they did it. But still, it was over, and Tory had been able to get her there to make it happen.

She moved down the street, holding on to the leash with one hand and feeling as proud as if she'd tamed a lion. *Look at me!* she wanted to crow. *I'm walking a dog!*

Barbra bounced ahead of her, so light against the leather lead that Tory felt as if she were holding a balloon. Tory looked at her with affection. The dog had taken to her as if she owned her, despite Tory's nervousness. When the vet had come at her with the shears, Barbra had backed into Tory's body as if Tory could protect her. It had been all Tory could do not to grab the dog's shaking body and tell the vet to back off, the poor thing was scared to death. If it hadn't been for the obvious fact that the dog would be better off without the bone stuck on her chin, she might have done it.

For about the fifteenth time that day, Tory pulled her cell phone out of her pocket and checked it. Keenan hadn't called. She hoped his mother was all right, but the longer she went without news, the more dire she feared the situation was.

She should put something in the oven for him for dinner, she thought. He'd have been at the hospital all day, with nothing to eat but vending machine candy or cafeteria food. And Tory made a really good pot roast. It was one of the few things she knew how to cook. Simple, but good.

Besides, it would be a nice gesture. Something to tell him that she was his friend, even if she didn't have it in her to be his girlfriend. Friends lasted longer anyway, didn't they?

She approached Keenan's building remembering the time Barbra had bounded out the door and jumped up on her. Had it only been a month and a half ago? Knowing what she knew now, she must have looked pretty silly standing there in terror while this gentle animal threw her affection at her. For the first time in her life, Tory felt liberated from a fear that had had her in its grip for years. Not that she was likely to go up to any strange dogs and pet them. Nor go out of her way to even see another one. But this dog . . . *this* dog had wormed her way into Tory's heart.

Along with its owner.

She was nearing the door to the building when it swung open and out stepped Stewart. He glanced her way before turning the opposite way down the street, then stopped and whirled back to her.

"Tory?" he asked, stunned, looking from her face to the dog and back again. "Is that *you*? Walking a dog?"

She couldn't help it, she grinned. "I know. Isn't it amazing?"

He walked back toward her, taking in her face at closer range. "What have you done to yourself?"

Tory lifted a hand to her cheek. She'd forgotten all about the smattering of makeup she'd put on before going to Keenan's that day. She hoped it wasn't smeared all over her face.

"What?" she asked defensively.

"Are you wearing makeup?" He bent toward her, and if he'd had a monocle, she was sure he would have held it up to better inspect her.

She laughed and stepped back. "Stewart! Yes, okay, I'm wearing a little makeup. I'm . . . trying something new."

Stewart frowned. "You start hanging around with Keenan James and wearing makeup, I hardly know you anymore. And you're walking a dog!"

"No, I just . . . did a favor for . . ." She blushed, even though Stewart could not possibly know what had passed between her and Keenan. He already knew they were working together.

He looked down at the dog again, and bent to pat it on the head. Barbra wagged her tail perfunctorily. Tory thought the day had been too much for her. Poor thing needed to sleep.

"For Keenan James," Stewart said, awareness tingeing his voice. There was no question Stewart was impressed with her proximity to the celebrity. "This is his dog, right? Barbra Streisand?"

At that the dog barked once, lifting off her front paws a little with the effort.

So much for being able to deny it, Tory thought.

"That's right. He had to leave suddenly, his mother is sick, so I took her to the vet."

He shook his head. "And you're not shaking like a leaf. He must have done some pretty good psychology on you to help you over that phobia."

"It was very sudden," she said, looking down at the dog, who now sat at her feet. Actually, *on* her feet. "I, uh, didn't have much choice. It was pretty scary at first."

Stewart looked at her quizzically. "You could have come and gotten me."

Tory opened her mouth to reply, then realized she

had no idea what to say. It hadn't even occurred to her to call Stewart. And he was right there in the same building!

Come to think of it, she hadn't thought about Stewart in any but a passing way in days. Maybe even a week.

"I," she began, "I was fine with her. I guess I've gotten used to her. You know, working with Keenan and all," she fudged, even though she'd been to Keenan's apartment all of two times.

"I guess you have. I'm getting used to a new cat, by the way. A woman, one of the orchestra's biggest sponsors, has had me over several times now. We're kind of an item."

"Oh, how nice," Tory said, meaning it. She'd feel so much better if Stewart found someone else. "Do I know her?"

"No, she's not famous, like *some* people. You know I wouldn't like that, being with someone who needed to be in the public eye. It's not good for more than one person in a couple to be famous, you know."

"Quite right," Tory agreed. God, he was pompous. Had it always been this obvious?

"So how is the project going?" Stewart's face was polite, and Tory wondered if their conversations had always been this impersonal or if they were just responding to each other's distance.

She told him a little about the project and they chatted for several minutes like nothing more than neighbors, until Barbra lay down between them.

"I'd better go," Tory said, looking at the tired dog. "I should get her back upstairs."

"Sure," Stewart said, backing up a step. Then he bent down to pat Barbra, who had stood up when he'd moved, on the head again. "Tell Keenan I said hello."

She smiled. "I sure will."

And they parted. It was the strangest thing. After eight years of attachment, she'd finally broken the cord. She and Stewart had well and truly broken up.

All it had taken was her falling in love with another man.

And his dog.

Keenan sat in the hospital waiting room, his head in his hands. Why did these things always take so *long*? He'd been here the entire day with barely an update. Granted, they'd put him in the special, smaller waiting room, closer to where they'd taken his mother, and he shared it with only three or four other people, but it was the same plastic seating with the same mounted televisions showing the same news channel as the one downstairs.

A nurse had come in twice to let him know she had nothing to tell him, and he'd spoken to the doctor only twice, and that earlier in the day, about their diagnostic plan.

He wasn't ready to lose her, he'd realized. He wanted his mother to stick around, to read the book, see it published . . . maybe even meet that special woman, if he ever met her. His mind flashed to Tory, and he had a moment of imagining the two of them meeting. She would like Tory, with her soft looks and no-nonsense manner. But Tory had made it clear how she felt about him.

He wondered how she was doing with the dog. He couldn't bear the thought of anything happening to that dog today of all days. If he couldn't tell his mother that she was fine. . .

He pulled his cell phone out of his pocket, knowing as he did so that it would have no signal, just as it hadn't the rest of the day. If he could get an update, maybe he could step outside for a second to check his voice mail, but he didn't want to leave without knowing what was happening.

The door to the waiting room squeaked open and Keenan looked up, hoping to see the doctor. Instead, entering the room was his brother, Brady, with a pretty, brown-haired woman behind him.

Keenan heaved a sigh of relief and rose. "You made good time."

The brothers clasped hands and shook, looking at each other as if the situation could be assessed in the other's face.

"The boss lent me the plane," Brady said. "He's generous like that. How is she?"

"We still don't know." Keenan pushed a hand

through his hair. "They're going to do a CAT scan but that won't show a stroke within the first twelve hours. They're thinking it might be a reaction to the codeine in the medicine she was taking for her cold, in which case she should regain consciousness, I think on her own."

"That would be good," Brady said on an exhale. Then he stepped back, and raised his arm to put it around the pretty girl's shoulders. "Kee, this is—"

"Lily. It's a pleasure to meet you at last." Keenan smiled at her, liking the look of her. Pretty, but sharp. He also liked the way Brady looked at her. And to think he had advised Brady to dump her at the beginning of their relationship. They'd gone through so much confusion and trouble, Keenan had been sure it wasn't worth it.

Chalk another one up for Tory—her advice would have been much different than his, and right on target.

Lily gave him a smile, muted for the occasion, he could tell. "I wish it was under better circumstances."

"Thank you." He inclined his head.

Behind them, the door opened again and a doctor entered. Everyone in the room looked up, hoping the white coat belonged to their physician, but Keenan recognized Dr. Schluntz.

"Here's the doctor now," he said to Brady and Lily.

They all turned toward the athletic-looking man,

who Keenan thought didn't look old enough to be a doctor, let alone a specialist.

"Mr. James," Dr. Schluntz said, approaching.

"Dr. Schluntz, this is my brother, Brady Cole, and this is Lily," Keenan said, gesturing toward them.

The doctor shook hands with both of them.

"I have good news," he said, breaking into a smile. "Your mother is awake."

"Awake?" Keenan repeated, at the same time that Lily let out a little shriek and jumped up to briefly hug Brady.

"She came to about half an hour ago. We believe it was the codeine, as she's showing no other negative effects, but we're going to keep her overnight for observation to be sure. If need be, we'll do a CAT scan in the morning."

Keenan felt the weight of a thousand nightmares lift off his chest. He and Brady looked at each other with matching dopey grins and they clasped each other swiftly, pounding once, twice, three times on each other's backs before stepping back to grin at each other some more.

"She's asking for you," the doctor added. "Why don't you come on back? You two can follow in a minute."

"You go first," Keenan said, motioning Brady forward, knowing it was him that his mother was asking to see, as she always did when he visited her. "I'll come in in a minute."

"Uh, Mr. James?" the doctor said. "It's you she's

asking for. She wanted to know if Keenan was here, and she seemed very relieved when I told her you were, that you hadn't left since she got here. I think you should go first."

Keenan would have thought he was too old for the emotion that ambushed him then, but he was nearly overwhelmed by a long-forgotten feeling from his boyhood.

He blinked rapidly and bent his head as he passed Lily and Brady, swallowing over the sudden lump in his throat.

There was laughing when Keenan turned the key in the lock and let himself into the apartment. Tory looked up from the magazine she was reading and bolted to her feet.

He was with other people. And they were carrying bags of what looked suspiciously like food.

Barbra bounced over to the group and practically embraced them by winding her wagging body through the small throng.

The girl knelt down and oohed over the dog.

Tory felt immediately and irrevocably foolish. What had she been thinking? Helping herself to Keenan's kitchen and cooking a meal for him. Of course he'd have called his friends—his *real* friends—in his hour of need. He didn't need her and her homey little pot roast. She felt like an unwanted houseguest—or worse, a stalker.

"Whoa, smells good in here," the guy said, petting the dog the girl was fussing over and looking up at Tory curiously.

The girl's eyes lit on Tory, and Tory wondered if this was some regular girl Keenan saw. She was beautiful, Tory noted, even if she didn't look like a model.

Somehow that made it worse.

"I, uh, it's just a roast," Tory said, her face hot and pinpricks of sweat breaking out all over her body. She'd never felt so mortified. Her eyes sought Keenan's.

He was looking at her in something of amazement. "You cooked me a roast?"

Her eyes skittered away, looking for her purse and her jacket so she could grab them and get out of this awkward situation. "Well, I, um, thought you'd need *some*thing to eat after being at the hospital all day." Then she realized, in her mortification, she'd forgotten the most important thing. "How is your mother?"

Keenan broke into a breathtaking smile. "She's going to be fine. It was the codeine, from the cough medicine."

"Oh I'm *so* glad," Tory said, sincerely, momentarily distracted from herself.

Until the guy friend cleared his throat.

Keenan glanced over at him and said, "Oh, Tory, this is my brother, Brady, and his girlfr—I mean, *fiancée*, Lily." He was grinning as he introduced them. "They just got engaged, and there could have been no better medicine for my mother than that. You should have seen her when they told her. She looked like they could have checked her out of the hospital on the spot."

The girl, Lily, smiled with deep satisfaction. "It's nice to meet you, Tory," she said, moving toward her to shake her hand. "And how wonderful to come back to such a delicious-smelling dinner."

She glanced over at her fiancé, Brady, who was unloading king crab legs and champagne and what looked like a variety of gourmet-looking cheeses onto the table.

"Why don't you put that in the fridge, Brady?" Lily suggested pointedly. "We can eat those later. Who wants all that when you've got a roast?"

Tory wished she could disappear into the carpeting. *She* would eat all that over a roast. A stupid, easy, Lipton-soup-recipe roast. How in the world did she think a pot roast would fit into the glamorous life Keenan James lived?

She spotted her things on the floor next to the chair in the living room. "Well, I better be going. So glad everything worked out for you all."

She edged over toward the living room.

"No, Tory, you have to stay," Keenan said, moving toward her. "We've got plenty of champagne and lots to celebrate. Please stay."

"I can't."

"Come on," he cajoled, a captivating smile still on his face. "I'm so glad you're still here." Barbra wiggled over to him and leaned against his legs. His hand dropped down to scratch her ears. "We also have to celebrate the removal of the bone. How did it go at the vet?"

"Oh, I'll tell you later." She waved a hand and grabbed her things. "She's fine. It was really quite simple. They just snipped it off. Nothing to it."

Tory would sooner die than stay and listen to them all try to make nice about her roast while the king crab legs waited in the refrigerator. In fact, she didn't know what she'd expected, why she hadn't thought ahead. Had she thought she and Keenan would sit there over the roast like two kids playing house when he got back?

"But I owe you money, surely," he added, pulling his wallet out of his back pocket. "And you didn't have any trouble, ah, getting her there?" The question was significant, they both knew, but she was glad he didn't reveal her dog phobia in front of his brother.

"No, no trouble at all!" She pushed her arms blindly into her jacket, hoping it wasn't upside down. "And they're going to bill you."

"Well, that's even more reason to celebrate," he said, his smile gentle now, and his eyes penetrating. "Please stay, Tory."

"I can't, really," she said quickly, only vaguely

absorbing the low tone of insistence in the words.

She scoured her brain for an excuse, one they couldn't possibly talk her out of, because she couldn't get out of there fast enough. Then it came to her. "I have a date!"

Chapter 18

"I cannot *believe* you didn't stay," Claudia said for about the fourth time on the phone. "He asked you to dinner with his *brother*. That's family, Tory! That's like, a step toward commitment. You can't tell me you honestly think this guy has a problem with commitment."

"Claudia, you read the tabloids, you said so yourself," Tory said, wishing she didn't agree so much with her sister. "The guy has had about fifteen girlfriends in the last year alone."

Her sister sighed with great exaggeration. "Oh,

please. Don't tell me you're starting to believe the crap they write in those things."

Tory had nothing to say to that. Of course she didn't believe them, but she thought Claudia did. But what difference did it make if Claudia believed Keenan couldn't commit? The question was if she herself really believed it.

Or if she was just—

"Chicken," Claudia said. "That's what you are. You're afraid to get into a relationship with a guy you think is out of your league, even though you're in love with him and he might well be in love with you."

Tory's scoff was involuntary and heartfelt. "He is *not* in love with me."

"How do you *know*? Have you asked him?"

"Of course not!"

Claudia exhaled. "Okay, I'll give you that one. I wouldn't ask either. But you gotta give the guy a chance to talk to you, an opportunity to say it. You can't keep running out on him just because you get a little bit out of your comfort zone."

Tory thought about that, about how comfortable she had been that night they'd slept together at his apartment. And how *un*comfortable she'd been in the morning when she woke up. Out of her comfort zone. Then again how out of place she felt with Keenan and his brother and his brother's fiancée. Why was that? Because she didn't know where she and Keenan stood, what they were doing, what they *were*.

Of course that was her fault, mostly. Because she'd left that stupid, defensive note.

God, she realized, *she* needed to go to Keenan's round table for real. She needed some *Straight Talk* from the man himself.

"Okay, so I'm a little cowardly," she admitted.

"A little!" Claudia was taking a deep breath to expound on the topic when Tory's call waiting beeped.

"Claudia, hang on, let me see who this is." She pressed flash and said, "Hello?"

"Tory, it's Keenan."

Tory's stomach hit the floor.

"Oh, hi!" she said, with as much gusto as if he'd actually been there to catch her talking about him. "Hang on a second, will you?"

A pause. "Sure."

She clicked back over to Claudia. "Claudia?" she asked, to be sure it had actually switched lines.

"Blow off whoever it is, this is important," Claudia directed.

"I can't," she said, swallowing with a completely dry mouth. "It's Keenan."

"So I went out with a Jack Russell," Jan said, picking up her water glass. "And—"

"Remember, Jan, no real names," Keenan said.

Jan laughed. Keenan didn't think he'd ever seen her this lighthearted. Apparently confronting her about her secret had set her free. She'd given up on him and had moved on in the space of a couple of weeks.

"I know. But a Jack Russell is a terrier," Jan explained. "A little barky, energetic clown of a dog, just like this guy I went out with the other night. He was stocky, talky, and *very* energetic, if you know what I mean." She laughed again.

Martina rolled her eyes. "Oh we know what you mean. Did he do it doggy style?"

"Okay, okay, we're getting into pretty personal territory," Keenan said, glancing over at the entryway to the restaurant. He had called Tory yesterday to make sure she was coming, and to ask her if they could go somewhere afterward. He wanted to talk to her. *Needed* to talk to her. And she'd said she would be here. Said she had to come clean to the group and explain about her part in the book.

He'd been glad she'd had other reasons to come. It meant she had more reasons not to change her mind.

After they'd come home from the hospital Friday night to the dinner she had made—which had tasted like a home he'd had only in his fondest imaginings as a boy—his brother's fiancée, Lily, had convinced him that a woman didn't do something like that if she wasn't interested in a man. Then she'd pointed out how completely intimidating Keenan's life was compared with just about anyone else's, and the fact that they'd come home with champagne and gourmet food probably didn't add anything to Tory's perception of him as a regular guy.

She also didn't believe for a second that Tory had a date.

Keenan wasn't so sure about that. For one thing, her ex-boyfriend lived just a few floors away. For another, she could get a date with just about anyone she chose, if she wanted to.

It didn't, however, go with what he knew of her character to be dating someone else while sleeping with *him*. That was about the only thing that gave him hope.

Then again, she'd called a halt to that.

The bottom line, though, was that the advice he got from Lily—corroborated by his own brother—was the advice he would have given to someone else in his situation. *Tell her how you feel.*

He paused, thinking that wasn't the advice he'd have given a couple of months ago. Back then he would have said, *Move on! She's not worth the trouble! Plenty more fish in the sea.*

Talk to her would have been Tory's advice, and he saw now how right she was. He had to tell her how he felt, even if it meant getting shot down.

"I have an announcement," Martina said, a big

smile on her face. She was dressed up today, Keenan had noted.

"Do tell," Angelica said, sipping her Perrier.

"I met a man," Martina said, her smile growing. "And he's *so perfect* for me. But the most amazing thing is, I'm perfect for him! At least he thinks so."

Now Keenan really wished Tory were here. Martina was a success story. He hadn't given her bad advice; he'd freed her from the trap she'd laid for herself. At least he could feel good about that.

"I can't tell you how wonderful it is," Martina continued, "not to feel bad about myself every day. Not to wonder what's wrong with me that Rex doesn't like, or what it is that's holding him back. And this new guy, we've been out on three dates already and he thinks I'm wonderful!"

"That's great," Keenan said with a smile. "Really great. You see? When a guy really likes you, he lets you know."

He, apparently, was the exception. He hadn't let Tory know how he felt at all. Was *all* his advice bullshit?

Finally the maître d' appeared with Tory at his side. He seated her in one of the two remaining seats—Ruth Bitterman hadn't come—across the table from Keenan.

She was greeted by all and she smiled at them in turn, looking small and sweet and less sure of herself than he'd ever seen her.

"I have an announcement to make too," Angelica said, with a swift smile at Keenan. He knew what was coming, and he hoped it didn't rock the group's boat too much. Especially not with Tory's news yet to come.

"Ruth won't be coming today," Angelica said, folding her hands on the table in front of her. "You see, her husband died."

Gasps shot round the table, but Angelica held up a hand.

"*Four years* ago," she added.

"What?" Martina demanded.

"I don't get it," Jan said. "Then what was she doing here?"

"I recommended the group to her," Angelica said. "To work out the issues she had with him that she'd never worked out while he was alive. She could also see that the problems she had with him were somewhat universal, part of the natural push and pull of male-female relationships, and not solely his fault or hers. You see, I used to be a psychiatrist, and Ruth was my patient." She glanced at Tory. "She gave me permission to say that."

Keenan's eyes shifted to Tory also. She sat up straighter and her mouth opened, her cheeks reddening. "What?" he heard her say breathlessly.

"Keenan is an old friend of mine," Angelica explained, "and when these round tables started getting bigger and more numerous, he asked me to join him a few times a month just to make sure he wasn't doing anybody any harm." Angelica smiled at Keenan. "And it has been my joy to see that not only is he not doing any harm, he's done a great deal of good."

There were some nods around the table, some murmurings, but Tory sat still as if she'd been electroshocked.

"Ruth, for example," Angelica continued. "She has been dealing with her marriage and her husband's death so much better over the last year, when she's been communing with all of you about your problems, and hearing Keenan's perspective on the male point of view, that she actually went out on a date last month. She's feeling much better about herself and her future. So she won't be joining us anymore."

Choruses of "That's wonderful!" and "Good for her" were joined with "So you're not here for yourself?" and "I wondered what you were getting out of straight talk from a guy."

Keenan smiled wryly. His eyes flicked back to Tory. She stared first at Angelica, then moved her gaze to Keenan.

Finally, she stood up as if propelled by a geyser under her seat, her chair scraping behind her, and propped her fingertips on the table in front of her. The waiter arrived with his pad and she glared daggers at him. "We're not ready yet."

The waiter backed off as if she'd bared her teeth.

"So, Angelica, you're a *psychiatrist*?" Tory asked.

"I *was*," Angelica corrected gently.

"And you're here because Keenan . . . ?"

"Because Keenan asked me to come. To check up on him," she explained. "Make sure he wasn't hurting anyone."

Tory's eyes moved to Keenan's. "Why didn't you *tell* me?"

"Why didn't he tell all of us?" Jan asked, then turned to Keenan. "Did you think we wouldn't act natural or something?"

"I didn't think it needed to be mentioned," he said. "Angelica agreed to the same confidentiality we all did. She was just here as a voluntary consultant. In the same way we don't know all the many reasons that each of you came here"—he passed his eyes from Jan, to Martina, to Tory—"everyone didn't need to know all of Angelica's."

That seemed to strike everyone as fair. Except for Tory, who looked at him as if she'd caught him in a lie.

He smiled calmly and tilted his head as he gazed at her. If he'd lied to her, it was no worse than the lie she'd told him when she'd gotten here. "Now I believe, uh, *Vicky* has something to say."

At that, the correlation obviously struck her too, and she lowered her eyes to the table.

"All right. I do have a confession to make," she

said, looking around the table. She paused, then with a deep breath jumped in. She explained about the book deal, about her skepticism, about her name and who she was, and finally, about how she'd taken the book deal and that she and Keenan would now be working together.

"For the record," Keenan added, "I did not know why she was here at first either."

Discussion swirled around these events, the waiter ventured back and took their orders, and they were just starting to settle down when a woman came rushing over to the table. Keenan recognized her as Tory's friend, the one he'd met the evening they'd been at the nightclub.

"I'm so sorry to interrupt, but Tory, uh, Vicky, told me I could come," she said breathlessly, winding her scarf from around her neck and bunching her gloves together in one hand. She edged around the table to the empty seat next to Angelica but kept talking, "You see I have kind of an emergency situation and I really need some good advice. Pronto."

Keenan frowned and looked over at Tory, wondering if this was more about the prenup that had been brought up that night. But the expression on Tory's face made it clear that she had not been expecting her friend to show up.

"See, here's the deal," the girl began.

"Wait, what's your name?" Angelica asked, putting a calming hand on the frenetic girl's arm.

"Oh!" She trilled a laugh. "Claudia. My name is Claudia. Sorry. Anyway, I'm like totally in love with this guy, but I'm also scared to death of getting involved with him. You see, he's kind of famous. Like an actor, that kind of famous. And I'm just a nobody. But we've been together a couple of times, if you know what I mean—"

"Oh we know what you mean," Martina said again, and the table laughed.

All except Tory, who plunked back down in her chair as if her legs had given out.

Claudia smiled. Her resemblance to Tory was unmissable. Keenan wondered who else might have picked up on it.

"Wait, your fiancé is an actor?" Keenan asked. He didn't remember this part of the story, and the young man who'd shown up at the bar that night had definitely not looked like someone from Hollywood. He had CPA written all over him.

Claudia shook her head with a smile that urged him to keep thinking. "I don't have a fiancé. I had a boyfriend, for a long time, *eight years*," she said significantly, looking at him, "but we broke up. And I got involved with this other man, but I'm afraid to tell him how I feel. Because he's famous, see, and I just can't believe he'd be interested in someone regular like me. I'm terrified he doesn't feel the same way, so I run away every time he gets close. Get it?" she added, in a tone of voice like a two-by-four to the head.

Keenan felt the light dawning. She wasn't talking about herself. She was talking about—

Tory stood up again. "Claudia!" she said sharply, leaning forward as if she could reach across the table and clap her hands over the girl's mouth. "What are you *doing*?"

"Wait, are you guys sisters?" Jan asked. "Because you look a lot alike."

"Oh we're *really* alike," Claudia said, looking back at Keenan and nodding her head. "In fact, you might say we're *exactly* alike."

Tory bolted to her feet again, this time turning to grab her jacket and purse. She pushed out of the seat, away from the table, dragging the tablecloth a foot or two so that everything on it jangled and shifted and people grabbed for their water glasses.

She headed straight for the door, ignoring the short grip someone had had on her sleeve, from which she easily broke free.

She was going to kill Claudia. It had been obvious to everyone—most importantly *Keenan*—whom she'd been talking about, or rather, pretending to be. That she would think Tory needed her to come and *playact* it all out—it was too humiliating!

She took it as a sign that escape was the only option when a cab pulled up in front of the restaurant and discharged some people just as she emerged from the front door. Practically elbowing them aside, she threw herself into the backseat.

"Brooklyn Heights, *now*," she said, slamming the door behind her.

As the cab pulled out, she looked out the window to see Keenan coming out of the restaurant and scanning the street. She sank back in the seat, wishing she were dead.

She took a deep breath.

Well, okay, not dead. Just somewhere else. Some-*one* else.

By the time the cab had reached SoHo she realized she'd been a fool. She should have dragged Claudia away, told her to shut up, then she should have explained everything to Keenan. Someplace private.

Not that anything really needed explaining, not after Claudia's performance. Still, she just needed to *talk* to the man, and quit running away. What was it about her that made her run instead of facing up to her own feelings?

Because that was it, she realized. It wasn't Keenan who made her uncomfortable, it was *herself*. She was trying to run away from herself, and that's why it never worked.

She leaned forward in the cab. "I've changed my mind. Take me to West Eighty-sixth Street, please."

She would go to Keenan's apartment and wait

for him there, even if she had to sit in the hall all day until he got back. They could at least talk there in private, and she could lay her cards on the table, humiliating as they were.

⁂

The elevator doors opened and Keenan stepped into the hallway, his eyes immediately arrested by the small figure on the floor next to his door. Her coat and purse were piled beside her.

He nearly laughed aloud, but settled for a huge sigh of relief. He walked toward her down the silent hall, unable to squelch the grin on his face.

She rose slowly to her feet, looking at him as if he were some sort of executioner.

"I have spent the last two hours in a similar position next to your door," he said, pushing his hands in his pockets.

The look in her eyes went from wary to surprised. "You did?"

He nodded. "I only left to come back and feed Barbra."

She swallowed, then looked down and laughed slightly, her cheeks coloring. She was so pretty, he thought. He wanted to reach out and cup those smooth, pink cheeks and kiss her tenderly all over, so she could feel his love, feel *him*. Not the cardboard image his fame made him.

"Streisand," she said, looking back up.

He paused. "What?"

"I discovered you don't have to call her by her whole name, she'll respond just to 'Streisand.' I guess that was the only part she attached to herself when she heard it. The rest was too long." She shrugged, smiling a little more confidently now. "That's probably why she wouldn't respond to 'Barbra.' I guess dogs don't get the whole first-name last-name thing."

He laughed then. "You can't imagine how glad I am to see you."

She looked away again.

He fished his keys out of his pocket and opened the door, gesturing for her to precede him. "Let's go inside, okay?"

She nodded and entered, head bowed, in front of him.

"Tory," he said, after closing the door behind him.

"No, Keenan, wait," she said. "I need to explain."

He smiled and shook his head. "No you don't. I need to tell you something I should have told you that night in the coatroom. And a dozen times afterward."

As he watched, her cheeks reddened again. He moved toward her, and this time he did cup her face in his hands.

"Tory, I'm falling in love with you," he said, looking into her wide, upturned eyes. "Me, just me. Not celebrity me or tabloid me or whoever else you think I am. But me, the man in front of you. I love you, and I want to be with you and no one else. Won't you please give me a chance? I know I'm not perfect, I'm not what you would have chosen for yourself, but I'm hoping you can overlook all of that. Because my feelings are real, and I'm hoping yours are too."

Tears welled in her eyes and dripped over her lower lashes.

"Oh, Keenan, I *do* love you. The real you. I really do. I just couldn't see how you could—"

He silenced her with a kiss, then drew back. "Don't finish that sentence, not unless you want me to think you've got me confused with some guy on television."

She looked up at him and smiled, silent.

He smiled back. "Well, that worked. Now tell me you love me."

"I do love you." She was grinning now, her hands rising to encircle his neck.

"And tell me you're not with me because I'm famous, or rich, or anything like that," he ordered, enjoying this.

She scoffed. "Hardly. Things would have gone a lot smoother for us if you hadn't been any of those things."

He laughed. "I believe you."

She sobered. "But I do have to confess something. There is one other reason I want to be with you, and it doesn't have anything to do with how I feel about you. You could call it shallow if you want, but I need to warn you."

His brows lowered. "Really? Warn me about what?"

She looked up at him with mock-guilty eyes and said, "I've fallen in love with your dog too."

Avon Romantic Treasures

Unforgettable, enthralling love stories, sparkling with passion and adventure from Romance's bestselling authors